Master and Favorite

Rachel Cherry

Copyright ©2023 Rachel Cherry. All Rights Reserved

Cover Design: Damonza at Damonza.com

Edited by Michelle Hoffman

Formatted by Amanda Empey

No part of this book may be reproduced in any form without express written permission from the author, except for the use of brief quotations in a review.

This book is a work of fiction. Any references to historical events, real people, or real places are used fictitiously. Other names, characters, places and events are products of the author's imagination, and any resemblance to actual events, places or persons, living or dead, is entirely coincidental.

Contents

1. Chapter 1 — 1
2. Chapter 2 — 4
3. Chapter 3 — 7
4. Chapter 4 — 11
5. Chapter 5 — 16
6. Chapter 6 — 20
7. Chapter 7 — 26
8. Chapter 8 — 30
9. Chapter 9 — 36
10. Chapter 10 — 41
11. Chapter 11 — 45
12. Chapter 12 — 49
13. Chapter 13 — 55
14. Chapter 14 — 61
15. Chapter 15 — 65
16. Chapter 16 — 69

17.	Chapter 17	72
18.	Chapter 18	77
19.	Chapter 19	80
20.	Chapter 20	85
21.	Chapter 21	93
22.	Chapter 22	98
23.	Chapter 23	101
24.	Chapter 24	103
25.	Chapter 25	107
26.	Chapter 26	112
27.	Chapter 27	117
28.	Chapter 28	125
29.	Chapter 29	129
30.	Chapter 30	133
31.	Chapter 31	137
32.	Chapter 32	140
33.	Chapter 33	145
34.	Chapter 34	150
35.	Chapter 35	156
36.	Chapter 36	160
37.	Chapter 37	166
38.	Chapter 38	170
39.	Chapter 39	176
40.	Chapter 40	183
41.	Chapter 41	187
42.	Chapter 42	191

43.	Chapter 43	193
44.	Chapter 44	196
45.	Chapter 45	198
46.	Chapter 46	200
47.	Chapter 47	206
48.	Chapter 48	209
49.	Chapter 49	211
50.	Chapter 50	214
51.	Chapter 51	220
52.	Chapter 52	223
53.	Chapter 53	225
54.	Chapter 54	231
55.	Chapter 55	234
56.	Chapter 56	236
57.	Chapter 57	240
58.	Chapter 58	245
59.	Chapter 59	249
60.	Chapter 60	254
61.	Chapter 61	257
62.	Chapter 62	260
63.	Chapter 63	264
64.	Chapter 64	266
65.	Chapter 65	268
66.	Chapter 66	270
67.	Chapter 67	275
	Historical Depictions Disclaimer	280

Acknowledgements	282
About the Author	283
Inspiration	284
Next Books	285

CHAPTER 1

Class was dismissed. Kallias followed his young master Rufus out into the crowded street of the Forum. They didn't head straight home. They liked to wander the city when Rufus finished his lessons. Rufus said nobody at home would miss him and he always had money. Kallias, chosen to accompany him everywhere, liked that. Home was boring and they were fourteen, old enough to walk where they wanted.

They stopped at the Syrian's bakery just outside the Subura. The Subura had a reputation as a rowdy neighborhood, but Rufus liked the thrill of going near it—this little shop was the closest he would go. They stood in line behind two women and a man who looked like a soldier. One of the women glanced at them and smiled. The line moved up. The soldier, sturdy with a white scar under his right eye, moved last.

"Wonder how he got it," Kallias whispered. Rufus only shrugged. Sometimes Rufus responded when Kallias spoke without being spoken to. Other times, especially more recently, Rufus wouldn't answer. It was impertinent for a slave to always be voicing his opinion. Kallias was aware of this but sometimes ignored it. It hadn't been that way until this year, Rufus getting irritated like that.

They stepped to the counter. The Syrian, friendly and gray haired, was serving customers. They didn't know his name, only that he knew them. He leaned over the counter, smiling, and asked what they wanted. His slave girl assistant stood watching with her arms folded. She was older than them and Rufus was always stealing glances at her.

"We just want honey cakes," said Rufus. "Two, please."

"Always the honey cakes." The Syrian smiled. The girl placed them on a little tray.

"Kallias, do you like them?" said the Syrian. Kallias nodded eagerly. "Everytime I see you, I just see Malika all over again." The man shook his head.

Kallias didn't know how they knew his mother and never bothered to ask. He only wanted the cake. The Syrian's wife walked out of the back room. "Malika?" she said. And then, "Oh Kallias! How are you doing?"

They were always like this to him. It was because of his looks. For as long as he could remember, people gushed about his beauty. It all went straight to his head and puffed him up. He naturally began to believe he was the prettiest person to ever exist. Here he was now, standing beside the son of a very rich man, and they were focusing on him, the slave.

"You can try a cake made of wine," said the Syrian's wife. She gestured to the girl, who gave her a little round cake on another small tray.

"You take that," said the woman. "Take a bite, before you take the whole thing, to see if you like it."

He tasted it with the tips of his fingers. He said it was good. The wife laughed. "I'll give you another one," and she did.

Rufus watched, silent and blank, as he paid for both of them. Kallias followed him out, already eating some of the sweets.

"They're really good," he said, holding out a piece of it to Rufus. "You can have one." He was on the verge of celebrating until he looked at the other boy.

"I don't want it," said Rufus. He pushed ahead of Kallias and started down the street without looking back. Kallias shrugged and paused to rearrange the bag on his shoulder, which held both of their school texts. He unwrapped the second cake. He'd eat as much of it as he could before arriving home.

Kallias didn't think it strange that he was so favored above his master. That was how it was everywhere. Rufus, whose father lent money to the government, only received the feigned respect due a rich man's son. People assumed he'd be rude because of his father and treated him with a mild, friendly caution.

But Kallias, with his perfect face, long lashes, and shiny dark hair, invoked something next to love. And that was how it was everywhere they went. He thought it was natural. He was pretty and people loved it. Rufus was too sensitive. If he had anything extraordinary about him besides his father's money, he'd understand.

They entered their home and crossed the atrium, neither of them meeting eyes with the servants. They went around a serving woman mopping the bright tiled floor and continued down the hall to the stairs. Rufus stormed ahead of Kallias, straight to his room where he flopped on his bed in the corner. He didn't eat his cake. He didn't even want to talk. He wanted to go to sleep and ordered Kallias to sleep too.

But Kallias didn't sleep, and soon he quit pretending to. He got up from his pallet at the foot of the bed and left the room. It was too early anyway.

Besides, he didn't have to do something just because a boy who called himself his master said so. Kallias thought increasingly about this now. They were the same age and the same size. It was stupid how Rufus tried to lord it over him, master or not.

These days, all Kallias could think about was how much he hated being a slave. He had no idea how he would change his lot in life, but he would find a way. One day, he would look Rufus right in the eye—as his equal.

Chapter 2

Kallias snuck into the mistress' bedroom where he knew he would find his mother putting things in order. He told her what happened while she folded clothing and stacked it on a shelf.

"You shouldn't make him feel bad," Malika said. "They never like that."

"But I offered to give him some," said Kallias. "I really did."

"I just don't know why you two are doing this, all of sudden. Do you want him to be your enemy?" She paused with a garment in her hand and looked at him.

He hoped Malika would laugh at his story but of course she didn't. She said their competition was unnecessary. It wasn't a good thing for Kallias to revel in his preferential treatment or find little ways to goad Rufus.

"He's no better than you," she said. "And you're no better than him. It's just that you both feel that way." She sighed, wiping her forehead with the back of her hand. "And that his father can make it very hard for us, if he wants to."

Kallias said he wasn't doing anything, not really. He just thought the story was funny. Couldn't he laugh in secret with her? Did they have to be subservient in private too? Malika ignored that and said that she only wanted him to be safe.

She was always giving Kallias advice, which mostly annoyed him. She was his mother and he loved her but she was a fearful slave. She was clingy and so afraid something terrible would happen to him.

One day, Kallias and Rufus had been surlier than usual. It was hot and they were both annoyed at having to stay in the classroom longer than normal. As soon as they were home, Kallias dropped the bag on the floor of the vestibule and Rufus lost his temper. Kallias picked up the bag and apologized but, inside, he seethed. He'd gone and told Malika.

"You have to be more careful, Kallias," she'd said. "Please. I don't want you to get in trouble." She said that all the time.

Kallias didn't think too deeply of anything. In their better moods, he and Rufus still occasionally played games. Rufus pointed out girls and Kallias looked where he pointed. In two years, Rufus would don his toga of manhood and go to Greece to complete his education.

"It's taking too long," Rufus said. "I'm ready to see the world by myself without my father always telling me what to do." Unlike his master, Kallias wouldn't get to choose what he wanted to do, so he said nothing. Still, the prospect of Greece was exciting.

"You won't just be traveling," said Lucius Spinther. They jumped and looked up, wondering if he heard the first thing Rufus said. They were in the sitting room, with Kallias sprawled on the floor while Rufus wrote on a wax tablet. His father looked at them and frowned. "You have to learn while you're there, too."

"Yes, Father," said Rufus, focusing again on the tablet.

Spinther told Kallias to sit up. It was bad manners for a slave to slouch.

Kallias got to his feet, stood straight and bowed his head.

"Remember, soon you'll enter the public with Rufus. You have to look good beside him."

He tousled Kallias' hair. Rufus sat staring after his father when he left. "He acts like we'll be in public tomorrow. He's so critical. He scares me a little bit."

He scared Kallias a little too, but that was because Rufus' father was the real master of the house. Spinther wasn't so bad up close. Kallias was born and raised in the house. Besides his mother, Lucius Spinther was the first person to pick him up.

The boys played marbles and Kallias won. Malika sat on the garden steps in front of a fountain. At thirty, his mother was still youthful. She looked like Kallias and everyone said so. Her main job was to keep the mistress' cosmetics in order and keep up with her chambers and she was thankful for this role. It could've been so much worse for a slave.

Whenever her mistress was away, she found Kallias.

"You won twice," said Rufus. "You've been winning a lot more than usual." Kallias couldn't think of anything to say, so he was quiet. Rufus scooped the marbles up and stuffed them in his bag. "These games are dumb. I'm tired of them."

Kallias stood looking down on Rufus, who jerked the bag tight by the strings and got to his feet, brushing at his dirtied knees. "I'm going inside to study," he said. "Stay out here so you don't distract me." He disappeared down the path toward the house.

Malika, chin in her hand, shook her head. "You're not supposed to win," she said. "You're never supposed to win."

"It was just a stupid game."

She shook her head again.

"He acts like he's the consul."

At that, Malika laughed and the bruise on her neck flashed into view, dark and purple. Kallias was almost startled into speaking but his mother waved her hand and her hair was back into place. "The boy grows into the consul, you know?"

"He could grow into a donkey, for all I care. Wouldn't it be nice if he were an animal? Then I wouldn't have to bow to him."

Her face was solemn. "I wish I was as stupid as you are, when I was your age."

She had him when she was only a year older than he was now, by the most famous gladiator in Rome at the time. Back then, she was fit for only the greatest heroes in the arena. His father was the Phoenix. She spent one night with him after a huge victory and then Lucius Spinther sent her back home. On the first day of the next year, she had Kallias.

"You almost killed me," she told him once. "But you were such a perfect baby."

Chapter 3

Rufus' two older brothers, who were in their twenties and helped their father run his business, were coming that evening with their father and a guest for dinner. Rufus stood near his couch waiting for them to arrive, while Kallias stood just a few paces from him, and they both fidgeted from boredom.

When the brothers walked in, one following the other, the first one flicked Rufus on the forehead and said, "Why're you so sweaty?" and grinned. Rufus turned bright pink. His brothers usually only acknowledged him to tease him.

Kallias looked at the floor to hide his face.

Later during the dinner, he gazed absentmindedly at one of the lamps. There was never anything for him to do in the dining room but show up and stand beside Rufus. When he looked up, Spinther was watching him. He made a gesture for Kallias to move beside his wife, so Kallias went to the other side of the room.

From where he reclined, Rufus rolled his eyes.

"I don't know why you left me," he said in his room after. He lay on the floor while Kallias sat on the couch, swinging one leg and chewing his nails—they were always informal alone.

"I was just obeying your father," said Kallias. "I had to listen to him."

"He saw you laughing with my brother."

"No he didn't."

"So you were laughing."

"I wasn't, I swear!"

"Just leave," said Rufus.

Kallias jumped up and went out. He slammed the door and stood in the hallway. Then he thought better of it, opened the door again and shut it lightly this time.

But again he didn't go to sleep, and he went and found Malika. She was in the cold room of the baths, lighting candles for when the mistress Annia arrived. Annia liked to come in late so that she could sit in her bath for hours alone and undisturbed.

Kallias said, "I'm sick. I'm sick of it."

She didn't look around at him.

"He hates me. He's always saying I did something wrong even though I try so hard. But I hate him too."

"You need to fix that," she said. "You have to."

She moved to the other candle. Then the steward peeked in, looking crossly at Kallias and the two other slaves who were dallying with placing the towels and perfumes near the pool, and they all dispersed.

Kallias didn't fix it. A few weeks after Rufus started going to the rhetor for his speech lessons, he went to his father in his office and said he was fed up with Kallias and wanted a different slave. Every time they looked at each other, it was with so much loathing and competition.

"I'm fifteen," he said. "I've outgrown him."

Spinther glanced at Kallias. "It's a bad choice, he will know you better than anyone new. And he's expensive."

"But that's what I want, one that's new. And how is he expensive if he was born in the house? You got him for free."

Spinther looked at him, clearly irritated at being disturbed at his work.

"If you sold him, you could buy me another slave as a replacement. Please, Father. Please?"

Kallias forgot to have a blank face as his mouth fell open. He said, "Sell me?"

"See, you just can't shut up," said Rufus, and snorted.

"Both of you be quiet." Spinther hit the table, making the boys jump. "Kallias, some masters would beat you for that."

Kallias said he was sorry, but Spinther didn't answer. He studied Kallias for a moment, and as he did, he got this strange look in his eye like he'd just noticed something important, something he hadn't seen before. Kallias shuddered and dropped his gaze.

Spinther called the steward over. The man went through some papers and found what he purchased Malika for. They spoke to each other in low voices without looking at the boys. Kallias could hardly breathe, while Rufus scowled with crossed arms and shifted impatiently. Then the steward moved the papers and looked up at them, face neutral.

Spinther gestured for Kallias and he came closer beside them and Spinther said, "I'm going to do you a great favor. I'm going to sell you. Someone like you will be worth a lot. You will go to one of the best houses in Rome, no doubt."

"I don't want to be sold," Kallias said. He couldn't help it then—tears welled up in his eyes and slid down his cheeks. He looked at the man who had watched him grow from a child to a youth and he couldn't believe it.

"Stop it," said Spinther, shaking his head. "You will go to a great house and it'll be better. You and Rufus aren't made for each other anymore."

"My mother," he said. His shoulders heaved.

"It's alright. I won't sell her. She'll be alright."

Annia, with two of her serving women trailing her, walked in just in time to witness this scene. She halted in her tracks and looked back and forth at all of them. But she didn't challenge her husband. Annia never disagreed with him.

"Poor boy," she said, making a little sad expression. "You're too young to be this stressed! He's right, you'll go somewhere good."

Kallias wiped his face, suddenly realizing that everybody was looking at him.

"Don't worry about your mother," said Annia. She drew closer to him and put her hand on his cheek, which was drying. She had never been affectionate with him, unlike Spinther, and Kallias didn't want her pity now, but he said nothing.

"She's just fine with me," she said, stroking his cheek.

He stared at the floor. All he could think of was when he was a little child and Spinther striding into the atrium, and looking down at him, and then lifting him high and swinging him around and making him laugh and laugh.

CHAPTER 4

Spinther sent him to the dealers hardly an hour later and he was sold before he could even say goodbye to his mother. It was the steward Zeno who purchased him. He was Greek like Kallias, and thin and graying. Zeno looked as if he were on the verge of halting a disaster, but for what? All the stewards of great households had the same harried look.

Zeno said that Kallias belonged now to Gaius Sulpicius Calvinus. But Kallias didn't meet Calvinus the first two days. He was taken to the house, which was even more grand and beautiful than Spinther's house had been. He thought he could disappear in there to avoid doing any chores, not that he had any.

Kallias did nothing all day. It was a strange new environment. There were slaves assigned to keep the place clean, but most of them seemed bored. They spent a lot of time outside in the gardens throwing pennies into this one fountain with a naked nymph statue next to it.

When Zeno would walk up, everybody would slowly disperse and try to look busy. They weren't afraid of him, but it was more that they didn't want to hear him scolding them. The reality was that there was nothing to do but clean things that were already cleaned. There was no mistress and no children. They were maintaining a house for a man who didn't seem to live there.

"He just got divorced." Kallias heard one of the slaves say. "He has a little daughter but she's at another of his houses and you'll never see her. That's why everything's so quiet."

"She cries a lot, about everything, if she doesn't get her way. But she's six, that's why. He spoils her, too. Even though he wanted a son, he still spoils her."

He heard this last part from Elpida, the head cook's daughter. She was a little older than Kallias, but she had a stupid and childish gaze, and he hated her as soon as he looked at her. She wanted to talk to him and show him everything. He thought she was ugly, and whenever she spoke to him he would stare at her without blinking.

"When he comes in," someone else told Kallias, "he likes to drink with his guards and his friends. If you're behaved, he won't notice you."

Calvinus had replaced his entire house in Rome, except for the cooks and the steward. He had given his former wife most of the slaves when she left, and sent his little daughter to another house. The new slaves Zeno had bought for him were mostly young and well-trained in domestic settings.

But a few days later, Calvinus was there and the whole atmosphere changed. No one loitered and everyone tried to look busy. Kallias saw the slaves rushing through the halls, touching and moving things for nothing. Zeno found Kallias and said, "Come with me to see your new master. He wants to know who's in his house."

Kallias followed Zeno to the study. There were a lot of people standing around and crowding the entrance. He figured these must be Calvinus's freedmen and clients. They always came to rich men the first thing in the morning to ask for favors and do business. Zeno pushed through them.

A freedman stood in front of the desk, where Calvinus sat. But Kallias couldn't see him. The freedman was gesturing animatedly, wringing his hands—and Calvinus seemed to be saying nothing. Then Calvinus said something very flat, and the man turned away, almost colliding with Kallias as he left.

With a nudge from Zeno, Kallias found himself facing Calvinus. He looked very patrician, with his close-cropped hair and straight-cut features. He was sitting back, with his head tilted, almost as if he were tired. But his dark eyes moved with a keen regard. Where Spinther was in his late fifties, this man looked to be in his early forties.

Calvinus said, "Are they adjusting?"

"Yes, master, " Zeno said, bowing. "I only pick the best for your house."

Calvinus sat straight, put up one hand, on which he wore a large signet ring, and gestured to Kallias. His slaves and secretaries swirled in the background, but like a lead player, Calvinus stood out and they were invisible. He looked as if he might sum anyone up with a glance, but he studied Kallias for just a little longer than necessary.

"I don't bite," he said. "Come closer."

When Zeno pushed Kallias forward some more, Calvinus leaned towards him and said, "What you do, boy? Zeno give you a job?"

Kallias glanced at Zeno, who stood with his hands folded, and then back at Calvinus.

"I'm educated," he blurted.

"I know," said Calvinus. "Zeno saw it on your placard. That's good."

He looked down for something on his desk. He held up a wax tablet and stylus, on which he made Kallias write out the menu for that night's dinner as he listed items.

With a slightly shaking hand, Kallias held up the tablet. Calvinus looked at it and said again, "That's good."

So at first, his job in the house was to write the menu and take messages for Calvinus. This was so very different from following Rufus around everywhere. Now Kallias had the freedom to walk in and out the house without anyone stopping him.

He was excited the most about the messages. The first time he was called, there was Calvinus standing in the hallway with Demetrius, his best secretary, and another man who looked Roman.

Calvinus said, "I have something important for you to do."

"I can do it, sir," he said.

"If you fuck it up, I'll break your hand."

He smiled at the face Kallias made. Then Kallias knew that he was joking and it made him blush even as he tried to smile in return. Meanwhile, Demetrius sized him up.

"He can do it," he said. "It's just a simple job."

Calvinus held out a sealed letter. Kallias didn't even look at it as he took it. He didn't want to seem nosy.

"Take it to Numerius, you understand? Just take it and give it to the doorman."

Kallias, who had been running all around the city for the past two years with Rufus, knew exactly where to go when given the address. He was glad he did because he wanted Calvinus to think that he was smart and this was his chance. His new master wouldn't have any reason to despise him. He would see that he was good and mannerable and attractive and then he'd value him.

After Kallias delivered the message, he took a detour and slipped to Spinther's house. He begged the doorman to let him in.

"I don't think Lady Annia would like that," said the doorman.

"Please," Kallias said. "Just for Malika."

"I can tell someone to call her."

So they didn't let him in, but the doorman got a slave to call Malika and she came out to the street to talk to him.

They hugged each other for a long time. He hadn't seen her in two weeks.

"He's very rich," he told her. "Richer than Spinther! I've never met anyone like him. Can you believe Spinther was right? I went to a good house."

"Try not to get in trouble, whatever you do."

"Of course I won't. He likes me, he speaks to me."

"Why are you out now? Does he know?"

He told her why he was out.

"You shouldn't have come to me," she said, and reached for him again to hug him. He let her, just for a few seconds, and then he pulled away.

"I'm so glad you're alright," she said, still trying to hold him.

As he looked at her, at her slender frame and soft eyes and her dark hair tumbling across her shoulders, she was suddenly pathetic to him. She was the opposite in every way of Calvinus, he thought. She had nothing in her life but the mercy of her mistress. He would not be like her. He would not be her age and still a lowly slave, not with Calvinus.

"I have to go," he said.

"Always come back," she begged him. "If you can."

He did not acknowledge this. He ran back to Calvinus' house and he hadn't even been missed when he returned two hours later.

Kallias was so excited. Gaius Calvinus was rich, handsome, and no doubt could have whatever he wanted, all the time. Kallias felt that in him he had found the key to his own life, in this man who was the literal image of all his dreams.

One day, he thought, he too would have all the money and power he wanted. He would have everything. And now was his chance to get it. All he would have to do was appeal to his new master.

CHAPTER 5

His heart always beat faster when he saw Calvinus. He had seen him three times now, and each time his face warmed up. Kallias was so impressed by him, he wanted Calvinus to look at him and be impressed in the same way. He was pretty and everyone said he was, and he wondered if Calvinus thought it too.

He was walking into the house one day and realized with a little jolt that Calvinus was right behind him. He could feel the gaze boring into him. Kallias had to look back then. He couldn't help himself. And Calvinus was staring right at him, and his eyes were dark, intent. He smiled at Kallias, who was so surprised he just turned around again immediately. And the skin on his neck was hot.

He ducked into a side room and pretended to be looking for something. He heard the footsteps pass by without slowing.

The head cook was a skinny older woman named Petra, and she liked Kallias. He knew it was because of his looks, because he never really said anything to her, except to ask for extra food. She had not yet witnessed him ignoring her daughter.

He didn't mean it in a bad way with Elpida. She annoyed him, that was all.

Kallias was trying to get Petra to give him extra food then, and she probably would, if he stayed around until everything was done. Then Calvinus walked into the kitchen, and Petra rushed from standing over her assistants at the oven to greet him. Everyone was probably trying to understand why the master was all the way back here, where only the slaves came.

Calvinus smiled at her. When he smiled, it was at once dangerous and friendly. Kallias could not take his gaze off him.

"Make me a surprise tonight, Petra," he said.

"Yes, sir," she said. "That's exactly what we're doing."

"Your food's still the best in Rome. Everyone else should take a note."

"You're so generous, master."

Kallias, standing in the background, stared. Calvinus walked right to one of the tables where the slaves always ate, and sat. The other four slaves in the kitchen stopped what they were doing to look at him in surprise. He acted as if he didn't notice, and maybe he didn't.

"Petra really does cook better than anyone else," he said, tapping his fingers on the table. The hand with the signet ring. "It's hot out. Bring me a cup of water, Kallias."

Kallias hadn't realized he'd noticed him. He rushed to get him some water and brought it to him. He was careful to set the cup down and not hand it to him. He didn't think he could handle touching him.

Kallias was so attracted to him. He liked his sturdy, masculine frame, and the power that radiated from him and how whenever he walked into the room everyone stood straighter and worked harder. He liked his even tone when he spoke, the way he didn't need to repeat himself or raise his voice to be heard.

Calvinus had the additional accents of three aggressive-looking guards to always accompany him. They were probably ex-gladiators, and maybe the Phoenix was similar to them, in the impression that he gave.

To Kallias it all seemed so violent and wonderful. Calvinus was who he wanted, and who wanted to be, all at once. And he could not stop gazing at him. He was transfixed. He wanted to be exactly like him.

One of the guards stood now at the back of the kitchen, near the door. He was a big Gaul with a tattoo of a twisting snake running down his right arm.

"Come outside," said Calvinus to Kallias, without looking at him. He stood and went out with the guard.

Again, they waited for him in the hallway.

"You want to see my rooms?" Calvinus nodded towards the hall.

He didn't wait for Kallias to say yes, because it wasn't a question after all. So Kallias followed them all the way. No one talked. He couldn't have spoken if he wanted to. Or at least not in the best formed sentences. The guard pushed the doors open and Calvinus gestured, and Kallias walked in ahead of him.

It was literally, the master's private rooms. There was a couch and table and a few chairs and it was well lit. There was a game set on the table still, and Calvinus' personal slave, Nestor, was stacking everything into a gilded box. He glanced up at them when they walked in, and then he seemed to have a prompt excuse to leave the room. Everything was opulent, like everything else at the house.

Calvinus sat on the couch and Demetrius sat at the table.

"Tell Nestor to come back," said Calvinus. "I did not dismiss him."

And the guard brought him back. He stood beside the guard with his head down and his gaze fixed on the floor.

"You see Nestor?" Calvinus looked at Kallias. "He's a good slave. He goes with me everywhere and he knows how to not talk. You see that?"

"Yes," said Kallias.

Demetrius and the guards just watched.

"One day I'll take you to the Forum with me. You have to be a perfect slave though. Nestor never shows what he's thinking, even though he always is."

Kallias stared at Nestor. He was young and good looking and so expertly silent and blank.

"I bought Nestor five years ago," said Calvinus. "He was your age."

The door opened and the other guard, the bald African, walked in. He sat and looked at all of them back and forth.

"Enough about Nestor. This is Jafari." Calvinus pointed to him.

Kallias nodded.

"He kills people who cause too much trouble."

Jafari laughed like it was the funniest thing he'd ever heard, with his head back. Even Demetrius smiled. Nestor was still looking at the floor and the Gaul was fiddling boredly with his knife. But he wore a half smile.

"Oh and that's Atis," said Calvinus, pointing to him. "He'll make you hurt before he kills you. He's good at it, too."

Kallias nodded. That was all he could do.

And the third guard, sitting near the back and looking—to put it simply, very mean—Calvinus only introduced as Linux.

"Well," said Calvinus, and spread his hands. "All of that is to say, you can stay in one of my rooms with my attendants. I'm going to dinner now. Talk to Nestor."

And then they all left.

Chapter 6

Kallias didn't talk to Nestor. He didn't like Nestor. Nothing anybody said could make his face change. But no one at the house had anything bad to say about him. And Kallias realized now that every time there was Calvinus, there was Nestor. Silent, catering, nearly hidden but there. The perfect personal slave. At the old house, Kallias had always heard Spinther say that the slaves who followed their masters everywhere had to be the most obedient, and loyal, and Nestor certainly was.

Once just after Kallias moved into Calvinus's rooms, he heard doors of one of them closing later than usual, so he got up from his pallet and sneaked to the main room and there was Nestor, naked and slim, and holding his tunic. He and Kallias stared at each other for a second, and then Nestor pulled on the garment and smoothed his hair and walked right by him without a word.

Then Kallias realized how everything had been so quiet before, as if something was happening. A lot of men enjoyed boys the same way they liked women, and it was probably unusual not to. Nestor was getting too old to be a boy, though. He wondered what Nestor thought, but there was no telling because Nestor never looked like he did think.

All this was only after a few nights. They came in, guards and all, and they did like to drink and talk, just as the slaves said. It was always about something that Calvinus owned and Kallias never understood it. But now he learned Calvinus had four houses, and Kallias had never really imagined that, although every summer he went to Spinther's Pompeii house.

Then there was a new development. Calvinus wanted only Kallias to pour his wine. It used to be a job for some other dining room slave. But Calvinus told Zeno, "Never send anyone but Kallias to pour my wine."

So then, every day when Calvinus came home—he was back in Rome to settle for a while—Kallias was first to go to him in the dining room and serve him.

He was always shaky when he did it. He had just learned to pour and how to mix just the right amount of water with the wine.

"Don't be nervous," said Calvinus. "You're better at anything if you're not nervous."

Kallias nodded. He put down the pitcher.

"I'm sorry."

"You like my rooms? You like it better than sharing a room with thirty other slaves?"

"Yes, I do, sir."

"You're not used to that are you?"

"The communal room, sir?"

"Sharing it."

"No, sir. I was only with my master."

Calvinus asked him why he'd been resold. Kallias thought he misheard, and blinked at him. But he realized it was a real question and Calvinus was waiting for an actual answer. And so Kallias explained, the sentences spilling out in a rush. He didn't have the sense to not reveal all of it. He told it all.

"Poor little house slave," said Calvinus. "They never love those children like they think. Are you rebellious?"

"No, never!"

"Good, that's not going to help you."

Gaius Sulpicius Calvinus had long stories about him. The few servants who knew him well gossiped in the lowest whispers that could be heard, but still they talked. With the encouragement of his father, who was now dead, Calvinus had first become a lawyer and pursued a political career, as was typical of a man of his rank. His father also was a prominent senator, close to the former emperor Augustus.

But the real family business was controlling operations through their network of numerous freedmen and associates, and keeping out any competition as far as they were concerned. And this was centered in Pompeii and Ostia particularly, maybe because of the commerce there.

And yes, Calvinus was so, so rich. Everything involving him made money.

He'd also stopped practicing law years ago.

Kallias had to pick it up using context. There were a lot of other details the servants didn't know, and of course they weren't talking all the time in chronological order.

But one thing was easy to see. Calvinus was popular in his circle. He knew a lot of people. He kept a few of them particularly close to him. And for some reason, always seemed pleased when he gave someone something, whether that was advice, money, or even a pen.

One day, a very important man came to the house for dinner with Calvinus. He was the prefect of the Praetorian Guard and his name was Lucius Aelius Sejanus. The servants said he was very good friends with the master and Kallias believed it. He'd never seen Calvinus actually laugh, but Sejanus slapped him on the back after a joke and Calvinus did then.

The prefect had the kind of stance only a soldier has. He looked as if the only thing missing was a helmet under his arm.

"I'm doing well," said Calvinus to him later during dinner. "I think soon the emperor will give me a province."

There was another man, too, some senator named Appius, who nodded. And Sejanus said that Calvinus was certainly due for a province, if not this year then the next.

"I think he will send you out soon, maybe when a place opens up."

"Someone needs to retire," said Calvinus. "Don't you think the days when you could remove someone because you were tired of them being in the way, don't you think those days were more exciting?"

"Gaius!" said the senator, and laughed.

"But it was. Just imagine, when you had to be afraid for your life all the time. I think that makes your mind sharp. Gives you something to do."

"Maybe so," said Appius. "But then what good is your mind if you're dead because your enemy hates you?"

"Everyone has to die, eventually," said Sejanus. And they all nodded. Sejanus had very blue eyes, an even demeanor, and made everything sound easy and wonderful when he talked.

The freedman, Demetrius, who dined with them, said, "I think Gaius means that the sharp mind is supposed to be put to use before all of that."

"Thank you, thank you," said Calvinus, extending his hand.

Sejanus held out his cup to Kallias, who stepped forward to refill it. Kallias hadn't imagined that he'd be listening to the dinner discussions of the men who ran the government, but now his head was full of those conversations. He couldn't even sleep because of it. He'd never really listened to the things Spinther said, but he listened to what his master said now.

Everyone he met had an important position of some sort, and all of them wanted more and more power. They were very open about it. As for Calvinus, all he wanted so badly was to be the governor of a province. Calvinus thought having a province would be the peak of his career. But all of the provinces were taken and there were other men standing in his way.

Kallias often wondered about Rufus. Their times together were much simpler than he'd realized. It felt like a long time ago that he wanted to be equal with Rufus, to be able to look in him the eye not as a slave, but as someone with respect, and all that was so paltry in comparison to his desire of being like Calvinus.

Once, instead of watching the guests signal for more wine, Kallias listened to a side conversation between two guests, and he didn't notice the third man holding up his cup until he glanced to the side and saw Calvinus frowning at him. He rushed forward and poured the refill. That look from Calvinus made him want to gag.

He didn't want Gaius Calvinus to think he was bad at anything. He wanted Calvinus to think he was perfect. Kallias would be better than Nestor, who was so boring, unambitious, and never even spoke to the master. Nestor probably couldn't even hold a conversation, and Calvinus was probably tired of him.

When Kallias went to the Forum with the entourage, he realized it wasn't about walking through, but it was about following his master to the important places. That was what Spinther was trying to say to Kallias before. He understood it now, as he walked with the guards, the secretaries, and Nestor and two other attendants.

The era was the height of peace in Rome. There was nothing for the Senate to do now but advise the emperor and for senators to come through the city in their beautiful litters and block up traffic because their entourages were so long and important.

Calvinus' own litter had the purple-striped lining and the opulent, white-gold curtains. As Kallias walked with the entourage, he realized how many people were looking at him. As they stood outside the Senate house, various individuals wandered over to speak to them or tried to hand them papers to give to their master when he was out.

Demetrius had instructed Kallias on this beforehand. Ignore them, or say that Calvinus is not responding to information. He had a lot of experience with this, being his most important secretary. Even people who had nothing worthwhile to say, still wanted to have a word with someone close to an important man.

It was exciting.

These were men at the center of everything that was happening in Rome, and that meant that they were the most important people in the world. They had everything they wanted and all they had to do was speak and have an order fulfilled. And Kallias was in their midst. It was so intoxicating.

He was a slave that was true. But Kallias felt that even being adjacent to them made him important. His master favored him and one look from him could make his heart race. And Calvinus was not an angry boy who had to fight to have his older brothers respect him. He wasn't trying to carve his way into the world. He could give Kallias anything he wanted.

Kallias had stopped in front of a mirror to gaze at himself. He didn't know Calvinus had just come into the hall until he heard his voice. Kallias spun around and saw him standing with his guard, Jafari. They paused in the middle of their conversation.

"Can I have a headband?" Kallias asked.

He wanted it to look like one of those older youths who had just won a race and been crowned for it. But Calvinus didn't answer, and when he and Jafari walked ahead, Kallias scolded himself for trying his luck. It was inappropriate and improper for him to request things, even something small. He didn't even know where he got the courage from, blurting it like that.

But he got something better. He received a dozen new outfits and more, delivered by a slave to Calvinus' rooms in a heavy trunk. He couldn't believe the generosity! He went wide-eyed as he looked through the clothes, and felt very lucky. Then from under all the other things he pulled out two skinny headbands.

Chapter 7

Kallias knew he wanted something from his life that was more than what he could imagine now. That part was a given. But the method of getting there, that was what he couldn't figure out. He passed the busts in the vestibule that showed off the master's ancestors, his father, grandfather, and on. An old family, old wealth. But Kallias didn't have that kind of background, so how was he supposed to have all the things he wanted if he didn't have a starting point?

The freedman Demetrius was something of a guide. He'd been a slave and he'd grown up with Calvinus. He was the only person in the house allowed to call him Gaius now, and he didn't have that obsequiousness that the other slaves and freedmen had when talking to him.

Demetrius was so successful because he helped Calvinus throughout his political career. As Calvinus got richer, so did he. Demetrius must've been useful and respected, to now call his former master by his first name.

Kallias stood looking around Demetrius' house. He was stunned that this man was so rich. And he even had a few slaves. And that was such a turnaround, when he was born a slave in Calvinus' father's house. They were in the library talking about the book Demetrius wrote, which was on good studying methods for learning Tironian shorthand.

"Nobody was smarter than you growing up," said Calvinus, turning the pages on the codex. They said it took hundreds of hours to make each one, with all the men they hired working on it. And Demetrius was selling a single copy for hundreds of sesterces.

"You wrote the most expensive book in Rome."

"If you understand how much work went into it," said Demetrius. "You would say I'm underselling it."

Calvinus had helped him pay for most of publishing it. He was always willing to throw his money behind other people's projects. His own hobby—studying the designs of roads and buildings—was free. (He liked the way it all made so much sense, he said, and it didn't hurt that researching it never cost anything.) But he didn't mind spending on something useful for a friend, providing he made his money back. Which he always did.

Kallias could tell they were proud of themselves. As a celebration of their work, they sat in Demetrius's library and had wine that Kallias poured for them.

When they left the house, the success of the freedman was all Kallias could think about. They came home late and went straight to the master's private sitting room. Calvinus walked out to speak to Zeno, while the guards hung around.

One of the newer slaves, Gaia, walked into the room. She was a little older than Kallias, slender, and very pretty. She wore a silver bracelet, which was a lot for a slave. The guards ogled her. She ignored them as she put two scrolls and some papers on the table.

"That looks like a lot for a girl to carry," said Linux, the third one who was here today. But she didn't even glance at him.

She had never been nice. She always looked at Kallias as if he made her nauseous.

"It's for the promotion of the book," said Calvinus, when he got back to the room.

He saw Kallias staring at them. Calvinus asked him if he thought it was interesting.

"I just didn't realize you could make a book on how to learn shorthand," said Kallias. "I thought you just had to learn it by studying it."

The guards laughed. As she left, Gaia gave him a reproachful look.

"You can make a book on anything," said Calvinus. "Nestor, go and start trimming the lamps in the other rooms."

Nestor turned away immediately.

Kallias still stood there, with two other servants. Calvinus told him to go and wash in the baths in the house.

When Kallias came back, hair still damp from his bath, the guards and servants were still there in the room.

"I saw the light go out of a man's eyes," said Linux. "When I twisted his head around until he couldn't breathe. Then I heard his bones crack."

"You will scare my slaves, Linux."

"I just think about it. I snapped the life right out of him."

Someone had been murdered. That was what they were talking about—and what Linux was making his comparison to. And Calvinus said that was just an everyday thing in some parts of Rome, but the only difference was this man was a gladiator and so a lot of fans were upset. It was bad to upset the fans. The drawn out investigation was making things worse.

"They'll get over it," said Linux. "Just like I did."

Kallias stood before Calvinus. The other servants had been dismissed, and the guards were talking, but not to them. Calvinus and Kallias were in their own conversation.

"I just want to learn it," Kallias said. "I know it's a lot to ask."

"People train for a long time. It's not easy."

"I would study really, really hard."

Calvinus nodded. "That's good, yes. But those books there are for sale. We won't keep them."

Kallias wasn't sure what that answer meant, or how to respond to it. He fiddled with the fabric of the end of the couch where Calvinus sat. He could feel him staring at him. Exciting as that was, it always made him nervous.

"Maybe," said Calvinus finally. "I'll tell Demetrius tomorrow you want to learn. How about that?"

"Thank you, master, thank you so much! I promise I'll do my best."

"You're very eager."

Kallias could have kissed him in that moment. "I just think that you have the best life," he explained. "That's all, and I hope I can be useful for you and be like you and—"

He was rambling, he stopped himself. After a long pause, Calvinus stood and walked over to his guards.

Chapter 8

They hadn't spoken this much, not since the first time Kallias came to pour wine for him. Calvinus always seemed distracted by something or headed elsewhere. Even in the dining room, he didn't really focus on Kallias. But Kallias couldn't keep out of his way forever.

When the guards left the rooms, it was just them. Calvinus turned to him then, laid a hand on his waist, and then dropped it lower and squeezed. Kallias went blank. But he moved when he was nudged forward.

In the bedroom, everything was still lit and the bed was soft when he settled in it.

He could hear his own heart. He watched Calvinus secure the door and cross the room. Calvinus said, moving in next to him, "Take off your clothes," so he did. Everything seemed to slow as the realization descended: he was in bed with his master.

His instinct was to draw away, but Calvinus was so close to him. And had locked his hand around his thigh. His hand was heavy. Kallias had often imagined this moment when looking at him in the day and standing apart from him. But now he was frozen.

"You're the most beautiful boy in Rome," said Calvinus. "Do you know that? I could look at you all day." He'd propped himself up on one elbow while he stared at Kallias. He was still fully dressed. Kallias could only gaze back at him.

"You're the most beautiful boy in Rome," said Calvinus. "Do you know that? I could look at you all day." He'd propped himself up on one elbow while he stared at Kallias. He was still fully dressed. His hand was heavy. And Kallias could only gaze back at him.

Calvinus took his hand from his thigh and stroked it through his hair, and Kallias told himself over and over that this man could give him anything he wanted in the morning.

"I know you've never been fucked before," said Calvinus suddenly. He patted the place beside them. "This is good in some ways. Turn around."

Kallias did as he was told and there was a shifting of weight on the bed. He glanced back at Calvinus, who wasn't looking at his face. He turned around again, blushing.

He felt ridiculous, and the pressure as Calvinus touched him was a strange hurt that made it hard to breathe. He would never be able to face a mirror again after this, he thought. But then he had no more time to think, because Calvinus was coaxing him into a position, making him lie flat.

He was in tears as soon as Calvinus pushed inside him. But Calvinus didn't stop, he went all the way. Slowly, through every resistance, then moving. Kallias lay with his cheek against the soft sheet, sobbing through agonizing, searing pain.

Then Calvinus put a hand on the back of his neck, and Kallias cried harder. He thought for a moment he would suffocate and throughout all that he remembered when Linux said he saw the light go out that man's eyes when he snapped his neck, and thought that maybe he would be just like that now. And he was just fifteen.

He wept silently, exhausted, when Calvinus took his hand from his neck and gripped his hips, pulling him to a slightly higher angle. He was still wearing his ring, Kallias could feel it digging into his flesh. Just another pain, one after the other. Calvinus pinned him with ease. He was steady and even with the way he moved. He said to Kallias, "You're hurting yourself, you stupid boy. Relax."

He didn't stop, while Kallias just lay there and took it.

Afterwards he lay on the bare floor of the baths and Patroclus knelt beside him with his things to tend him. The household doctor was Greek, like everyone else there who did an important job. He was flushed and there was sweat on his hooked nose. "Oh it's just minor," Patroclus said. "Falls can do that."

Kallias closed his eyes, but immediately in his mind he was on the bed and it was happening all over again. Something in him was all at once stunned and falling apart, all at the same time. He blinked and focused on the high ceiling with the swirling painting of Jupiter fighting Neptune.

Patroclus patched him in the few places where everything hurt and said that it wasn't a good idea to run in the dark. And Kallias only nodded, unable to speak a word.

He hated himself then. He had a bruise on the back of his leg and he had bled. Maybe he should've said something, told Calvinus that it hurt, asked him to stop. But he hadn't. He had just froze. Why hadn't he said anything? So he brought it on himself.

But that wasn't really true either, he thought. Calvinus knew he was crying.

So Kallias didn't know what to think. And mainly he couldn't believe it all had happened so fast and left him so hurt.

But trembling, he still poured the wine the next day. He didn't want to stand too close to Calvinus, but he had to in order to serve him.

Calvinus acted no differently than before. He barely glanced at the bruise, though Kallias knew he could see it and was aware of it. Once, Kallias turned and saw his gaze on the spot. Calvinus must have felt him looking at his face, and looked away immediately with no change of expression and asked Zeno about his guests for today.

Kallias just couldn't believe it had turned out that way. He had always assumed that because of his looks, he'd have fun when he eventually went to bed with his master, not be casually harmed. People always treated him special.

When Demetrius walked in, Kallias couldn't even look him in the eye. There was no mention of learning shorthand. Kallias was in too much pain to talk about anything anyway. He still felt as if he were in a bad dream.

The guests that Calvinus had asked about finally came to the house. One was a merchant, and he had an associate and two burly guards with him. The other was also of the same occupation, but only brought a servant.

Calvinus was supporting the last man, and did all the talking.

Calvinus wanted the others to shut down their company in Pompeii, because he and his friend there wanted to end their competition.

As Kallias stood there, he was certain that everyone could see how shaken and tired he looked. But no one was looking at him. Or Nestor, who stepped forward to right an upturned bowl on the low table. Calvinus put out his hand, the barest gesture, and Nestor moved back into his place near the wall.

"We'll buy the company," said Calvinus then. "We'll buy it and the problem's solved. Just like that. Then you get the money and there's no more issue."

"You mean your problem's solved," said the merchant, seated across from him. "I would only get a lump, you would get my business. This is bullshit, Gaius, and you know it. And besides, we don't take offers under pressure."

"It doesn't matter what you take. It's the best choice," said Manilus, when Calvinus did not say anything. Manilus was one of the merchants. He had an ugly, pockmarked face, and he kept drumming his fingers on his lap. But Calvinus said that if they were thinking about it well, they would take the offer.

Their voices rose. The first man, Endymion, said something particularly sharp and then Calvinus tilted the bowl up and drew out a dagger.

All at once they were talking over each other.

Endymion leapt up, pulling a knife from his own sleeve. Calvinus was still sitting. The other two men scrambled to their feet and backed against their couches—they had no weapons. Their guards, who did, moved in close, blocking them.

And everyone was talking at once.

It was Demetrius who calmed them. He said that none of them were being logical. And that obviously if they all sat and thought about it a while longer, they would come to a better conclusion. Which was obviously to sell.

"Gaius always pays well," he said. "And Manilus was there first after all, so you two can't stay." This he said as if it were the simplest thing in the world, as if his patron's friend's competitors were small children being taught to add.

They put the knives away and the guests sat again. The guards of all the men stepped back with folded arms, to loom near the perimeters of the couches. Calvinus put his dagger down by his side.

Kallias would have thought before that this was all so fun and exciting, but not today. He turned away, blinking puffy eyes.

He waited over the next few days for Calvinus to say something similar to an apology. Masters didn't apologize to their slaves, but this should have been different somehow. The man had fucked him through tears and not once bothered to stop. He thought Calvinus would look at the bruises on him and say, I didn't mean to hurt you, or I should've been more careful with you, but this never happened.

Kallias waited, and waited. They walked past each other, he poured the wine, he stood before the mirror and remembered Calvinus saying: You're the most beautiful boy in Rome. That had to mean something, Kallias thought. Didn't that mean anything?

Kallias had no friends at the house. The other servants saw him as stuck up, someone who was too busy identifying with the master. When he first arrived he had tried a little to hide his disinterest in them, but now he didn't bother. After everything that had happened, they were the people he could afford to be angry with. He slammed doors, never spoke when anyone greeted him, and absolutely could not be convinced to do any sort of chore around the house. Not that he'd ever intended to. But now he had a new and stronger disdain for everything and everyone.

Once he even argued with Petra because she wouldn't give him the cut of bread that he wanted. She had since begun to look at him with a frown on her weathered face. But that was because one day Petra saw her daughter sweeping the floor near where Kallias walked by, and when Elpida spoke to him and touched his arm, he jabbed her in the ankle. He'd known Petra wouldn't like him anymore after that, but he hated everything anyway.

"I'll tell the master you starved me," he said.

"Tell him," she said. "Since you think he loves you so much."

He stormed out, but he didn't tell Calvinus.

Chapter 9

This time when Kallias slipped to see his mother, the doorman let him into the house, where they stood hidden near an alcove. She held him tight and he let her. He'd never admit it, but he wished he could crawl back into her arms and stay there forever. She was the most familiar scent, soft, and warm.

"You look different!" She drew back to take him in. His eyes kept darting away from her gaze.

"I know what it is," she said. "Your hair is longer!"

It was flopping over his eyes and he had to keep pushing it back.

"And you're taller."

When he asked about Rufus, Malika said he'd gone to Greece early.

"Oh," Kallias said. It hurt him that Rufus got to go on and live the life they were supposed to both experience, at least in a similar way.

"He wants to be a man. The master says he's too emotional. Lady Annia was upset because she was thinking it would be later. So we both lost our boys after all."

There was a moment of silence while he fidgeted.

"When you had me, did you hate me?"

"Did I hate you?"

"Yes, did you feel forced to have me?"

"I had a child by someone I worshiped. I never hated you."

They stared into each other's eyes for a moment. Then she knew, and she said, "Oh Kallias," and took him into her arms again. "No, I'm so sorry."

Malika cried as she held him tight and rubbed his back. She told him that men like Calvinus were usually cruel, especially with sex, and that Kallias should try to avoid him in the house.

"I can't," he said, pulling away from her. "I pour his wine."

There was nothing more to say. She stared at him with teary eyes, and pulled him close again. He didn't return her embrace. She was so weak and she couldn't help anything.

But now he was certainly his master's favorite. He was in the dining room every evening, hearing everything that happened, and all the guests got to see him. Calvinus' friends would touch his arm or his side when he stood close to them to pour the wine, and sometimes say things like, 'Where did you get this one from, Gaius?' or 'This one is perfect.' And Calvinus would agree.

"Kallias!" said Sejanus to him one day, as the prefect was leaving the house and Kallias was lounging against a wall near the exit. "You tell your master he has my support all the way for getting that province. Alright?"

Kallias nodded. Sejanus had spoken directly to him, looked him right in the eye. He had spoken to him. So, Kallias thought that there was benefit to all this, still.

And he was given another gift.

Calvinus made Nestor move out his room, which was adjacent to his own. Nestor had to move in with other members of the entourage, and Kallias had a whole room to himself. Nestor kept a blank face as he took his few things and left. Kallias was sure that he complained to Petra and Gaia later, but he didn't care. He didn't need their approval and they had nothing to give him.

They snubbed him, and he walked through the house, flipping his hair and shooting them dirty looks. He heard them say that he was dumb to fall for these gifts and a man who was clearly using him, but they had nothing at all, so who had really won here? When he was free, and elevated above them with an important job, and money, then they would really see.

The only people in the household the master acknowledged were Kallias, Zeno, and Petra. The rest of them were just fixtures and furniture to him. He had the habit, when entering the house, of tossing the nearest servant his cloak and striding away without looking back. They said, If Calvinus has no interest in you, he won't speak to you. He won't even look at your face.

And the boy he's so obsessed with is just as rude as him.

Calvinus was drunk, seated on the couch in his main room, while Kallias poured wine for him. His eyes were red, but he wasn't sloppy because that would've been undignified, and men of his status were never undignified. That was a sin to them. But he was drunk and his temper was always even then. He said, "Come here," and Kallias sat beside him.

"Are you afraid of me?" said Calvinus, drawing him close.

Kallias said no. But his chest was rising and falling fast. He thought it was the wrong answer, although saying yes might also be offensive.

But Calvinus only nodded. He flicked his hand at the silent slave in the corner, and the woman hurried to leave. The door shut, Calvinus turned back to Kallias. There was a towel and oil brought by the servant who had just left. There was always a servant in every corner of the house, waiting inconspicuously to provide something.

Sitting drawn up against the couch arm, Kallias watched Calvinus casually discard his own clothing. Kallias had to admit it, a man should look like that. Fit but not bulky.

Kallias didn't want to upset Calvinus and he didn't want it to be like the first time. He parted his legs willingly. And Calvinus was more patient this time, although he still maneuvered Kallias as if he weighed nothing, and he probably didn't care if Kallias liked it or not. But Kallias tried not to think about that, or anything at all, and went along with it.

In the morning he woke late in his master's bed. He hadn't been kicked out, and he thought that was a good sign that he was rising in favor. Well, secured in it. He was already the favorite, wasn't he? He looked around. Calvinus was gone and the house was no doubt already astir. Kallias sat up, and shrugged to himself and out of a sheet. He felt he had done something wrong, but clearly he hadn't.

Then the memories of the previous night returned. He'd done all those things he did last night with a man who had given him a whole room, and clothes, and a good job in the house. That man was not bald or fat or physically disgusting. And when they first met, Kallias would have done anything for his attention.

But the fantasy was a world different from the reality.

He'd left the wine in the other room when Calvinus invited him to leave with him. It was probably still there in the same pitcher and cup. He wondered how he would feel if he drank. After all, he'd never had expensive wine before. All those times, pouring it but never tasting it. As he crept out the bedroom, he saw a single silver cup on one of the tables.

He gulped down water instead of the expected wine. He threw the cup on the floor and kicked it. He gazed at it upturned, and thought maybe that was the way things would be. Every man was doing that to at least one of his slaves. Since he'd experienced it he noticed it all the time now.

No one would care if he did hate it. He couldn't even decide himself what he felt about it. He couldn't forget either, when Calvinus hit a place inside him that felt so shamefully good, and made his breath catch. His body had betrayed him so easily. He didn't have a choice, and he liked it, anyway.

He'd told his mother too much. She must be making herself sick with worry. The next time she saw him she would probably try to make him tell her everything. That would be horrifying, and of course soon, she'd guess that he enjoyed it. He could never tell her that.

He went a year without seeing her.

She found the house in the end and Zeno came to him while he was in the dining room collecting trays and said, "Yesterday, when you were away, this woman who called herself your mother stopped by with someone called Lady Annia Spinther."

All he said was, "Oh."

Zeno said he'ld find a way to get them together, if Kallias wanted to.

Kallias said he didn't want to.

Zeno raised his brows. "It took them a lot to do this, you know. The trip over here."

"I don't want to see her," said Kallias.

"Your mother, you don't want to see your own mother?"

He stopped with the trays and gave the steward a hard look.

"Kallias, now, there's no need to be spiteful."

"I'm not being spiteful. I just don't want to see her. She's annoying. They both are, and I don't want to see them."

Zeno threw up his hands.

Kallias knew Annia brought Malika to the house out of guilt, because he should have been in Greece with Rufus. He was a house slave, and Spinther watched him grow up. So he should have been in Greece with Rufus.

But Annia and Malika watched their sons do the bidding of the men in their lives who held all the power. And they would not say a word of their own wishes.

Chapter 10

Kallias wouldn't ask Demetrius directly about learning to write shorthand, since that would seem like going over Calvinus. Kallias knew not to try that. Besides, Demetrius worked for Calvinus, not him. And the secretary never seemed friendly, with his narrow eyes and critical musings.

Asking Calvinus was hardly easier, but this time, Kallias would bring the proof that he was really fit for something better. Over the week, he used a new tablet each time he wrote the menu for dinner. The day he decided to ask, he stacked them all and brought them into the dining room and set them on the low center table.

"Master," he said, when Calvinus walked in. He'd just come home. He told the steward to tell the cooks that he had already eaten, but maybe he would have wine. He sat on his couch and looked at Kallias blankly. He glanced at the stack of tablets on the table, but didn't seem to take them in.

"Does Demetrius have to be paid before he does anything?" said Kallias. "Any kind of work, I mean."

"Everybody wants to be paid," said Calvinus. He made a gesture of confusion.

Kallias picked up the tablets then and held them up to show him.

"I really am good at Greek and Latin," he said, "and I just thought, well, that I could be good at shorthand too." He set them down again and put his hands behind him and took a deep breath. "Demetrius could teach me? I know we talked…"

Calvinus took a drink, and put the cup down. He said, with no change of face, "You're very young, give it some time."

"I'd learn fast. I swear it. And then I could help him too, with stuff for you. Or I could go to Tiro's school."

"Take the pitcher back to the kitchen, and don't use that many tablets again. Zeno!"

The steward rushed into the room as if he had been waiting all along.

"Close the house up," said Calvinus, rising and brushing past Kallias. "Early. I'm tired tonight, long day."

"Absolutely, sir," said Zeno.

The conversation ended just like that.

It was so frustrating. Kallias poured wine daily for one of the most powerful men in Rome, and he had nothing real to show for it. He could enjoy all of the things in the house, but he still wanted his freedom and to make something of himself.

He'd have to wait, that was all. Calvinus wouldn't renege. Eventually he'd see that Kallias was capable of more and promote him from the dining room to something that really mattered and give him his freedom.

Meanwhile the book on studying sold well, and Calvinus was very pleased with the fact that all the copies left the house.

Impulsively once, Kallias threw his arms around the man's neck and kissed him square on the lips. They were about to leave for the Games, Calvinus was in a great mood and had just promised to teach Kallias how to bet on the races. The moment was perfect. But instead of an embrace or a kiss back, Calvinus put his hands on Kallias's wrists and peeled him off.

He said, "What are you doing?"

He stammered. He thought it was a nice sign that he was open and receptive to his master. If he were Calvinus, he'd want to know that the slave he was always taking to bed didn't hate him and thought he was nice enough to kiss on the lips.

He thought he should love this, for all the many times he touched him.

"What's wrong with you?" said Calvinus.

"I'm so sorry," said Kallias, and stood back from him and lowered his gaze.

Calvinus stared at him as if he had grown two heads and turned into Janus, and then he turned and Kallias followed him from the room. Kallias touched his fingers to his own lips. If they had a perfect equal relationship where Calvinus liked these kinds of things, they'd do this all the time.

It was so maddening that everything in this situation was going so wrong.

Kallias had never figured out how to talk to him. Because it wasn't that kind of relationship. He poured the wine and he lay on the couch when his master wanted him and he tried not to offend him. And Calvinus smiled at him and ruffled his hair and called him good things. Calvinus always gave him gifts. But he never talked to him like he did his friends or his freedmen or even the steward.

But then Kallias felt he had no idea what to say if he would talk to him because he simply had nothing to offer. What would he say, the wine is very red? My mother says my father was a gladiator? None of that would be interesting to Calvinus and he probably wouldn't appreciate the slave speaking without being spoken to.

So they didn't have real conversations, their interactions could be perfunctory, and Kallias often had the feeling that he was rushing to keep up with him. But he didn't allow himself to focus on that. Once he overheard Calvinus in his office telling Zeno, "Kallias was an excellent purchase, he's very fun and good."

Kallias stood behind the adjoining wall and listened without moving. He thought that was an amazing compliment. Zeno replied, but his voice was quieter and hard to hear. Calvinus said something in return, lower, and they went back and forth until Kallias realized Calvinus was talking about his ex-wife.

"That's the difference between women and boys," he said, very clearly. "Lavinia's just a cold bitch. Some things don't change."

Zeno said something then, but Kallias walked away. He wasn't interested in the divorced wife or whatever comparison Calvinus was making of women and boys. He had heard the compliment for him and that was all that mattered.

Chapter 11

Calvinus got what he wanted: a province. The emperor summoned him and said he was giving him a commission. The prefect Sejanus congratulated his friend on this and said that it had finally happened. He wished him a safe trip.

Tiberius Caesar was the most powerful man in the world but he didn't look like it. He was frail and wrinkled. He lay on a gold-colored couch, propped up with half a dozen pillows. The only robust thing about him were his eyes. Every time anyone in the room shifted, Caesar's eyes would follow the movement.

The Praetorians watched Calvinus hard, even if he was close friends with their prefect Sejanus. Calvinus seemed to note this, and he moved slowly, even when shifting in his official chair where he sat directly in front of Caesar. Calvinus had remarked to Demetrius earlier that Caesar was paranoid of someone taking his spot.

When the Praetorians showed them out, Kallias knew he had to go and see his mother. He had learned that Moesia was far away, north of Macedonia and near the Rhine. Calvinus was taking over after Poppaeus Sabinus, who had run things very well, and Calvinus was expected to leave soon. If Kallias didn't see his mother now, the next time would be four years from now. He couldn't do that even in spite of everything.

He rushed to see her in the morning while the house was still distracted.

His first words to her were, "I'm leaving Rome with Calvinus."

They moved from the hall, behind a column on the edge of the peristyle. He could see people walking in and out of the house. He told her he would be gone for four years. Her face, a series of expressions, finally settled on hurt. She said she'd tried to see him and even the mistress tried to help her.

"I never knew," he said.

"He doesn't hurt you?"

"I'm fine. Stop worrying."

"How can I not? I just want you to be alright."

"Forget it, will you? I'm fine, he likes me."

She folded her arms and stared at him.

"He'll give me my freedom one day," said Kallias. "He really will. He has everything."

"What does that have to do with him giving you your freedom?"

"Well you wouldn't know, would you?"

She tilted her head, and opened and closed her mouth. There was silence. And then. "If only you knew. You think I haven't tried?"

He shrugged.

"You don't understand men like him. I was young as you once, remember? Don't you think I know about his kind? How they use you, discard you?"

After another moment she said, "I wasn't the one who hurt you, Kallias. It was him. You should hate him, not me."

He didn't say anything. Finally she hugged him, held him tight. Then she took his face in her hands. "You know your father was the Phoenix? I hope you're lucky like that. Maybe you're lucky."

He turned, but she was right behind him. "Kallias," she said. He looked at her. She grabbed his arm. "I love you."

He shrugged again, and then he ran out.

The household servants gathered in the atrium while Calvinus explained his commission to them and when he was done they all clapped politely.

"I know some of you will be relieved to not see me for this long," he said, and then laughed at his own joke. No one else did. He ignored the awkwardness and went on talking. Then he pointed out Petra and one of her assistants and said he wanted them with him.

"I'll take Kallias, too," he said, and put his arm around his shoulders. Calvinus was always open with his favoritism. Both out of pride and shame, Kallias made sure not to meet eyes with anyone.

He stiffened when Calvinus pointed out Gaia. Kallias tried not to show it, with his master's heavy arm draped over his shoulder. Calvinus had a casual interest in her. A few times she got on her knees for him or in his bed. He always kicked her out of his room immediately when he was done with her.

She thanked him too loudly. Zeno gave her a hard glance and she went silent.

This pesky little side situation was so irksome. Gaia had dropped flirting with the doorkeeper's son to focus on their owner. Kallias thought it was ridiculous. Gaia was just a girl, so she was unimportant, she could never be promoted, could never be the favorite like him.

He forced himself to keep a blank expression.

Calvinus said that Praxus would oversee them while they were gone and that he could pick whoever else would come, and he left.

After that, Praxus said that nobody had better disappoint him.

"We are not going on a fucking vacation," he said. "Don't even think that you will go there to be lazy birds. We still run a house."

He had a strap on his belt and a house key Zeno had given him. They knew he would enjoy playing Zeno's job in Moesia. Praxus was a big man, constantly huffing, always suspicious of something. He assisted Zeno in running the house in Rome, but liked to overstep by beating on the slaves whenever he was in a foul mood.

He especially didn't like Kallias. He always looked at him with narrowed eyes.

But he was very humble when Calvinus was nearby. He bowed even more than Zeno.

When Praxus was around, Kallias did not tarry. He was also in the habit of leaving whenever his master did. No need to endure their reproachful looks. He rushed from the room.

Earlier that week, Demetrius had brought in a copy of the shorthand textbook and gave it back to Calvinus. The rest had sold. They left the single on the table in the library, and congratulated themselves.

Kallias had been thinking about this ever since. So later when he saw that the main hall was empty, he stole into the room. If Zeno saw him here he would scold him. The servants were not encouraged to poke around these extremely expensive texts. Kallias took the book and slipped out.

Chapter 12

In Moesia, the quaestors came during tax season and Kallias witnessed something unforgettable.

Calvinus and Demetrius had spoken earlier about what they would do.

"I will make me richer, and you richer," Calvinus had told Demetrius, as they stood at an office table and looked through some official papers. Every governor before him, in this province and others, had done what he was going to do, he said. "They'll say Rome is a tyrant," he went on. "But they'll say that regardless. Every ruler's a tyrant to poor, stupid people."

The next day, the quaestors—two fresh, snappy officials recently appointed by the Senate, sat before him working. At first they did their jobs without any disturbance. Then Calvinus told them the current percent that stood already was not enough. He cited the building projects and everything else that needed to be done to keep building up the province.

The quaestors lost some of their confidence. But they obeyed, exchanging glances.

When he ordered them to allot a percentage of this money to his accounts, they stopped. The first quaestor said, "Your account?"

Calvinus made a gesture as if to say, Of course.

"You were already paid on the Kalends of January," said the man, scratching his face.

"And this is for the construction projects," said the second quaestor.

Calvinus regarded them for a moment. Then he said, "Yes, that's what you'll put on the books, but a portion of the money goes to me."

"The people won't respond well to this sudden hike in taxes."

"I have two legions who can put down any revolts from here to Macedonia." Calvinus handed them a paper. "But that won't happen. And the Prefect Sejanus gets his cut, too."

The quaestor looked at it. He looked at it for a very long time and no one moved. Then Calvinus stood. Kallias imagined he saw the lictors move, too, if only a half an inch, with their weapons. Just like all his guards, the lictors were always in tune with Calvinus's movements.

"So," said Calvinus, "how about you get something, too?"

When the question registered, the change on their faces was instantly evident. There were little smiles all around. The second quaestor said, "We were only interested in not being called down for corruption. But we have no issue complying with you."

"Who's going to call you?" Calvinus shrugged. "You set the rates."

The other one laughed and rubbed his forehead. But they had already given in.

Calvinus leaned over and scribbled something up for them on a tablet and handed it to them. They said they would take care of all the rest.

"Now that's how you steal when you do it." Demetrius came in just as they were leaving. He knew it worked when Calvinus made a sign with his hand. But the freedman was staring at Kallias, which made Calvinus glance over his shoulder.

"Don't call it that," said Calvinus, smiling. "Stop gawking, Kallias. They're just a little on the edge about their careers."

He turned from him. "I thought it was strange they tried to refuse. I was surprised."

"They just needed the gentle prodding of a good offer," said Demetrius, standing at the door. "And besides, it's your province. How can they tell you how to run it?"

Calvinus laughed at that and said he was going riding.

"So you can just do this," said Kallias after he went out.

He looked at Demetrius, who was all but gleaming.

"I didn't know you could do that."

"You can do anything you want," said Demetrius. "If you have a legion."

Kallias had never personally met anyone poor, but he was sure they would despise the new taxes and now he understood why rulers were always annoyed with their subjects and calling them trouble-making masses. It was because men who had power did things like this. And then people inevitably hated it.

It was awful. It was equally exciting.

It was exciting and it made him a little more in awe of Calvinus, because it was so deliberately wrong and yet Calvinus did it. He always did what he wanted and took what he pleased. And Kallias wanted to be the same, wished he could go through the world that way too, with no one ever stopping him.

After that, his slavery and his position felt even more frustrating.

Calvinus said the merchants and random travelers passing through would love an invitation to party with a governor, so he began to throw monthly parties. He and his tribunes and his first centurions were always the hosts, and Gaia and Kallias were always in attendance. And there was never any time for Kallias to read the book he stole because he was always trailing Calvinus for all the events.

During the third party, Kallias realized they were out of wine. It was Praxus's fault because he stocked items, but he was nowhere to be found. When Kallias came into the kitchen and saw no wine there, he panicked. He ran down a few hallways and looked into a few rooms searching for Praxus. As he came back to the kitchen, he nearly collided with Calvinus. For him to leave in the middle of his own party was a bad sign.

"Why aren't you in your place?" said Calvinus. "You're late. And where's the wine? People are waiting."

"I was looking for it," said Kallias. "I was—"

Calvinus hit him hard on the side of the head. Kallias saw stars as he sank to the floor to dodge him. He was in a tight space, wedged between him and the table.

"Where's Praxus?" said Calvinus.

While Kallias still crouched, Praxus rushed in to explain. He said some servants were bringing more from the cellar. He apologized profusely, bowing up and down. They ran out because they had already served them three times, but he would make up for all of it with the next course.

"I will fix it immediately, master," said Praxus. "Swear, I swear."

Kallias held his face in his hands and didn't look up.

Calvinus didn't respond and left.

As soon as he was gone, Kallias grabbed an empty pitcher from a shelf and hurled it against the wall. It shattered with a bang that made everyone jump. All eyes were on him in shock. And Praxus came back at just that moment. He scolded Kallias, who didn't reply as he grabbed the wine. Another servant rushed to sweep up the bits.

After the party, Praxus tried to get Calvinus to give him permission to strap him.

"The slaves can't break things, master," said Praxus. Always that wheedling tone. "You know that, they can't break your things."

They'd stopped in the hallway outside the dining room where they had all the parties.

"Just let me give him some strikes, master."

"Absolutely not," said Calvinus. "You touch my boy, you'll be the one getting the beating."

"Forgive me," said Praxus quickly. "Forgive me."

Calvinus glanced at Kallias, a few steps behind him, jerked his head in the opposite direction, and Kallias followed him down the hall.

No one talked about it after, how Kallias lost his temper and broke a cheap pitcher. But by the way they eyed him, clearly they'd been waiting for him to be punished and were disappointed he hadn't been.

But of course not. He was the favorite.

He'd been hit anyway. And it was so unfair that Calvinus could commit actual crimes, while Kallias could be struck for something that wasn't even his fault.

Calvinus was not to be corrected either. Not too long after that, he got a letter from Caesar. Caesar said that he had heard questionable things about him and that he should focus on managing his province with fairness. It was a very scolding letter and should have been enough to crush anyone. Demetrius read this out one morning.

"Who's spying on me?" asked Calvinus, and took it from him and looked at it.

"Always at least someone," said Demetrius.

"It's irrelevant," said Calvinus, tossing the letter across the table. It fell on the floor. Nestor stooped and picked it up and gave it back to Demetrius, who threw it back on the table.

"I'm all the way on the other side of the world, almost hanging off," said Calvinus. "He should be grateful I'm keeping these fucking barbarians off his back. What does he do?"

Meanwhile his friend Sejanus held the capital under his control. They had another letter, this time from him, bragging about how he had saved the emperor's life when a caved ceiling collapsed on them. He wrote that Tiberius Caesar had retired from Rome for good. Demetrius read it out at breakfast.

Sejanus was the most powerful man in the empire now. These days, no one even got an important post in the empire without his favor.

"Caesar's out of the way," said Calvinus. "He's ancient anyway. Sejanus does all his work."

And so Sejanus had said, later in his letter.

"Anyone in the capital can see I'm running it," he wrote. "Tiberius has given up."

Calvinus said, "Everyone but the emperor is running Rome."

Tiberius had been an outstanding general in his day. But he'd never wanted to be emperor, and the men who ran his empire now loved to say disgraceful things about him behind his back.

Chapter 13

Kallias and Calvinus had the same birthday. Kallias found out from a conversation in the kitchen. Petra told Praxus she hoped Calvinus wouldn't make her cook for another party so close to the Saturnalia, but said that he probably wouldn't, because he never did celebrate. Praxus said it was because it was the Kalends, and Kallias said, "That's mine, too!"

They gave him odd looks.

Later that day, Gaia caught Calvinus as he was leaving the governor's residence to go to the fort at Viminacium, only a mile from there. It was a good time, he was alone. His guards and lictors were outside waiting. She said she thought Kallias was lying, while Kallias tried not to laugh, knowing exactly what would happen. She never stood a chance next to him.

"I would happily help you celebrate," said Gaia.

"You already have a bracelet," said Calvinus.

"That's really my birthday," Kallias told him as they walked on, after she left. "I didn't make it up."

"No, I believe you. I believe you."

They came to a portico and the guards stood in the distance. Kallias took his chance. "I didn't know it was yours, too, because you never said."

Calvinus looked at him. Then he said, "I'll get you something."

"You will?"

"We have the same day, of course I will. Am I not always good to you?"

"Always, master," he said, and looked immediately at the ground.

"It'll be a surprise," said Calvinus. "How about that? I'll get you something special. Something you'll love."

Kallias nodded and left.

He was suddenly certain that the gift would be his freedom.

There wouldn't be anything else that could be so special as a single gift, and he was sure that Calvinus knew how much he wanted it. It made perfect sense that it would be his freedom.

Every first of the new year, the legions stood in the fields and renewed their oaths to their legates. Calvinus renewed his own oath to Caesar, and offered sacrifices and wrote letters home. He sent his daughter a large sum of money, arranged by Demetrius. Then he came into the kitchen and talked to Petra.

"Did you know Kallias was born on the same day as me?" he said. "That's a nice coincidence, isn't it?"

"It is," she said.

"My perfect boy, born on the same day as me. I like that."

He told Petra to bake a cake. He was giving Kallias a birthday party. His guards looked on blandly as usual, but the slaves all stared. Kallias caught eyes with Gaia, looking like she'd tasted something sour. He didn't care. He turned around. He was glimmering with satisfaction.

Praxus and Kallias were called to the dining room after Calvinus had his own meal. After Praxus brought the cake, Calvinus ordered him to fetch the gift. Praxus nodded meekly and rushed away, while Kallias sat on the couch close to Calvinus.

Kallias tried the cake. It was still warm, and tasty. Calvinus had cut it in even slices for him. And Calvinus told him he should enjoy his special day. "So yes," he said. "I got you something." He put his arm around Kallias. "You'll love this, you'll love this."

Kallias was eighteen—and it was the first time he'd ever celebrated his birthday. He said quickly that he'd be grateful for anything. Calvinus looked pleased.

Praxus returned, carrying a little ornate box. He wouldn't look at them. Kallias thought now, disheartened, that it was probably not his freedom papers in there. He didn't think they'd fit in a box that small. He was trying to tell but it didn't look like it.

Calvinus went over to where Praxus stood fumbling with the package. Kallias followed him, and stared over his shoulder, hopeful. But Praxus got the box open and Calvinus held out a gold necklace. He put the necklace on Kallias, his fingers lightly brushing his skin.

"Praxus, you like this?" Calvinus turned to the steward.

But the man had already slipped away, leaving them alone.

"Well," Calvinus said. "I like it. I should've given you a necklace a long time ago." He adjusted it on Kallias. "That was what you needed. Now you're complete."

They returned to the middle couch. Kallias held the out necklace as he wore it, studying the links. One of them, engraved in a delicate inscription, had his master's name. Shining gold but not his freedom.

Kallias thanked him, though, as genuinely as he could. He said that it was the best gift he'd ever received and that he'd wear it all the time.

"Of course you will," said Calvinus. He twisted the necklace and examined it himself, while Kallias sat tensely beside him half breathing and unmoving. The door opened again and they looked up at Petra's assistant entering, carrying a plate of food. Wordlessly, he placed it on the table and bowed out.

Calvinus dropped the necklace and turned to drink more wine. Kallias inched forward, reaching for the food, but just as he did, Calvinus pushed the plate out of reach.

"The assistant always cooks too much," he said. "Petra will have to tell him."

"Can I have it?" said Kallias quietly. "I mean, to not waste it..."

"You don't need it, he'll take it back later. And you have cake."

The cake was very light, and Kallias hadn't eaten since noon, and only a little at that, so he was very hungry. But it didn't matter. He stood to pour the wine as usual. He'd just go to the kitchen later and have that plate—and make everyone sick when they saw his shiny expensive gift.

Calvinus pointed to the pitcher then and said, "Drink some. I know you want to."

Kallias drank the wine. It was sweet. He'd tasted it before, but never not furtively, and never this much. He drank it all. Maybe it would make up for his hunger now.

Calvinus said he should drink more, and so he did, until his forehead was hot.

"You just might be the only slave whose master ever said, today is my servant's birthday, I will give him something."

"I'm so grateful. But it's yours, too. Your birthday."

"Yes, that's what makes it good," Calvinus said. "Drink some more."

Kallias poured himself more. He downed two more cups, even as he poured for Calvinus. When he sloshed the last pour, and there were drops on the table, Calvinus told him to sit again. The room was spinning now.

"When I was your age," said Calvinus, gesturing to the wine. "I only drank after I studied. So my father wouldn't be angry. I couldn't fail and make him upset."

Calvinus was getting drunk too, since he only was this conversational when he was. He glanced at Kallias at his side, who nodded with eyes he felt were unnaturally wide. Kallias was trying his best to seem sober, because he didn't want to look stupid in front of Calvinus, who could drink as much as he wanted without falling over.

"I was his only son and his favorite child. So he had these very high standards for me. He was a hard man, the only person I listened to. But that was necessary, certainly."

Kallias didn't say anything. He never knew what to say to Calvinus.

"You know," said Calvinus. "Everyone loved me because of him. I had lots of friends, everyone except my two sisters. We all hate each other, long story." He poured himself his own wine this time and drank. He went on, "But as long as

I studied, and listened to him on the serious matters, he let me do whatever I wanted. Ah, fun memories. Eighteen is a good year."

He gave Kallias another cup. It was just his thoughts out loud, and Kallias probably didn't need to say anything anyway. So he said nothing and he twirled the necklace around his finger and he laughed at something that Calvinus told him. Everything was blurry, he was happier than he had been since forever, and he just couldn't focus. And Calvinus kept talking.

Kallias drank more and more, and in between, Calvinus encouraged him.

Then somehow, he was lying down. There was only the taste of the too-sweet cake in his mouth and the wine and he was drunk for the first time. He was very, very drunk. The only thing he still had on was the necklace, now gathered in a glorious, shining pool on the deep-red cushion beneath him and he lay with his face on the couch.

He couldn't even form a clear thought, he was so drunk. But he understood he must have drank very quickly, and maybe that was bad. He said something that he wasn't sure made sense. He was kneeling now, with his master's hand tangled through his hair, and he imagined a stunned servant, standing in the doorway gaping.

"The wine makes me sick," he said, or at least he thought he said.

Calvinus said something in reply.

When Kallias could finally keep his eyes open, there was a heavy feeling in his head and he was still drunk. In his line of vision sat the plate of uneaten food on the table. He didn't want any now, he was so nauseous. He pulled himself up straight and looked around at the quiet empty room. He really shouldn't have drank so much.

He went to the running water in the baths where he stayed for a long time. He didn't want to leave, he didn't want to finish the night. Everything was flat, weird, and blurry. The necklace felt like a weight around his neck. He swayed for one moment before he steadied himself with a hand on the wall along where the lamps set. He was still drunk, but he would be sober soon.

He lay with his eyes closed too tight when he heard his name being called. He threw off his blanket and went to the entrance of his little room. Calvinus and Jafari and a tribune, all of them looking very tired and quiet, sat slumped in a circle in the sitting area while Praxus stood by the door holding the rest of the uneaten cake.

"You left this," Praxus said, paying special attention to the top of it, like he didn't want to have to look at Calvinus.

"You want it?" said Calvinus, glancing boredly at Kallias.

He shook his head.

"Throw it out."

Chapter 14

At first Kallias was disappointed, but then he thought he was finally succeeding. The gift was clearly expensive, probably the most expensive thing Calvinus had ever given him. So Kallias was certain that now was the time to ask for what he wanted. There couldn't be a better time to appeal to him, when he was at the prime of his youth and beauty and had been given something costly. He didn't let himself focus on other things from that night, how he had been too drunk to think or speak through things he couldn't quite remember.

He went to Demetrius's room and knocked. The secretary let him in, and didn't smile. "What do you want?" he said as a greeting.

Kallias gave him the shorthand book, told him he was sorry he had taken it, and explained why. "I think Calvinus was going to tell you, eventually," he said. "But maybe he forgot because he has so many more important things."

Demetrius grunted, looking at the book. "Maybe." He added, "This is a curious thing to take. I went to Tiro's school and you wouldn't believe how boring it was, the training. But I see you want to learn, hmm."

"So will you teach me? All those things?"

"Ah, well. I write for people who'll understand."

Kallias stared at him. "I'd understand it, why wouldn't I?"

"What does Gaius think of this? Does he know you took his only copy of a very expensive project?"

Kallias didn't say anything.

"I'm not a slave tutor, you know. And if Gaius wanted this for you, he'd have simply told you so, don't you think?"

"I don't know." This came out sullen.

"Well if you don't know, then why don't you just ask him?"

"I already did," said Kallias. "He just forgets."

Demetrius didn't say anything, so Kallias walked out. He couldn't believe it. All this time he thought that he'd simply ask Demetrius and the man would agree to teach him. Because that was the impression Calvinus gave.

He tried to figure out how to mention it again, but it was Demetrius who brought it up later that evening. The dining room was empty and it was just Kallias, waiting with the wine for Calvinus, who studied an official paper, when Demetrius walked in with the book.

"Did you tell him that I'd teach him shorthand?" He sat across from Calvinus.

"What?" Calvinus looked up.

"Kallias thinks you and he made some sort of agreement? For me to teach him."

"Oh," said Calvinus. "There was no agreement."

"But we talked," said Kallias, hating the begging tone of his voice. He gripped the wine pitcher with all the frustration he felt now. "You said to wait, that's all."

It had been three years ago since he first asked. The shock hit him. In another three years, he wouldn't be the wine boy anymore. He would be too old for it, not quite youthful enough to impress the guests. He would probably be too old for Calvinus. He didn't want to be a random slave whose master did not look him in the face. He had seen how it was for Nestor.

He couldn't imagine walking through the house past Calvinus and thinking of how he used to go to him all the time, and then not even being acknowledged by him.

He would rather die. He felt his eyes swimming.

Calvinus said, "You're just so serious about this shorthand thing."

"I have to learn it," Kallias said, blinking back tears. "I can never help you if I don't know how to write it."

Calvinus held out his hand and beckoned him closer until he stood right next to him.

"Tell me, why does my wine boy need to know shorthand?"

A pause.

"You're helping me already."

Kallias nodded, and the lump in his throat swelled.

"You're pestering him," said Calvinus, gesturing to the freedman. "He doesn't want to teach you, he has a lot to do, he's busy. Don't pester him."

"Yes, master."

"Everyone has a place in the house," said Calvinus. "When everyone knows his place, the world works in order. And so does a house. If a cook had to watch the door, the food would burn. My guards don't pour my wine. You understand?"

"I understand."

"You really have to. Everyone has a place, a position. And you have to be where you fit, for everything to work."

Kallias nodded.

"I have as many secretaries and freedmen as I need for whatever that requires shorthand or anything else important. They're intelligent and capable and will take care of whatever I need done. You don't have to worry about it."

Calvinus tapped the pitcher. "You have one very simple job, to pour the wine. Just do that, alright? That's all you need to do. Don't ask this again."

Kallias hadn't gotten anywhere at all since being here. They'd already done the things they wanted to do in their lives, and he was just someone who happened to come along late, begging to join them. And Calvinus could not be impressed, because he already had everything. He didn't care that Kallias wanted to do things now.

He was in his forties and so was Demetrius. None of their associates were younger than that and none of them were just starting out. Meanwhile, Kallias had just turned eighteen. So he was just the wine boy and to them that was what all he would always be. Just the boy who came to the house and inevitably got tangled with the master.

He'd never changed in their perceptions since the first day. He'd waited and waited for Calvinus to treat him better, to speak to him about things that really mattered, to value him for more than his looks. It never did happen. It wasn't going to happen either, because that wasn't the trajectory of this relationship. The necklace he wore, he received on a night when he'd been made to drink to the point of helplessness and then used as nothing more than a plaything. All those other times too, he'd been used easily, casually, without regard—like a plaything. That was really what he was, and there was no future here.

For the first time, he saw it for what it was.

Chapter 15

There were merchants who came through the fort everyday and talked about the travel routes. Listening to them, Kallias realized exactly how close this location was to being on the edge of the empire. He got an idea then and he knew he had to do it. He would do it regardless of what happened to him after.

He found his first opportunity when he went to take a message for Calvinus. He detoured after and stopped by a jeweler in the city. He figured it was the right shop. The man took the necklace and smiled and said, "I sold this to the governor seven months ago! He gave you this?"

"How much is it worth?" Kallias asked.

The jeweler told him. His jaw dropped.

The necklace was worth enough money to last him for a year.

Maybe more, if he was close with it.

Regardless, he could live on it without working and until he reached a safe place. And so he decided he'd run.

He had to be free of Calvinus. He could hardly stand to look at him anymore.

He allowed himself to thoroughly soak in his resentment. This resentment was so palpable, so physical, it was like a wall between them. And Calvinus knew it too, must have felt it, but had the upper hand, as he always did, so didn't care.

But Kallias could no longer disguise his sullenness. He wouldn't speak. He stood stiffly when he served the wine. He could have gazed at his master's solid chest while Calvinus was in bed above him, could have glanced up at his intent blank expression, but he would turn his face away. He would look at nothing, hating himself, hating Calvinus, hating these meaningless physical acts that always made him hate himself and Calvinus, each time even more than he thought was even possible.

His life would be wasted, he'd go crazy if he stayed. He had to run.

When the next merchant caravan came through the fort, he befriended the man's son and asked where they were going.

"Philippopolis," said the son, Amenos. He was around Kallias's age, and maybe they would have been friends if he were a normal boy who could have friends.

"I want to go," said Kallias, standing across from him, at the back of a wagon. His father came through to the fort because he wanted to know if he could make a contract with the legions, said Amenos. And he was delivering some fabrics for his father because he wanted to travel the world and not just sit at home.

"How will you go?" Amenos asked. "Do you really think you can pull that off?"

"Yes," said Kallias, laughing and faking confidence. "I know I can. I just have to move quickly. Let me go with you, and I'll give you a fifth of the money that this necklace is worth."

Amenos gazed at the necklace. "I've never even had something so expensive myself," he said. "And my father is doing very well in business!"

Kallias shrugged.

But Amenos said he would sneak him with him. He liked Kallias and he thought he was very worldly because he was from Rome and he was associated with the governor of the province. Amenos had never been to the capital. Kallias wouldn't tell him everything, and he certainly wouldn't tell him that sometimes the city was not as beautiful as everyone said it was, and that there were parts that were filthy and poor.

He also didn't tell him that the necklace that was going to be his freedom was really just a symbol of his servitude and not a real gift at all. People who were never in that kind of situation wouldn't understand that gifts were never free.

"You can come," said Amenos to him the next day, and Kallias said he only had to know how. They came up with a plan. Kallias would have to wait until the very last minute when they left to leave with them, or else he would be missed.

The next morning, Kallias faked illness. Patroclus looked at him, and said that he did look unwell, and so everyone left him alone. After that, Kallias got up and took a heavy cloak and put the necklace into its pocket and slipped out. It was hardly daybreak. Calvinus was probably in a meeting. No one would be checking on him so early.

Kallias was sad thinking about it. He'd never see his mother again, and he'd failed in every way. There was none of the glory he had imagined when he first came to the house in Rome and looked at a man who made him feel real awe for the first time.

Amenos waited for Kallias at the end of the street. They went to Amenos's house, where his father paid them no mind. They had a handful of slaves helping load materials. And Kallias blended in well as everyone rushed around to finalize the start of the journey. It was time for them to leave almost as soon as they arrived.

Amenos had a cart and Kallias rode with him all day until they reached Serdica.

"You have such an accent," said Amenos, flicking the reins. "It makes me really want to see Rome even more."

"Maybe you can go one day," said Kallias.

"Where will you pawn the necklace?"

"When we get to Philippopolis, I thought you knew. I said it before."

"Oh I see."

"I can't do it anywhere near here. His name is on one of the links."

They rode on. It was exhilarating, except for when legionaries passed by them and Kallias would lay on the floor of the cart. Amenos laughed and laughed at this. He said, "I can't believe I am doing this, but I always wanted to do something extremely foolish."

And it was extremely foolish. He'd be in a lot of trouble if it was discovered that he had aided a runaway, and one from the governor's household no less, but Amenos was up for it anyway. He wanted excitement.

"If we're caught," said Kallias. "Just say you're returning me."

The other boy thought this was a good idea.

The caravan went on for miles.

"Soon," said Amenos, "we'll be in another province!"

They didn't stop. They lumbered on with the men who helped move the caravan, and the horses, and the rest of the goods. Every time they passed legionaries, Kallias leaned down low.

Chapter 16

There were too many soldiers in Remasiana, so Kallias made the decision to split with Amenos. They agreed to meet again in the next city or on the road. "I hate to leave you," said Amenos, but Kallias knew he was thinking about the money. Nobody ever did anything for anyone else for free.

"Remember, I'll meet you two hours from now," said Kallias.

"By the city gate."

"Yes." And they looked at each other for a while, before parting.

At this point, he believed might actually escape. He tried to imagine how it would be when he was really free. He looked at the road and the sky and he wondered why some people had to be born in positions that made them under the will of others. That would not be him, not any longer.

Legionaries caught him on the road with a man and a cart—he told the man that he was a merchant's son and would pay him handsomely, but he had been waylaid by the thieves—and stopped them.

They pulled the man off the cart and kicked him while he lay in the dirt. They searched Kallias for the necklace, and took it and the cloak and dragged him back to a nearby fort where they kept him for the night.

In the morning, he leaned against the iron bars of his cell and felt stupid. It wasn't as though he was going to ever get very far, and his master controlled the whole province. He slid to the floor and held his head. There was no one around here either. The outside of his cell faced a bleak wall.

He got strikes with the strap instead of the whip, but it still hurt. He was lying on the floor. The centurion who ordered the beating said something and then he left and the door clanged shut. Then it opened again and someone else said, "My apologies again, sir, for his trouble..."

Calvinus was there, like the worst vision.

Kallias knew it was him by the way he was standing. And the voice. Always used to giving the orders. He said, "A damaged slave's a waste of money. He must not have a single scar. Welts will go down easily."

Someone murmured a yes, and then snapped at his assistant.

Patroclus the doctor. Here to patch him up again. There was rummaging, and then either Patroclus or the assistant rubbed a salve on his back.

Kallias sat alone after that, having a queasy feeling that there was something else coming, because for all he'd done, he'd only been strapped for it, and he was still in this cell.

The day turned into another. He wondered what would happen to him. He tried not to think about it.

Jafari and Atis stood at the cell door, unlocking it. They were carrying thick silver chains. Kallias shrank back against the wall, which was cold, but he was sweating. They didn't look at him. They lay the chains on the floor. He had watched them hard, and closed his eyes when they dragged him forward. They hung him from a hook in the ceiling, his wrists in metal connected to chain.

"No, no," he pleaded, when they stepped back.

Jafari grinned. "Your master don't like that you take his gifts and try to sell them."

"You don't ever make him mad," said Atis. "That's the first thing you should've learned, not to make him mad."

He kicked Kallias in the shin and they left.

For the first few seconds it seemed endurable. A minute later Kallias thought he was going to die. His arms burned in a tight ache that spread all over to his shoulders. Combined with the pain in his back it was unbearable. Every time he tried to stand and put some of the pressure on his feet, he was held by the chain, away from the floor.

He didn't know time like this. He was sobbing. He thought of his entire short life in that moment, and as the agony burned through him he wished he'd never lived. He wondered how he went from the boy whose master gave him the set of brand new clothes, to swinging from his wrists by hooks in the ceiling.

He had no idea how long it was when Jafari and Atis came back and took him down. He dropped to the floor, sobbing.

"It was only ten minutes," said Linux, who was with them this time. He squatted next to him, and shook his head. "And you acted like you were dying. You would've if we left you up! But that's what he wanted you to think."

"He'll be here in a bit," said Atis. "Smile at him when you see him, you know he took a lot of time just to come back up here, don't you?"

Calvinus came in a few seconds later, with Praxus and two real soldiers. Kallias was sitting on the floor, wiping his face with his sleeve and his hand.

"I kept looking for you," said Calvinus, "and kept remembering that you'd run off." He paused, hard-eyed with something else in his gaze. "You know I was all about you, Kallias. You were special. I liked you."

Kallias blinked at him, focused on the floor.

Calvinus stepped closer. The guard pulled Kallias to his feet. Cradling his wrist, Kallias raised his eyes to look at his master. Calvinus took his chin in his hand.

"I gave you everything," Calvinus said. "But you were so ungrateful."

"Please don't hurt me anymore," Kallias whispered. "Please."

"You did it to yourself, boy."

The room was quiet for that moment.

Calvinus waved his hand. "Praxus, get him presentable."

Chapter 17

They didn't sell him in the provinces. He was a runaway, but the dealers thought they could wait and get the most for him in Rome. So Kallias came back to Italy again. He was sold within two days, to the house of Lucius Domitius Ahenobarbus. Kallias heard the name and figured just another powerful and wealthy Roman, although where Calvinus had his connections with Prefect Sejanus, Ahenobarbus was close to the imperial family.

In Ahenobarbus's house, Kallias was a regular slave. He stayed in a communal room with other slaves, and learned to wash dishes, mop floors, and dust furniture. It was a far fall from his former position, and he realized how little he had worked before. Bringing wine and carrying a message was hardly work.

Whenever the steward, Polycarp, would assign him to a task, he would say, "Yes, sir," without the slightest hesitation. He was not about his looks so much more either, seeing as they had never really bought him anything but pain and abuse. He worked hard, and walked fast.

He saw Ahenobarbus in the house one day. Ahenobarbus was looking for his cloak because he was going to take his chariot out. He had a cold and he blew his nose in his hand and then wiped it on Polycarp's sleeve. Polycarp didn't flinch. He said Kallias was one of the new slaves. Kallias didn't even try to get a good look at the man. He just said, "I am happy to serve you," and kept his gaze on the floor.

Ahenobarbus wasn't interested in him in the least. He only liked a few things, mainly his chariot and wine and some of the slave girls. He just waved his hand at Kallias. And all for the better. Kallias didn't desire to be noticed by Ahenobarbus. He had no reason to want to accompany another master and learn his ways. He'd served an envious little boy and a cruel man, what would he want to do with a boor like Ahenobarbus?

Kallias knew he should see Malika, but put her off. He couldn't let himself worry, he didn't have a place in his heart for any more pain. He tried not to think of anything. He was so beyond any real feeling by then that he was just walking and doing things out of habit. He told himself that one day he'd find her, but not just yet.

He had to let it wear off, everything that happened. It would be so humiliating on top of everything to tell her just how hard he failed with Calvinus. The first few days of being there and thinking, he is going to like me and trust me because I'm pretty. That was the thinking of a child.

The other servants were interested in him. They wanted to know where this good-looking boy with the impeccable manners came from. He'd learned by then to be nice even if he was agitated, and when they plied him with (what he thought were inappropriate) questions he told them his old master died and he was simply resold again.

"Fate," he said.

They said, "Oh yes, that is how it is. Be thankful regardless."

He said, "Yes." Even though he did not believe this and never would. He would never believe in being thankful for his lot in life beneath others.

There was a boy named Dion who clung to him.

Kallias was neutral to avoid making enemies, but he tolerated Dion. He was eleven years old, had been born in the house, and was self absorbed, which was to be expected at his age. But he was extremely friendly and everyone liked him and Kallias didn't mind him.

Dion moved his sleeping mat next to Kallias's and constantly tried to talk to him. He wanted to be around him all the time.

"What's your secret?" he asked Kallias one day.

"What secret?" Kallias said.

"Being perfect," said Dion. "Everybody wants to know about you because you seem so perfect."

Kallias had been popping his knuckles, standing back to examine the Lares he had been cleaning. He had not heard Dion coming. He glanced back at him.

"People aren't perfect," he said.

When Dion stood before mirrors, he lingered long. He was in love with his own face. Everybody pointed out how his cheekbones were so high and fine and how his dark skin was so shiny and clean looking. The pretty house girls tickled him and petted him and told him they wished he were a doll so they could carry him around. His hair was the tightest little coils in a low shape on his head, and they touched it all the time too.

He would put his arm beside Kallias's arm and say, "Look, I'm the moon and you're the sun. See?"

Kallias looked so white beside him, and he always laughed when Dion did that.

But when he saw the boy before the mirror, Kallias would shake his head and say, "No one cares about that but you."

Dion always complained. He put his tongue out when he had to sweep. He groaned when he was sent to the cellar to bring wine. At night, he wanted to sneak out for food in the pantry and when Kallias advised him not to, he pouted.

"You want them to whip you?" Kallias would ask, joking. Nobody ever lost patience with Dion because he was a child and they excused him for everything.

He broke a vase once—he was very clumsy—and the steward Polycarp just said, "Run away before you get in trouble."

"The master wouldn't have it," Dion would say. "He always gives me the pomegranates on his plate. Besides, it's not really stealing. I'm just hungry."

Dion thought Ahenobarbus would never hurt anyone. It was going to be an interesting day when the boy began to see beyond just a pomegranate. He probably hadn't noticed yet either how often his sister was called to the master's rooms. Or if he did, he didn't care.

Irene was probably seventeen, and had the same stark beauty as her younger brother, except her hair was much longer than his, and always swinging in braids. She could never sit still around the other servants—she was always tapping her fingers or her sandals or fiddling with her dress. She wasn't talkative either, like Dion.

Ahenobarbus would give her arm bands—she had a new one all the time—and she would exchange them for coins. Kallias knew it because he stepped down into the cellar once and interrupted her counting her stash. She hadn't been able to even attempt to hide it. He said, "I saw nothing, you love his gifts."

"They're just bangles," she snapped, but she was clearly wrecked with nerves.

He turned and left without taking the case he had come down for.

He thought Dion definitely didn't know about all that.

Ahenobarbus kept a cold, and had sneezed on Polycarp and Kallias several times.

That was probably on purpose. Ahenobarbus thought it was funny when other people were uncomfortable. The thing about Calvinus, he wouldn't hurt his slaves unless they crossed him, but other than that he ignored them. But Ahenobarbus liked to hurt his slaves for fun. And when they heard his heavy footsteps rounding on them, they would flee. No one wanted him to casually bop them with his meaty fist, just for having the wrong expression. So they all cowered and avoided him.

Except Dion, because every time Ahenobarbus saw him he gave him a penny or a fruit. To him, Ahenobarbus must have been something paternal. Brusque, gruff, but paternal. Dion must have thought that as long Ahenobarbus treated him well, there was no reason to care about anyone else. And Kallias understood it, he understood it all so perfectly.

Chapter 18

Ahenobarbus came striding into the house one day with his tunic spattered in blood. The household slaves looked at him aghast, and no one moved. His attendant came running in after he left, with his hands over his mouth, and blurted, "He ran over a child, he hit a child in the road and didn't stop. He ran over a child."

They were all gaping at the man, who looked as if he might burst into tears. He said, "His bones! You heard it crunch."

Dion, next to Kallias, said, "Do you really think that happened?"

But the master's clothes had blood all over them. And, of course, it was true, because then everyone was talking about it, and the mother of the child came to the house and wanted to speak to him, and she was sobbing and pleading in the entrance.

The doorkeeper told her to get the fuck out of there before he put his foot up her ass. She sobbed and begged, on her knees.

"No one cares about your brat," he said. "Now go on before I really do it."

Later Kallias went down to the street where they said it happened, but by then someone had gathered the mangled body.

He ought to speak to his own mother soon. But he still didn't have the courage to look at her.

Polycarp found out he could read. This was because he was in the kitchen and he wrote something on the tablet for the cook who told him to remind her to ask Polycarp for something later. Polycarp said, "I didn't know you were literate!"

When Kallias was sold, he read his own placard that stated he was temperamental but good for a household. That was nearly the exact description. For some reason nothing about his literacy, and of course the dealers hadn't told people he was a runaway.

Then Polycarp said, "Well, it's no more dirty dishes on trays for you."

"It isn't?"

"Of course not. You can help me around the house. We'll make a good team."

Kallias walked out past Dion, leaning on the doorway and chewing on an apple core. His brown eyes were wide.

"You can write?" He fell in step beside Kallias. "That means you won't be doing simple things anymore?"

"Not really," said Kallias. "I just help where I can." He was supposed to go to the pharmacy for Ahenobarbus to get something for his stuffy nose.

"Can I come with you?"

Soon Kallias did all that Polycarp dreaded, and all that Ahenobarbus' secretaries would not do. He mainly wrote the shopping lists and tallies for inventories, so Polycarp could simply stroll in and say, "Oh, it looks right. That's the amount of the supplies we have."

Kallias learned he was good at counting. He could remember numbers in order. When he discovered this he began to feel better about himself in general. Then he started to carry a wax tablet to write down the costs of all the household purchases.

It had been one of Polycarp's jobs, but then the steward told Kallias that the less he documented, the clearer he could think, and the clearer he could think, the smoother he could run the household.

"That makes sense," said Kallias, although it really didn't.

And he did his job. How was the condition of the roof of the house? Polycarp would send a servant up, and the servant would bring a report. Kallias would write it, Polycarp would give it to Ahenobarbus. How were the servants' clothing? Kallias would go around to check, Kallias would write a report, Polycarp would give it to Ahenobarbus. And that was how it went with everything.

The only things Polycarp would not allow Kallias to touch were the account books. No one touched them but Ahenobarbus, his secretaries, and Polycarp. "You just focus on helping me," the steward told him. "And don't you worry about the major stuff."

He was still a lowly slave, just one who could help with some things around the house. But he didn't mind this. He wanted more than anything now to be left alone and to do his work without being noticed.

Chapter 19

The first time Kallias ever laid eyes on Julia Agrippina, she'd come to the house to visit. She was engaged to marry the master, and when the steward was notified that she would come, he made everyone clean the house from top to bottom. Julia Agrippina was important. She was the emperor's niece and the daughter of the famous general Germanicus. The household's presentation must be excellent for her.

That meant every alcove swept and every column polished. Kallias, tasked with marking off completed assignments, knew better than to play overseer. In each room, he set aside his tablet and joined in the work.

He'd once heard a slave say to another, "The new Greek fellow they brought in is really decent. Helps Polycarp, but nothing like him."

Kallias liked to keep that picture of himself. It would never do to seem like a lazy cat, spoiled and full and worthless.

He also couldn't bring himself to slow down from working. If he took a break, he might start thinking about old, bad things. He wanted to forget the last house as soon as possible.

Then Julia Agrippina came. It was noon, earlier than what she had suggested, and Ahenobarbus was not home. Everyone gathered around the door to see her. As she descended the litter, one of her servants offered her his hand but she waved it away and half leapt down, not bothering to pretend to be a delicate daughter of Rome.

For the emperor's niece, she was dressed plainly. No jewelry, clothes of excellent material but simple style. No elaborate hairstyle to put her neck in a cramp. But she had a pretty little dignified face.

In the atrium, standing behind a flustered and pandering Polycarp, Kallias could see her clearly.

She was so young! She was just a girl.

She played with her hair a few times, but still she was far more composed than most children her age, and then she smiled at Polycarp's bow, and said in a clear voice, "It's fine. I never told Gnaeus I'd stay. I'm going to visit my sister anyway. But this feels foolish! He's very busy?"

"Oh, oh, I'm just disturbed," Polycarp said. "You took your time to visit and he's not here!"

"I said it was alright," said Julia Agrippina. She met eyes with Kallias just then, for a long moment. Then Polycarp offered her a cup of water or wine.

But she was already turning around and her servants swallowed her up.

Later, one of the slaves gossiped that she was only trying to be polite. The emperor ordered her to marry Ahenobarbus and she was nicely trying to visit him, but when he was absent she hadn't taken it to heart because she hadn't cared about him.

She had been ordered to marry him. She had no choice. Of course she didn't care about him.

November of the next year, they were married in a joyless ceremony. Agrippina's face was a frightened shade of white throughout the entire event. She had none of the performed confidence from her first visit. And her new husband looked annoyed every time he glanced at her, as if she were an interruption to his life.

"She didn't look happy," Dion whispered to him later that night as they lay on their mats close together.

Kallias opened his eyes. "She was fine," he said. "She's just young."

Dion paused, and then giggled. "Do you think Ahenobarbus has her Herculean knot untied yet? He has thick fingers. He might be struggling."

Kallias began to laugh, then he thought about probably how she was feeling, and stopped himself and said, "That's rude to say. Go to sleep."

At first she was a regular girl who had nothing to say. She was proper and polite as any high-class girl would be. She never really changed her expression, which was this keen stare. But she loved wine: the servants were always bringing different samples to her.

"Really," Kallias heard her saying once when he passed the dining room. "I may as well do everything I couldn't do before."

And she enjoyed her matronly privileges, ordering servants about the house, drinking whenever she wanted, and sleeping past noon. There was no mother-in-law to keep her in check, to remind her that she needed to get out her loom or keep up an appearance of virtue. Her husband didn't know that she was drinking and sleeping in, because he was usually away throughout the day.

Whenever he returned home, she would be standing appropriately somewhere near the dining room waiting to greet him politely. Once he said, patting her on the head, "Is this what you do all day, stand here like a little, weak-eyed, lost puppy?"

Her face drained. "I thought that's what you wanted, I..."

He grunted and strode past her.

Julia Agrippina was truly on her own. She was fourteen years old. Maybe she didn't love her husband of six months, but marrying him brought its benefits. She kept on drinking the same amount of wine and sleeping past noon everyday. And trying her best to appear perfect and domestic before her Ahenobarbus. And she never talked too much.

Kallias thought she was simply going through every day the same way he was—without much thought.

As Kallias walked by the sitting room one day she called him. She lay on the couch with an empty plate near her head. As he came close, she saw the tablet in his hands and said, "Oh, never mind. You're busy."

He said it was alright.

She wanted him to kill a fly that kept buzzing around her head.

He sucked in a sigh and glanced around for something. Agrippina's maid stood behind the couch, and Kallias thought Agrippina should make her find the fly.

She must have felt some of the impatience he thought he hid so well, or maybe she felt guilty for stopping him from doing what looked like important business. "No, go ahead." She sat up. "Call one of the little boys doing nothing."

As he turned she stopped him again.

"Aren't you Polycarp's assistant?"

He affirmed it.

"What's your name?" she said. "I see you all over my house."

She held his eye and studied him with a clear gaze, as if she already knew him well. He did not find it hard to look back at her, either.

In May, she and Ahenobarbus packed up to travel to their second home in Anzio.

"Polycarp," Ahenobarbus said, "you and your fellow here keep the house. Agrippina and I want to be out of the way of the heat."

Agrippina took half the kitchen staff with her, saying she couldn't trust the cooks at Anzio because she'd never eaten their food. Dion, who somehow secured himself a place in Agrippina's group, slipped away with them. Maybe it was because his sister Irene had found herself a spot as one of the new mistress's personal attendants. But as he was, Dion probably only wanted to be away from Rome for once.

With the master and mistress away, the house was very slow. Finally, Kallias went to find Malika. He walked to Spinther's house—he still remembered the way. And there was a new doorkeeper, younger and friendly and more understanding.

All Kallias wanted to tell her was that he really did love her, of course he did because she was his mother. And that he was sorry he treated her so badly. He also wanted to tell her that she was right, that she was right about everything and he should have valued her more.

But there was no Malika, not anymore.

"Oh," said the doorkeeper, after he went and found out for him. "She died two years ago. There was a fever everyone had."

Kallias walked home with his head down. But there was nothing to really do for it, and he had to move on. He felt guilty for even wishing she were still alive. He'd acted as if he didn't care when she was.

He did nothing that summer but meander. Once, he got with a young senator and let the man fuck him in the hot room of the baths. It was a simple decision, made by a few long glances and a shrug. But he hated the way the man gripped his hair, and then he realized he hated the whole degrading thing. That was the day he decided he would never again be a man's boy. He would never have power just by being with someone who had it. He wanted his own.

So he cut his hair short, and when he put his hand on his head he did not miss what used to be there. He had to grow up at some point. It didn't matter that he was a slave, and that submission was expected of him. He was not like Gaia, or Malika, or Irene, they had to take it regardless. He would grow into a man.

He would never again take the shameful lower position. And with this new look, no one would mistake him ever again for that type of boy. No matter that he was a slave. He was going to do something different in the household of Ahenobarbus.

Chapter 20

Instead of staying only for summer as Ahenobarbus had said, he and Agrippina did not return to Rome until the fall of the next year. The servants gathered in the atrium and Kallias only looked for one person, his little friend with high cheekbones. He only cared about Dion because there was no one else to care about.

Kallias was not the only one who changed. He saw Agrippina before he saw Dion, and she was a shock, so tall and grownup. It was the first time he had ever seen her so expressive. She had her hand on her husband's arm and she laughed at something. Ahenobarbus grinned, too. Even the maids wore soft smiles, and the attendants glowed. When the chatter mellowed, Ahenobarbus said, "Polycarp! Been keeping house?"

Polycarp bowed again and again, beaming. Ahenobarbus, in his usual way, interrupted him. He clapped Polycarp so hard on the shoulder he sagged.

"Agrippina brought your cooks back," he said. "I thought somebody was going to get killed, up there in Anzio."

Agrippina giggled. They were joking with everyone. "Our trip was good for Gnaeus. He hasn't had a cold in months. It was the fresh air."

Polycarp cleared his throat. "If I may say, you stayed away for a long time."

"We went to Greece," she said, laughing.

"We went to Greece!" The first thing Dion said when he greeted Kallias by flinging his arms around him. "It was so exciting!"

Kallias kissed him on the forehead. He said, "I know. Sounds fun."

"See, I pierced my ear?" Dion turned his head to show him the little silver stud. "Irene got it done, we went to this shop. The mistress paid for it. She'll get me whatever I ask for."

Then looking at him. "You look different! You look old. Not in the bad way, Kallias. Old in a good way."

Agrippina had changed with her husband. Servants talked about seeing them strolling through the gardens together, flowers in Agrippina's hair, Ahenobarbus whispering Propertius, giggling and laughter. And the house was light with their bawdy jokes. The first time Agrippina cracked a raunchy quip, Kallias had reeled, but now he figured Ahenobarbus had found, despite its arrangement, his match.

Because the servants never stopped gossiping, he heard two things now: that she was pregnant, and that she was faking her happiness. He paid attention to the latter rumor, and decided that all the laughter and joking really was just an attempt for Agrippina to match her husband's humor, to keep him happy and avoid his displeasure. Often when they laughed, her face would change to straight again no more than two seconds later.

That gossip was true, too, because once the master said to his wife, "You know, Julia Agrippina, I made you a much funnier girl than you were before you married good old me!"

He slapped her arm. Agrippina smiled, laughed loudly, and the expression was gone in an instant.

So they were faking their happy marriage.

As for the pregnancy rumor, Kallias thought she seemed exactly the same, but he knew nothing about those things and didn't care either so maybe it was true.

One day Chloe requested him to the mistress's private rooms. Agrippina had never asked for him there so that was interesting. Chloe led the way down the hall, her sandals slapping on the floor. She always walked very hard, as if she wanted people to hear her coming. She was a typical slave, gossipy, always blank-faced in front of her masters, usually petty with fellow servants. He imagined she must be eighteen or nineteen years old, a bit older than Agrippina.

Agrippina's rooms had a sense of quiet and comfort, and Agrippina lay on a plump couch with two of her other girls and Irene leaning on either end of it.

The first thing Agrippina said was, "Were you busy?"

He assured her he wasn't.

"Wonderful," she said, clapping twice. "I called you because you can read very well." She smiled. "Obviously, I can too. But it's a good slave's job."

He was confused, and she held up a scroll.

At the first line, they all tittered. They were all laughing when he was done, and he had to smile at it too. It was so dumb.

"Sorry," he said. "But why do you read this? It's bad."

"Because it's stupid," she said. "Here, sit down."

She pointed him to the low stool in front of the couch.

"I'd like for you to read some more." She sat up, swinging her bare feet over the couch. "I couldn't get anyone to do it. You can forget Polycarp. Lazy, that one."

"It's not my place to say."

"Well, I can say it. I've been noticing how much he pushes for perfection in the housework. That's because he never lifts a finger himself to help. It's like screaming for a mountain to move, instead of getting to work digging. How did he get to be the steward anyway, I was wondering?"

Kallias said he didn't know.

After that conversation, Chloe smiled at him whenever she saw him. Since he cut his hair, he found that women assumed he liked them more, and so they began to acknowledge him in a way that was not just girlish admiration. In the past, they'd probably thought he wasn't for them.

Chloe was very pretty, and he'd never tried a girl. There had never been any chance for that. But he'd always liked them and he liked this one a lot and it was convenient. Agrippina thought that it would be funny. "She'll do anything," she whispered to him about her maid. "I've seen it myself."

So Kallias and Chloe got together over and over. They would sneak to Agrippina's rooms to have sex. He liked that he could switch it, and do to her all the things he used to have done to him, or what he watched happen to other slaves. She always smiled at him through the day, but he never took her as anything more than something to relieve his stress on.

He saw the way she gazed up at him when he fucked her, and he thought that was a bad sign. She was confusing the physical with the emotional. He never really meant to hurt her though. It was just something to do to feel good, and she was the instrument to use.

"You stay in the communal room?" said Agrippina, when she learned it. "What, an assistant to Polycarp?"

Sometimes, he didn't read and they just talked. Agrippina plied him with questions about the household. They walked through the rooms, and he introduced her to servants; he showed her where the pots were kept in the kitchen, and where the letters sat on the office table, and how the servants kept their quarters, and which keys went to which rooms, and how the bath was cleaned.

She said it wasn't fair for Kallias to stay in the common quarters, so she gave him his own little spot.

Ahenobarbus was busy with his consulship that year, so he was hardly at home during the day. When he did come home, for dinner, he often brought a prominent guest, some praetor or senator or even ex consul, to discuss some important law, and leave a trail of attendants lounging in the atrium.

Agrippina acted delighted to play hostess to these powerful men. She was always smiling and graceful, an appropriate wife. But her eyes never changed—she always looked at all of them as if she were trying to read them, as if staring long enough at them could make her see through them.

Since he was more perceptive now, Kallias recognized her look as calculating. "I'm so happy for Gnaeus," she said to Kallias. "But we have to know who our enemies are, that's important for our safety. "

In the meantime, Lucius Aelius Sejanus grew more powerful than ever. There were statues of him everywhere. Every time Kallias went to the Forum, he saw the prefect's name in the Dia Acturna. Sejanus's birthday had even been declared an official holiday. Most recently, Caesar had written a letter addressing him as 'my partner in toils.'

The men who came to the house talked about Sejanus often. No one seemed to finish a sentence without mentioning his name. Every time they did, a strange look would come over Agrippina's face. Once, a senator said that Sejanus was probably an inspiration to many men, and Agrippina stopped drinking her wine and sat still for a long time. She could fake loving Ahenobarbus, but she couldn't fake her expression when someone mentioned Sejanus.

There was something about that man that made her miserable.

She walked out of the dining room that evening with gritted teeth, and Kallias just so happened to be standing near the door now. They stopped and looked at each other. She said, "You're right, I'm not a good hostess."

"I didn't say that, " he said. "Why would I say that?"

"Because just the mention of him and I have to storm out without saying something."

He noticed she was shaking.

"You don't like Sejanus, do you?"

She took a deep breath. The attendants standing at a distance stared at them, but could not hear what they said. She said that was an understatement.

"I knew him," he said suddenly. "He doesn't seem likable."

That was not exactly true. It hadn't been true at the time anyway. Sejanus was charming and that was a part of why the emperor liked him so much. But he was the close friend to someone Kallias could barely stand to think of now.

"He's not likable at all." She stopped. "I have to go back in. But we have to talk about this later. You know him! I didn't know you know him!"

Kallias was breaking his rule of keeping his head down at the house. He wasn't sure if he wanted to know why Agrippina had it out for the Praetorian prefect. But he'd already said too much, and he did want to know what her issue was with him.

Agrippina came back after everyone was gone from the dinner. They stood in the empty vestibule. She laid it all out. She told him how Lucius Aelius Sejanus, this jumped-up equestrian, had made a name for himself by reforming the Praetorian Guard and squaring up opposite her father, who would have been the heir to the throne if he hadn't died.

"Everybody loved my father," said Agrippina. "Everybody. When we were visiting camps, people used to come out and scream and throw flowers."

Kallias did know that much. People used to say Germanicus was the best general Rome ever had. He knew that the man had died early. What Kallias did not know, and what Agrippina told him now, was that Sejanus was behind all of it. She was certain Sejanus had him poisoned. After all he was the one who made her family look like traitors.

He was the reason the emperor turned on her family.

"He killed him," she said. "Essentially that's what he did."

And all because of Sejanus, her mother had been exiled and imprisoned. The woman had ended up losing an eye fighting a guard, and later her life.

"So then," said Agrippina. "My father is dead, my family is all split up and I have to go live with my freak uncle who likes small children and—you know? Let's just focus on Sejanus."

"So he was really the beginning of all the bad stuff you had happen to you."

"That's exactly what he was, you couldn't have said it better."

She looked at Kallias, almost in wonder.

Sejanus had been cruel to everyone she loved and Agrippina, left behind, had suffered all the fallout. And throughout it all she was just a child. Helpless.

"He tried to wipe out my whole family, that bastard," Agrippina said. "So you see now. One day, I'm going to destroy him."

"It's terrible," said Kallias, when she was done. "Of course you should hate him."

He thought about Sejanus that day, clapping Calvinus on back and the two of them laughing and then striding into the dining room.

"I hate him too," Kallias said. "And all his friends. I hate him as much as you do."

There was a moment of silence as they both stood thinking. The single lit lamp made shadows on her face.

"So how well did you know him?" she asked then. "Or his friends?" Then she added, as he stilled, "Nevermind, I know slaves don't like to tell their stories. About who they belonged to."

He couldn't say. He just couldn't. But it was enough.

She ranted to him about Sejanus all the time after that. He listened faithfully and nodded. No one else understood her hate like him. No one else understood what it was like to have an enemy so powerful that fighting back felt useless.

"Of course you were wronged," he would say. "You have to get him back."

"Good night," she said to him once after hours as they encountered each other in the hall. But both of them had stopped walking, and neither of them had moved from their places in the hall. Even in the dim light it was clear she'd been crying. He took a few steps closer to her but made no other move.

She swiped her hand under her eye. "I'm alright," she said. "Really."

"What's wrong?"

"Why does Gnaeus have to be so mean?" she blurted. "I know he didn't want to marry me, but can't he at least be nice to me? All I did was light a lamp for him and he said it made me look like a servant girl. He treats me like I'm desperate and silly."

Kallias wasn't going to agree with her about her own husband, not when he was a slave. He was silent.

"I don't know why I tried to hope this would be different. I heard so many bad stories. On the day before our wedding, somebody had told me how he ran over a child and kept going. A child playing in the street. He didn't even try to slow down. Sped up, maybe, they said. All these stories. But I tried to be brave."

"You had your duty and you knew that was all that mattered."

"I did," she said. "I did. And the next day, I was alright. I thought, the blood of the Caesars runs in my veins. I'm not some cowering slave. I won't go to my wedding trembling. But I was so scared. I guess I never know when he's going to make fun of me."

She was tired and rambling. He nodded.

"At least he doesn't outright abuse me," she said finally. "Only Sejanus has that kind of audacity. But I get so tired of Gnaeus mocking me, and calling me stupid."

"You'll be better off than your mother was," he told her.

She looked at him.

"Your mother didn't win," he said. "But you can."

Chapter 21

Ahenobarbus had a single guest one evening. All the slaves were talking about him. Someone expressed surprise that such a close friend of Sejanus would be dining with Ahenobarbus. "Ahenobarbus doesn't care," somebody said. "It only bothers her."

Kallias found one piece of gossip particularly hilarious. This guest had recently been on trial for arson and corruption. But nobody was interested in the corruption part. They were talking about the merchant who had crossed him, a conflict which ended in this guest having several of the merchant's trade ships set afire as they sat in the Ostia docks. Or so he was accused, and of which he had been acquitted.

"Who is he?" Kallias asked. They were too busy talking to hear him. So he went to see. He and Dion walked in at the same time, and Agrippina called the boy.

Then the guest looked up and Kallias felt like someone had kicked him in the guts when he saw it was none other than Gaius Calvinus. Dion went to Agrippina while Kallias stood to the side and eyed his former master.

He had aged. His once dark hair had gone almost completely silver. His expression was harder than ever, about the cheeks and his eyes, but he was still good looking.

Calvinus didn't see him.

"They tried to string me up," he said. "A long list of bullshit charges. Why is it a practice to harass provincial governors the minute they step foot back in Rome?"

He went on. "Certainly there may be corruption in some other provinces, but just to draw up a baseless claim feels very targeting."

"Oh, I don't know," Ahenobarbus said, scratching his head. "Most of the things about me are true. They say I love women, and I beat people, and I ran over a brat. And that's all very true. But say, Gaius, you didn't steal a penny?"

"If I did, I wouldn't tell you," Calvinus said, after a pause. They all laughed, even Agrippina, whose own laughter was more brittle than humor. And that was when his gaze moved, and landed on Kallias. And moved again. He didn't even recognize him.

"Who was your lawyer?" asked Agrippina.

He ignored her, or maybe he didn't hear her. She was staring fixedly at him, toying with the stem of her goblet. Her cheeks were red.

"You think you're lucky, don't you?" she said.

"Lucky, I'm invincible. Sometimes it's boring. They should make it exciting, give me something to work with."

Kallias left and returned with the keys in his hand. When Calvinus looked at him, Kallias wanted him to know that he had the house keys and had been making something of himself. He was already so much more here than he'd been with him.

Because no one could avoid talking about the prefect, Ahenobarbus said, "Sejanus is going to be granted the tribunician powers, I hear in the Senate."

"Which he does not deserve," Agrippina added immediately.

Calvinus looked at her. "Do you think that's harsh? He's only shown unwavering loyalty to Caesar."

"Not my family, obviously," she said, raising one shoulder.

"Not your family, no. Pity. Sorry, Julia Agrippina."

She didn't say anything.

Ahenobarbus laughed. "Don't you say you're a friend of Sejanus. I'd have to throw you out of my house."

"I understand," said Calvinus. "This is delicate."

They dropped the politics conversation.

There had been changes. The servants that Kallias saw in the entourage in the atrium were no one he had seen before. The attendant with Calvinus was not Nestor. He was just a nondescript Greek servant.

And in addition to his heavy signet ring, now Calvinus wore a wedding band. But of course he had remarried, because men like him were always married, and men like him always wanted a son and an heir.

Calvinus prepared to leave. Dion brought him his cloak. A servant pinned it while Calvinus stared at Dion. He asked Ahenobarbus Dion's age.

Ahenobarbus laughed suddenly, and said he didn't remember. All he knew was that the boy had been underfoot since forever. He said, "Tell him your age."

Dion told him. Then Ahenobarbus said he remembered exactly who his mother was and said that fourteen was probably right.

Dion had his gaze on the floor.

"You must hear you're exotic all the time," said Calvinus. And the guests did indeed sometimes say this, or some other comment on his looks.

"Siblings," Ahenobarbus said, pointing to Irene standing near the wall. "A nice pair."

It was no secret that Ahenobarbus was taking the sister to bed and Agrippina ignored that. No wonder she was so angry about everything. Her enemies' friends came to dinner because her husband didn't care about her political grievances, and in the meantime he got with the slave girls in the house he wanted.

Calvinus turned to Ahenobarbus. "Want to sell him? I could teach him how to dance, he looks like he should learn to dance."

Dion looked from his master to Calvinus and then quickly again at the floor.

"Well, I don't think he has any skills," said Ahenobarbus.

"Everyone needs to learn something," said Calvinus. "Do you know the woman who trains dancers for her master? They make them a lot of money."

"You can have him for a very good price."

Kallias knew the dancer he was talking about. She was very lithe and harsh. She trained one of the slave girls who used to come to the house with one of his former master's friends, and the poor thing always looked terrified. He could not imagine Dion training with someone like her, and making money for Calvinus.

Kallias walked up and put his hand on Dion's shoulder. "I shouldn't interrupt, please forgive me," he said. "But it's untrue that Dion has no skills."

Everyone looked at him. And Calvinus knew him now. There was a sudden switch as he recognized him. Kallias could feel him staring hard. He could have burned him with that stare.

"Dion is so helpful in this house."

"Trying to tell me what to do, slave?" said Ahenobarbus.

"I would never advise anything, sir, no."

But he didn't back down, and he didn't look at Calvinus. "If you sold him, you would be selling a valuable servant."

Everybody swung from him to Ahenobarbus to Calvinus. Dion was still.

Finally Ahenobarbus said, "This is not your business. Mind your fucking business."

Calvinus began to speak, but Agrippina leapt up.

"I don't want to sell him either." She rushed to Dion and put her arm around him. "He's the sweetest and I'll be heartbroken if you sell him. I really won't ever be right."

"You can always buy a different slave," said Ahenobabarbus. "One replaces another."

"As many as you want," said Calvinus. But he was still looking at Kallias.

"I like him, Gnaeus," she said, addressing her husband instead of Calvinus. "I like him. Don't you see?"

"Yes, little dove, yes I see."

The servants began to move again. Ahenobarbus said, "If that's what you must have. It's amazing how you women attach to slaves." He looked at Calvinus.

"I would sell him, Gaius. But my princess here simply can't stand it. I like to indulge her sometimes, you know. Come on bird, don't get all angry, I do have to cater to your stupid female wishes."

"All of you are so disgusting," she said, cutting him off. "I would never get rid of someone who had been in my house for all their life. Don't you know you have to keep the good slaves around you so they can take care of you? They grow up and love you."

She looked at Dion. "And what if he can't dance and you wasted your money? You can't just say he's a dancer because he's skinny."

"Princess," said Ahenobarbus. She glared at him, but said no more.

After that Calvinus said, "What a nice dinner, nice talk."

He turned, almost colliding with the slave who had been pinning the cloak. The slave hopped out of the way.

Agrippina ordered Dion back to the kitchen, and he scampered. Calvinus cut through the space between two couches and made his way down the side of the room. He was going to walk right by Kallias—and Kallias could not bring himself to move or turn from his direction. As Calvinus passed him, they looked each other right in the eye.

Kallias dropped his gaze.

But in that moment he glimpsed both the anger in his expression and the man's surprise at the difference in his appearance. And that he remembered. In spite of everything they had once been so entangled, the master and favorite. And for those few seconds, Kallias wanted to believe that Calvinus carried those memories the same way he did. All that had happened, the good and the bad.

But Calvinus walked without looking back.

And then he was gone.

Kallias turned back to his duties.

Chapter 22

A servant was sent to extend gratitude for the meal. And in the aftermath, Ahenobarbus had angry words with Kallias and ended with striking him. Kallias said nothing to defend himself, but when Ahenobarbus strode away, he rubbed his face and uttered a string of curses. He was so angry in that moment he genuinely could have murdered someone.

He saw Dion creeping from around the column he had been hiding behind. "Gods," Dion whispered, "you made them really mad."

Kallias said nothing.

The boy fell in step beside him. They walked across the peristyle together. "Thanks for taking up for me," Dion said. "I didn't want to be sold."

"That woman who trains dancers is very cruel, and so is the man who tried to buy you. Start measuring up to all that praise I put on you just to save you."

Kallias had to tell Agrippina then. They stood in the doorway of her room, him leaning against the post to seem more casual about it all, and he told her everything. He told her the whole story, with no details spared, things he'd never told anyone. She listened with wide eyes. She didn't interrupt him once, even when she put a hand on his arm when he got to the part about running away. It was like vomiting, the way he couldn't stop talking.

When he was done she said, "It shouldn't be that they can do all these things and no one ever stops them."

"Of course not. But that's how it works."

"He knew you! He was thinking a lot. I saw it in his eyes when you were talking."

"I wish he didn't know me, I'd have been better for it."

"Well, he won't be coming back. Gnaeus likes to bring anyone to dinner but I can't have that one. His arrogance, just listening to him almost made my eyes bleed."

"Good thing you intervened."

"Well, I couldn't let him win. He sat at my table bragging about his crimes and how he could do anything he wanted, so I said one thing you won't do, is have a poor little slave from my house. I just had to show him he can't have everything he wants."

"That's what I was thinking too," he said.

"So what Sejanus is to me, Calvinus is to you."

He stood with folded arms thinking about that for a moment. Then he said, "Exactly right. They're friends and our enemies."

"Except you loved him. You loved Gaius Calvinus. When you met him the very first time, at least."

"I was stupid back then."

"But you did, admit it. I can tell. You know it's good to be aware of what it is you really feel about something."

"That doesn't make sense."

"But it does."

He walked away from her without being dismissed. He couldn't believe she'd said something so ridiculous. He was angry with himself too, for being stupid for so long, for being hurt, and for wanting Calvinus to look back at him just once before he left. He looked for something to throw, or kick, or squeeze.

But he had not gone more than three paces when he stopped beside a door and it all came to him as clear a vision.

He had to take his revenge on that man.

This man had walked all over him, dragged him, used him, tricked him, and he'd done it without any intervention. He'd made a complete game of young, dumb, pretty Kallias. There was never anyone there to make him stop. The entire situation had always been him holding complete power.

Kallias had never been in any position to take down Calvinus. He was not now. But he had to do something. He couldn't let it end this way. He would start, he told himself, by working his way out of his slavery and gaining the power to do something that he could get away with. And Agrippina could help him. She could help him because they had the same enemies.

He couldn't do anything now. That would end with him hanging on a cross. He wasn't exactly interested in dying like that. So he would have to wait. But he was alright with that. He was certain he would see Calvinus again one day. He knew he would.

Maybe Kallias would stab him or slit his throat. Or destroy his political career. He would have to be very, very good to do that. Calvinus would be old by then, and that would be all the better. The methods didn't matter too much. But when the time came, Kallias wanted Calvinus to know that it was him. He wanted him to look into his eyes and remember everything. Scene by scene.

It was going to take a lot of power to destroy someone like that. He would almost have to be the state itself!

But no time for details now. He was here, standing in the middle of the hallway, and Polycarp was calling him for a task. Kallias turned and replied. But in his mind he knew.

He was going to get power, as he had always intended, and he was going to get his revenge on Gaius Calvinus.

Chapter 23

To make Agrippina's rage worse, she found a spy in her household. The doorkeeper discovered it after the slave kept slipping out the house after dark. Sejanus's tactic, the gossip said, was to seduce his enemies' wives and then peck from them all the secrets about their husbands and their activities. But Agrippina was out of reach, so supposedly, he got next to one of the boys instead.

The doorkeeper sent a guard behind the boy twice, and the guard heard the boy telling one of Sejanus's attendants everything he knew. The next day, the boy spoke to Sejanus himself in the street, and Sejanus kissed him.

"Alright," said Ahenobarbus to the slave, as the guards held him struggling. "When you hang on your cross, you can shout all your lies in the sky."

Agrippina, in the process of licking the last of her breakfast from her fingers, laid a hand on her husband's arm. "Don't you think," she said, "the punishment should fit the crime? Isn't that how it works?"

"This'll certainly fit it," he said, smiling at her.

"But you are creative, Gnaeus," she said. "Make it fun, for what he did!"

He looked at her in confusion. He thought crucifixion would be good. He was annoyed now, too, at Sejanus poking at his wife. At first it seemed like an exaggerated rivalry, but spies in his household were too much.

"You know," she said, "he committed the crime with his tongue."

His eyes lit. Cleverly, she had allowed him to feel as if he made final decisions. A good Roman wife, lenient and imploring when her husband was cruel.

"Cut out his tongue," said Ahenobarbus.

Later, Agrippina fumed. "Won't he just stay out of our business? Out of our lives? Sejanus is like a plague, he's everywhere. What did my mother ever do to make enemies with that man? Why won't he just leave me alone?"

She threw a pillow. Kallias came behind her and picked it up and punched it. He said, "Taking them down will be the best thing we ever did."

"One day," said Agrippina. "One day."

Chapter 24

"Now, Kallias," Polycarp said to him that morning of the first day of the games that summer, "I am going to run out and see what's happening in the Forum. You're a trustworthy fellow, you'll make sure the house is locked up and everything is in order before you leave, won't you?"

He held out the gate keys to Kallias.

Kallias hesitated before taking them.

"I can't thank you enough," Polycarp said, shaking his head. "You don't know what you do for me." He patted his shoulder. "Just be mindful, won't you?"

Kallias reassured him. And with that, Polycarp rushed outside to join the rest of the people on their way to the crowded Circus Maximus.

The house was empty. Agrippina and Ahenobarbus had gone, and half the servants had slipped away before dawn. The rest disappeared before they could be compelled into any chores.

Holidays always made Kallias more irritated with Polycarp than other times. On those days, Polycarp was his most worthless. He never gave orders, not even for tasks needing to be completed, and as the servants slipped out the house, Polycarp sat and drank wine much too good for him. Then he gave Kallias the keys to the entire place, all the heavy responsibility on a neck string, and went out for fun himself.

Kallias understood now why the stewards of great households always rushed around wearing sour looks on their faces. He thought it was just an overexerted importance. But they were really unimaginably stressed. As he rushed through the empty house now, looking to see that everything was secure and that doors were closed and nothing was out of place, sweat welled up across his hairline.

But despite that labor he tried to stay kind and reasonable. When one of the slaves was lazy, he told him that things had to be done because it was necessary. He never wanted Polycarp to order any beatings, and he always spoke carefully. "I think that if everyone contributes and works willingly," he always said, "Things can get done fast and we can all be happy with each other."

He even, after he no longer wanted to get with Chloe, and she cried about it, decided to actually speak to her and explain himself. In the past, he would have simply ignored her. But he was trying not to make any unnecessary enemies. The ones he was going to go up against were strong enough, and there was no need to have conflict where none was necessary.

So he told Chloe they would talk about it. They met in Agrippina's room, just the two of them, both of them arms crossed. "It wasn't me trying to scorn you," he said. "I just don't see what is there to look forward to, with our stations, that's all."

She said, very low, "Yes."

"You have a lot to do, following Agrippina."

"Yes."

"And I have to help the steward."

"Yes."

"We have our duties, you know, Chloe?"

Not too long after that, Irene ran away. Agrippina knew the night she did it, but waited for a week to grudgingly admit to her husband that the girl was gone. Ahenobarbus grabbed the nearest slave, slammed the man again and again into a wall until the slave lay on the floor with blood seeping from under his head.

Agrippina had been quiet through the whole scene. Now she turned, and slipped from the sitting room without a word.

"Fucking liar," said Ahenobarbus, standing over the servant who had nothing to do with any of this. "I know you lied, damn you!"

Kallias and Polycarp and Dion stood against the opposite wall and dared not to make a sound. Ahenobarbus started stomping the man on the floor. Nobody was going to stop the master so Ahenobarbus kept on going. He looked like he would walk away but every time he did, the slave would whimper, and Ahenobarbus would turn on him with a new fury.

Dion wept silently. Beside him, Kallias forced himself not to look away. Then Polycarp cleared his throat, just the barest—the slave on the floor stopped twitching, and Ahenobarbus straightened and grunted. He strode away, and slammed the door behind him.

They all looked at each other.

Irene didn't deserve to be caught by Ahenobarbus. Even Polycarp, who generally looked the other way from whatever his master did, was in agreement with that. He said, though, that the poor thing would find there was only a crueler world waiting than the household she escaped.

Dion withered now whenever Ahenobarbus passed him in the hall and patted him on the head. He had been hesitant about Ahenobarbus since the man came close to selling him, but that incident seemed to shatter his illusions.

The girl had pluck, running away like that. And still they hadn't found her and at this point, they probably would never. She probably had those few coins too, from all that bartering.

"Hope she's luckier than when I tried it," said Kallias under his breath.

"We live good lives," said Chloe. "What's better out there? Agrippina lets me wear cosmetics, and I'm clean and happy."

"Well, that's good for you. But you ought to understand why she ran."

"I mean I do, and I wish her luck. But what if something worse happens? She's just a girl, going alone."

Chloe couldn't understand that some people actually had things they wanted, things that mattered. And he wanted her even less after she said that, knowing how small her thoughts were. She was going to live and die, delusional and comfortable, without ever doing anything for herself.

She sought him again, when he was in the office clearing the desk for Polycarp and Ahenobarbus.

"I just don't know what I did to make you not like me anymore, Kallias."

"Nothing." He looked up and shrugged, irritation flaring in him. "I told you, you did nothing." And he walked around her.

He helped run his master's household. He had a purpose and was building himself up. He'd never been so clear-headed in his whole life. It might've been that he was older now and could think straight. Or maybe it was that he was so driven by the desire to change his status again and again until he had all the power he needed to match Calvinus.

Regardless, one simple slave girl had no place in his plans. Nothing would distract him from his drive and make him content.

Love was useless anyway. Love had never conquered anything, not like power. A person didn't have to be a cynic to see that. Look at the world and those ruling it.

Chapter 25

Kallias and Agrippina wanted revenge on two specific men. But they had no plan and no one on their side. She was a woman handed in marriage as something of a pawn. He was a slave, and that explained itself. So all they had was their hatred and the hope that the opportunity would find them a way soon.

"What do you think we could do?" she said to him, day after day.

"We just have to wait," said Kallias. "For now."

And he walked around the house thinking to himself, What can a slave and a woman do to take down a powerful senator and the prefect of the Praetorian Guard? And in a way that publicly humiliates them and makes them beg for their wicked lives? What to do?

He kept coming up short.

Then the government stole their chance.

Sejanus toppled from power just like that, one day in the fall. Agrippina gathered her stola and ran into the house one day after talking to Ahenobarbus in the street. She rushed to her room and then someone called Kallias and said she asked for him. He had been cleaning the pool in the atrium.

"You won't believe this!" she said, when he stood in her doorway. She told him everything Ahenobarbus told her as fast as she could, hardly stopping to catch her breath. His mouth fell open.

Sejanus was found guilty of treason that very afternoon and executed. He had been so close. He had been close enough to have the kind of power that matched the emperor. They read a letter from the emperor in the Senate today that said he knew about a plot that Sejanus had to overthrow him.

"He was literally plotting to kill him! The senators sitting beside him got up and moved when they started reading it," said Agrippina. "Gnaeus says he looked so shocked, like he couldn't believe it. They arrested him and he said, 'Me?' Can you imagine that, Kallias? He thought nobody could take him down, and then he's down just like that."

Kallias rubbed his eyes and blinked.

"The whole truth came out," said Agrippina. "Everybody knows it all now, what he did to me. And he poisoned Drusus, too!"

"Are you sure?" he said. "This is all real?"

"Gnaeus was there!" She was nearly screaming. "It's going down right now!"

He turned to rush out, but she caught him by the sleeve.

"You can't."

Ahenobarbus said that no one could leave the house but him and his guards. She said, though, that maybe tomorrow or the day after they could see, or she would send a guard for more information. But that was all they could know for now.

"I fucking hate this," Kallias said.

It was a restless night. Ahenobarbus came in and went straight to his bedroom. His attendants whispered about it to Kallias. They said that all of a sudden Rome was wild about the story of the man who had gotten close enough to the emperor to murder his own heirs. Sejanus wanted complete power for himself. He wanted to be the emperor.

Kallias couldn't wait to talk to Agrippina in the morning. But he didn't see her at all the next day or after that. He tried to steal pieces of information. He heard about the trials going on and the emperor. And he wondered who was involved and what else was going on. But he did not see his mistress.

Polycarp told them to carry on as if nothing was happening.

"These are our masters' problems," he said, "Not ours. No more gossip."

But two days later, Agrippina called him again. She'd been away, at her aunt's house. He hadn't seen her leave or return.

"Gnaeus says we'll stay in Anzio for a while," she said, gesturing to their packed trunks and bags when they walked into her outer room. The servants scurried around them, preparing. "Says the Forum is dangerous. You heard about the riots?"

He had. Stupid people. What was there to riot about? Sejanus's treachery? That his cronies thought the emperor was unfit to rule? They didn't know any of these men personally.

"He's gone, Kallias," she said. She searched his face.

He thought she was talking about Sejanus. But then she said, "His friend. Calvinus."

Kallias was motionless. He said, "So he's not alive anymore?"

"He slit his wrists to avoid trial. You can't get acquitted every time."

The image was sharp in his mind, but all he said was, "Too bad. Too bad he did it before he went to court."

She waited for him to say more, but he didn't.

"Some others did that too. They were too quick for the government. His property went to the state."

"Didn't he have a daughter?" Kallias asked suddenly.

Agrippina said he had. She was certain the girl was dead. "Sejanus's daughter got it the worst, though," she said. "I don't even want to mention it. The poor thing, having to go through that before the soldiers killed her. But that's just her luck, because it was just my luck when it was my turn and her father was killing my parents."

Kallias just shook his head and stared at the floor.

"I asked about him specifically for you, I made sure I found out names."

He thanked her for it. Then he asked about Demetrius. She said he probably had gone to Greece to escape being beaten in the streets, she wasn't sure. She didn't know about him. But neither of them were interested in the henchmen of their enemies. That conversation died soon.

The second wife had never been charged. She remembered suddenly.

"He's dead now!" Kallias repeated. "He's really dead."

She thought Kallias was happy, but there went his chance to look the man in the eye while he gouged them out. He felt flattened.

"He won't brag about his crimes anymore," said Agrippina. "But Sejanus, that was the one I wanted! Come out here, Kallias, let me tell you—" He followed her out. "I wanted to go get my own kick at his head but Gnaeus told me I couldn't. I think Gnaeus likes seeing me suffer."

Suddenly she turned, and embraced Kallias. As she laughed through gritted teeth, she said, "I wanted to help them tear him from limb to limb! But he is dead now, and I feel so much better it is a relief—"

"Mistress, I know, I know. Listen, just celebrate it."

"I will, I will. I feel so much better. It took too long. Oh, gods. I can finally live."

Ahenobarbus and Agrippina left for Anzio the next day, and Kallias went out into the city. He decided he would go whether Polycarp allowed the servants to leave or not. He walked all the way over to where the house was.

He stood across the street gazing at it, his hand up across his brow to shield his eyes from the sun. Once upon a time, he imagined Calvinus had everything and always would. The power and money and friends and looks. But now he was nothing himself. And this thought put in him an odd feeling of emptiness.

One day, on top of the world. The next, he kills himself to avoid execution.

No one was there at the house, of course. The slaves must have all been tortured and killed or resold. That was the fate of slaves whose masters were involved in treason trials. The air was so still, Kallias could have heard a whisper from a hundred feet away. He stood for a long while, looking.

He thought about the people he met there and he wondered what became of them. And he had never met her, but he wondered what the daughter thought before they killed her. He wondered if she knew all about her father's crimes.

In the distance were the shouts of the city from the people running amok through it. He was going to go home and stay out of the way, but he really couldn't blame them. Agrippina said she wanted to kick the dead body of Sejanus. He wanted to kick the dead body of Calvinus.

A shame there was not a body to go and kick.

The government had stolen that opportunity from him.

Because he really would have liked to. He would have liked to do that more than anything else.

Chapter 26

When the terror died down Ahenobarbus came back to Rome. Around that time Agrippina miscarried and she was sad and silent. Nobody tried to talk to her, but Kallias came and read poetry to her. Ahenobarbus said, "Do whatever you can to get my bird's song back."

While she sat around depressed, he took servant girls to his room. Everyone tried to keep her from knowing. She and Ahenobarbus had separate rooms and as long as she was in hers, she was less likely to know. But she had to know, because it was all going on right in the house.

Clearly, her sadness was more than the miscarriage.

It was the fact that she felt her life had been frustrated. Her husband was a reckless man who said he cared for her but then mocked her and never listened to her unless she sweetened him with flattery. Her enemy had been executed by someone else before she could get her hands on him. She'd been robbed of her chance to hurt the person she hated the most. She had wanted to do it herself.

Kallias couldn't relate more to anything else in the world.

A pact between them, while she lay on her couch and he sat with her. She'd taken his hand. She said he was a very good listener, even if he refused to be introspective. She was always saying things like that about him, peering at him emotionally.

"Kallias," she said. "Of everyone, you understand my life exactly."

"Yes, I do."

"You know what?" she said. "Calvinus and Sejanus might be dead. Maybe we can never kick them. I've accepted that. But I think it'll feel very good to have all the power we want to do anything, and never have to worry for our lives again."

He knew immediately that she was right. And after all, hadn't that been his goal for himself all his life?

That clicked to him, it made sense like the most natural thing in the world.

"Whatever we do," he said, and meant it with all his heart. "Whatever we do. Next time, we'll be the terror. Not the ones terrorized."

She looked into his eyes, and her own were bright, and she smiled.

He accepted it too. Or at least he decided not to allow himself to dwell on the fact that he'd missed his chance at revenge. Now he allowed himself to be driven by the thought of one day owning himself, and answering to no one.

That would be his new and best revenge.

Kallias grew into a man in those years. A very good-looking one, but to himself and diligent. He never gossiped, he seemed to only care about the rituals of supporting the household, and no one disliked him because he was so thorough and hard working. If anyone needed help, they could ask Kallias.

Dion thought he was the best friend ever and hung around him every free moment he had. Kallias had seen the wide-eyed love in his gaze for years and thought it only childish. But Dion was not a child anymore, even if the house remembered when he was and could only think of him as that, and he was stuck on Kallias. Finally one day, he told him.

"I think what it is," he said, one time when he was strumming his kithara and sitting next to Kallias in the gardens. "I think I actually love you. In the serious way."

"You're young," said Kallias. "You don't know what you want."

Dion said, "Yes, I do. I do."

Kallias took the kithara from him and looked at it. Dion was always carrying the thing. Someone had gifted it to him last Saturnalia.

"Don't Greeks love boys?" asked Dion. "Do you love me?"

Kallias laughed and scratched his head.

Dion was seventeen. Kallias never took what he said seriously. But it was flattering to be so looked up to. And he thought why not, someone was going to do it anyway, so why not him.

Later, he and Dion went to his room. Dion was the first boy he ever had, and Kallias understood why some men were so obsessed with it. It was so much better than the other side.

They only did it twice. It was just a chance for Kallias to try what he'd never done before. And Dion had been the perfect eager choice for him to start with. And he was the first person Dion slept with.

Kallias told him he should find a girl, someone his age, but Dion had no interest in girls.

No one would ever take him seriously because of that, said Kallias. Dion said he didn't care. Why should he care? Nobody could make him like girls if that wasn't what he wanted.

Dion focused on someone else. It was one of the other boys in the house, and then another, and then a Praetorian. He never seemed upset when these things were over. He was too busy finding the next man. All he cared about was having fun.

Kallias went through so many girls. Satisfying something that could never be satisfied.

He rarely saw a man he really liked, but there was a time when he became obsessed with this other slave who looked physically very much like himself. He finally made a sly suggestion, but Philo politely declined.

Kallias met a serving girl from the next residence, and when that interest dissipated, he moved on to a new girl who had just come to the house. He was nice to her for a little while before dropping her for yet another girl. It always collapsed in the same way. He ended up bored with them, he made excuses why he didn't want them, couldn't love them.

He was twenty-six years old and he had to ask himself what was happening with his life. He used to wonder how he would become a man, but now that he was, he realized how he'd simply grown into it. He remembered how envious he'd been of Rufus, getting to go to Greece, while he was halted by his slavery.

For a while recently, he had been feeling not so halted. But then he realized.

He was at a standstill. Kallias, assistant to the steward Polycarp in the household of Gnaeus Ahenobarbus.

Polycarp had only grown lazier since he discovered that Kallias was so good at organizing everything. The steward barely bothered to really see to the house anymore. If there was any detail left forgotten, it was Kallias who would remember to set it straight. He had even planned banquets thrown by Ahenobarbus, where every guest had the best experience.

Polycarp was the steward but it was Kallias who kept the house running like water. And when it came to the money, and the household's budget, Kallias knew exactly what to spend on what, never overspent, and there was always some money left over.

He had been allowed to see the books ever since Polycarp realized he could add very quickly. Then Kallias sat down one day for four hours, and he looked over all the accounts and he realized that Polycarp was spending far too much on everything in this house.

After he proved these calculations to Polycarp and how to reduce it, he had been managing the books.

Polycarp said, "You sure are bright! Well, fix whatever then so we can keep going."

"Look," he told Polycarp one day, standing in the storeroom. They were throwing away so much food, shaking it into large baskets to tote away so some slave could put it into the Tiber or some disposal. "This is a huge waste!"

There was stale bread, wrinkled fruit, molded cheese. It hadn't been properly kept and it went almost as fast as it came into the house.

Polycarp moved a basket. It was already full from all they had thrown out. And the food was rotting and smelled terrible. Kallias ignored the smell as he worked. He said, "You have always bought too much of everything, Polycarp, and then you waste. Ask for less next time."

"It's alright," said Polycarp, burping. "We waste all the time. Our master is rich, it's what we do."

"I bet he would like to be richer," said Kallias, and rubbed his hands on a towel and walked out.

He hated Polycarp for being lazy. He said to him one day, "Do you never wonder that Ahenobarbus will think you're not dedicated enough to him?"

And Polycarp said, "Bah. He'd never say that."

But Kallias wished he would. It was unfair that Polycarp was the steward and was sometimes given coins by his master, while Kallias did all his work.

Of course, someone did notice all this, and it was Agrippina. She said, after looking at the account books one day for the first time, "So, really you are saving us thousands of sesterces every month. Kallias, what a difference!"

Kallias, standing before her at the desk, spread his hands. "It only makes sense," he said. "It's about understanding what should go to what and saving anywhere you can. It's a game. I like it."

"I had never thought of it this way. I just read what's written here and think it's correct."

"You can always save money," he said. "But the key is that you really have to watch where it's going."

She jumped up, her chair scraped the tiles. She ran around the other side of the desk and hugged him and kissed him on the cheek. He was stunned at the hug and the softness of her body. She said, "You really are so valuable!"

He pulled back from her and stared into her face. "Make me steward," he said. "If I'm so valuable. Demote Polycarp and make me steward of this household."

Chapter 27

Ahenobarbus wouldn't remove him because he disliked when his wife tried to undermine his authority in the household. He was partial to Polycarp, who'd been there for years, and he never had a word to say to Kallias. It wasn't a situation of proving that Kallias deserved the position either. Polycarp always took the credit for what Kallias did.

"It's just not right," said Kallias. "Lazy fuck."

"He is," said Agrippina. "It's really unfair."

They had long settled into this now, of validating each other's feelings. Soon it turned to them both agreeing with each other that Polycarp just needed to die. Kallias said it first, as a joke, that they should kill him, but Agrippina latched on to it.

One day she accosted him in alcove and held out a tablet. There was just enough light in the space for him to read what was on it. She could make him steward if he just went down to the beauty shop and got her a case of that. Pointing to it.

"What is it?"

She laughed. "It's a face cream, but it has lead in it."

He squinted. "Lead?"

"Yes, that's why I don't use it. I use a different kind."

"You want me to..."

Looking at it and then at her. "Are you really serious? He'll taste it. I'm sure it doesn't taste like food."

"You don't have to do that part."

"Why can't you get it then?"

"If you can't follow my orders, or you're too afraid to go for what you want, you don't deserve to be my steward, do you? What do you want? Do you really want to be steward?"

He snatched the tablet from her.

Did he want to be steward?

He might as well be. The plan made perfect sense. Polycarp was at the end of his life after all. Well, he might not be near dead—not yet—but he was in his fifties and he'd never done anything with himself besides serve his masters.

And there was nothing left for him to look forward to doing.

It would only be right that Kallias served himself. That was all a person could do, serve themselves.

Obviously neither Kallias nor Agrippina were expert poisoners. Neither of them even knew what would work as an easy way to kill a man, which was why Agrippina came up with the idea of using cosmetics to do it. No access to actual poison, and who would give them that anyway? That would be suspicious.

There was a little hesitation about who would be the one to put the stuff in Polycarp's food, but when it came down to it, one of them had to do it and they couldn't trust anyone else to. And Kallias had done his part of buying the lead item no one in the household even used.

So Agrippina did the other part—she walked into the kitchen and scolded one of the kitchen slaves for loitering, her distraction. And then she did it, when Kallias met her gaze and with his eyes showed her the intended food. She stirred it just a little, while no one was looking, and then later Kallias gave the plate to Polycarp. Dinner, as usual.

Polycarp was violently ill almost immediately. His stomach ache turned to vomiting and diarrhea. Kallias could not even find it in himself to say, "I hope you get well."

Polycarp disappeared into his sleeping quarters, and stayed there all the next day. Whenever anyone asked what was going on with the steward, Kallias just said that the man probably had the flu.

"It's taking too long," said Agrippina. They stood together in the hallway again, the both of them sweating, but he more than her.

"I don't think you gave him enough," said Kallias.

"Well I couldn't let him have enough to taste it. He'd know something was wrong."

"How much did you use? Because I think he might recover. What then?"

But before the end of the week Polycarp was dead. Two servants lugged the man's body out on a sheet, and Kallias watched them pass by without blinking. At the funeral pyre an hour later, no one cried, and least of all Kallias. His eyes were very dry. Dion, standing beside him, whispered, "What do you think he was sick with?"

Kallias said, "Probably old age."

There was no time for regret. He became the steward just like that. It was their first win in the house. Agrippina had someone in an important position who would side with her, and Kallias was no longer a little slave who could be made to do absolutely whatever.

Kallias knew how to handle money.

So that was what he was good for, and to think he used to believe it was his looks!

He'd been so stupid then, and no wonder he hadn't gotten anywhere.

He was valuable in the most valuable way of all, through being good with money. And he felt very good about himself. He wanted to feel bad about Polycarp, but he couldn't, not when he felt so good about himself.

"You are kinder than he was," said one of the slaves to him. All of them of course, ignorant about what happened. "You really do deserve to be the steward."

He had all the keys to the house.

Tiberius Caesar died also in the same month, and right after that Agrippina announced her pregnancy. There were false tears for Tiberius and real tears for the baby. All her siblings came to the house congratulating. They were all very touchy. Caligula crouched next to Agrippina on the couch, his ear near her stomach.

"I can't hear it," he said, straightening.

"Silly doll." She patted him on the head. "It hasn't quickened yet."

The other sisters broke apart, laughing at their brother. It was something to see the new Caesar be patted on the head by his sister and called a silly doll.

"Gnaeus just hopes it's a boy," Agrippina said, touching her belly. "I do too."

They all seemed very close, sometimes a little too close. But the two most vibrant of them, his mistress and Caligula, had their mean streaks and competition. They had argued over the directions for the litter bearers earlier that day. He called her a bitch, she called him an unhinged boy. Then Caligula apologized to his sister for disturbing her when she was clearly in a delicate position, and she said that she loved him after all.

"So, I did it for you," Agrippina said. She came into the tiny room where he stayed, and made herself comfortable on the edge of his pallet. He sat with his back against the wall.

"What are you saying?"

"He's gone."

"Polycarp."

"You have to be loyal to me now."

"I'm already loyal to you. And you know I am."

"I want something too," she said. When she spoke this time her voice was lower. "I don't think Caligula is capable. He's immature and he gets angry easily. Being the ruler of the world isn't the right job for him."

She'd helped him, she'd killed for him. They had done it together. But his reflexive response was anxiety. He pointed to her stomach. He said, "Don't you have that to focus on?"

She laughed and held her forehead. "You are very mean sometimes," she said. "We'll talk about it more. But come to my room tomorrow, I have another project for you."

And then she went to the doorway. "About Polycarp."

He looked at her.

"I don't regret it. Not really. I mean, he was just a slave."

He thought, Well, I'm a slave, too. But of course he didn't say that.

"One of us will have to be on top so the other is on the bottom," said Agrippina. "I'd rather be on top. Wouldn't you?"

He laughed this time.

"I mean, wouldn't you?" she said, grinning. "Wouldn't you rather be on top?"

Kallias went to Agrippina's rooms again. Chloe answered the door, blinking and then looking down. All this time and she still wasn't over him. He couldn't understand it. He'd never done anything for her to be so stuck on him.

Agrippina, sitting up on her couch, waved at him.

"The project. I want to write a biography of my mother. The secretaries won't do it."

After the Games were over, and the crowds returned home gorged on bread and sated with bloodshed, Kallias began writing the biography of Agrippina's mother. Agrippina would dictate and Kallias would write. It was a daunting amount of work. Agrippina wanted him to write rapidly, and she wanted copies in Greek and Latin.

But she spoke very quickly, and she wanted him to write at the same pace.

"Come on," she said. "You have to keep up, Kallias. I won't slow down just for you. No one slows down for their secretaries. I see the men, they speak without pausing and their secretaries always keep up."

This was when he began to learn shorthand, when she gave him a text to study just so he could keep up. Later, she said, he could transcribe it. He looked at the text first for most of the sentences and then he found he needed it less and less to help him. He was becoming excellent at it. He couldn't believe that he'd had to beg for this before.

They began the biography with a family tree. Arranging it was very confusing. Everybody had the same name, several spouses, and several sets of biological and adopted children, and everyone had married some other family member's spouse, for a political reason.

"I want to be remembered," she said. "Everyone will know those ugly, evil men for years and years later. They should know me, too."

In the meantime, she had started her own affair. She was pregnant and she said it was perfect because she could get away with it. Since Ahenobarbus spent more and more time ignoring her and doing whatever he wanted aside from her, his young wife was left to her devices.

The man was Lepidus, and he was married to none other than her sister. Kallias wanted to ask her why she couldn't find a man, any man who was not her sister's husband, but then again it wasn't his business. He was not Chloe or one of the others and he didn't have to trail Agrippina everywhere she went. All he had to do was write her biography and listen to her when she ranted.

But he couldn't escape it because soon she wanted him to write and deliver her love letters to the man she was seeing. He had walked to Lepidus's house several times and dropped the letters to him. He always sauntered away hoping that Drusilla never saw him and that no one knew what he was doing. He felt dirty, but he had done far worse things. There was no time for regret now.

Agrippina was getting too heavy to see Lepidus, and she worried that he would think she was disgusting with her shape. But she still wanted him to think of her all the time. One week, Kallias took four letters over to the man's house.

Kallias had to be careful not to make any mistakes, and he had to reword Agrippina's dictations as they were never concise enough. He didn't like it, but she'd killed Polycarp for him. She knew his secrets and he knew hers and they were tied together now.

One day when he came in, she said, "Kallias! I had this big idea. About our situation."

She shooed the girls. They went out one by one, Chloe glancing at Kallias before she shut the door. He sat on the hard floor and Agrippina sat on her couch above him. She could hardly move with her swollen wrists and ankles.

"If we can stop Polycarp and get away with it, I feel we could do it again. Truly."

He studied her face, feeling his own pale. Her features looked impassive, but there was a desperation and a hardness in her eyes. "You know about my thing with Lepidus. I think he loves me, or at least he cares about my feelings."

Kallias paused.

"He might be our key, Kallias. He's a senator. Rich. Influential."

"Willing to...do all of that?"

"He cares about how I feel. He cares that I lost something that should've been mine."

"I know you want it," he said suddenly, before she could speak again. "And I want it too, just as much. But then I think, What's the point if I end up crucified?"

There was a short silence.

"You remember we help each other," she said then. "And you are my slave after all."

"Of course."

"You should've let me finish telling you what I was going to say. You know you should listen before you respond."

That was true. And it was true that he wanted this as much as he was afraid—and it was true that if this worked, he would have what he wanted after all. He would have to risk his life. There was no other way.

He listened to everything she had to say. Then he took the things out of his bag so he could write for her and balanced the paper across his lap. He wrote what she dictated.

The very plain words of her message asked Lepidus to think about a plot to kill Caligula. Lepidus then could be emperor, and Agrippina would marry him. She just wanted Lepidus to think about it, to see how possible it was. But it would be wonderful for both of them—he the emperor, and Agrippina, empress of Rome.

"What are you going to give me for it?" Kallias said, after he set down his pen. He could go to Ahenobarbus, he could go out in the street, to the Forum, even straight to Caligula Caesar, and show him everything. "Shouldn't risking my life be worth it?"

She was reading over what he wrote, and holding the letter close to her face as her eyes scanned the words. She didn't look up.

"What do you want?"

"My freedom." He didn't miss a beat. "And a position in the palace with the new Caesar."

CHAPTER 28

The birth of the child paused the plot. His parents named him Lucius Domitius Ahenobarbus. Their first after so many years, and a son. Agrippina recovered quickly and the baby was healthy. A servant decorated the front door with an olive wreath and the household offered sacrifices.

People flocked to the house, congratulating them and bringing gifts. Rockers, toys, blankets, even money, none of which Caesar's sister needed. After the twentieth visitor, Ahenobarbus began to say, "I don't think anything made by me and Agrippina could be of any good to anyone."

The visitors would reel, and then they would laugh. Nobody believed that Ahenobarbus was a good man, and there were stories about Agrippina.

Agrippina let Kallias hold the baby when he was five months. As soon as the nurse stepped away, Lucius whimpered. "He feels your tension," the woman said. "Relax."

He gave it back to her in a rush. The thing was too delicate for the world. He had never appreciated delicate things.

"Did you get any letters?" Agrippina asked after the nurse left.

"Not for weeks now," he said. "The two that came were the last. From Lady Livilla."

She was thinking about it all the while, just as he was. These days all he could imagine was his freedom, and working with someone who was married to a new

Caesar. That would be real power. He and Agrippina could have whatever they wanted if that came true. They could have the world.

Still it made him uneasy. He'd slept restlessly those past weeks, plagued with nightmares about hanging from his hands, about being beaten and crying. Even about Polycarp. He didn't tell Agrippina—she knew enough of his secrets already.

"We have to keep going," she said to him as they sat in Ahenobarbus' study alone.

"You know it's dangerous."

"Don't tell me about danger. You're talking to me, Julia Agrippina."

"I only said from my experiences. I just want us to get them without them getting us."

"We were only speculating," she said. "Nobody planned anything. And you didn't read all the letters."

"It's just that when this stuff comes out," he said. "They always torture the slaves."

She looked at him indignantly. "We have to help each other, Kallias."

"If we're discovered, who suffers more? You, or me?"

"We might both die," she said. "It's not a scale."

Well, but it was. The law was that if a master was found murdered then all his slaves must be crucified. They were also tortured and executed if their masters were tried for treason. Not that Agrippina's risks were small! But regardless, Kallias had to worry for himself.

It was so funny how he had thought, when she first came to the house, that because she was a woman she would be passive and simple and sweet. And no doubt she assumed because he was a slave he was disposable. Well, they were learning some valuable things about each other.

"You can't abandon me now," Agrippina said. "Don't you dare."

"I was only advising you. I think that —"

"Save it," she snapped. "You're loyal to me, and you'll help me."

Kallias resumed the biography of her mother. The nurse took the baby. The plot solidified then and she told Lepidus that she would marry him when she was free of Ahenobarbus. All they needed was the money to pay off the Praetorians, and to figure out a way to involve the new Praetorian prefect. Agrippina didn't know him, and she couldn't exactly write to him and say, Will you murder my brother so me and this random senator can be the emperor and empress of Rome?

So that was a hangup.

She and Kallias and her other conspirators didn't know how to breach that. They'd never planned something this big before.

Kallias thought she should bluntly ask him and show him the money upfront.

"The money will make him move," he said. "I'm sure of that."

Agrippina said that was absurd. She didn't have enough money to pay off the entire Guard anyway. She had her inheritance, but that would leave her broke if she tried to pay herself.

"That's the problem with men," she said. "Everything is too dogged with you. You don't know how to be clever and careful."

Then the fever went through Rome. The plot was abandoned again. Agrippina made sacrifices everyday at the altar for the life of the child. Finally she was so afraid she shut herself up in her room and only allowed the servants to pass food around the door to her. Hundreds fell sick, even the golden new emperor.

Kallias was struck himself, and so was Ahenobarbus and Chloe and several other household slaves. Ahenobarbus stayed in his rooms and Agrippina would not see him or tend him. Drusilla died, and Chloe. When Kallias heard about it, he was relieved.

Caesar narrowly survived, and when he did, he was a different man. There were reports of his new bizarre and irrational behavior. Kallias recovered too, but he was already a different man.

"He's crazy," said Agrippina to him one day. She had come back to the house and she was standing in the atrium, whispering to him. "He looks at me like he doesn't trust me."

"What about the thing?"

"Well, one of our friends had wanted to wait. But Lepidus thinks we should do it as soon as possible now. We just have to keep moving to convince the people we really need. He says he will start talking to men in the Guard. And the Senate."

She could focus on it now that she was back on her feet and the fever was over. She wanted him to run a message from Lepidus to another senator, by way of mouth. He walked to the house on the Palatine and waited behind a long line of freedmen and clients, just to speak to the man Agrippina had sent him to. No letters today, just a phrase.

The man didn't look old enough to have that many clients, but maybe he was rich enough. He must have been influential too, being a friend to Agrippina and Lepidus. He was probably also sleeping with Agrippina. She had a lot of male interests these days.

But he was just another conspirator, and Kallias didn't want to be so recognizable. He half looked away while he conveyed his mistress's message. "She says, get your money ready for the Guard."

The man nodded, and Kallias weaved through the others standing nearby and made his way to the door. He didn't even nod at the doorkeeper. His heart was out of rhythm.

But he wanted to see this out. He wanted what he would get on the other side of it.

Chapter 29

The Praetorians came to the house late one night and arrested Agrippina. Kallias heard the commotion and came out of his little room and saw the doorkeeper and Ahenobarbus and the guards shouting all at once. His first thought was to turn and run, but he was planted where he was. Their eyes met as she was herded by him with her arms behind her back. The Praetorians knocked a few things over, shattering expensive turquoise glass, and then they were gone.

The next day, Ahenobarbus left and the soldiers came with the human dealers. They rounded up all the slaves and marched them out, but they made Kallias and the doorkeeper go into the cellar. They sat on the cold floor in the dimness. There was a smell of wine that spilled.

"The steward and the doorkeeper have to know something," said the Praetorian centurion, gripping his sword.

The doorkeeper shook like a limb. He was shaking so hard, Kallias thought something was going to fall off him. But Kallias was still. He stared straight ahead.

"Make them talk," said the officer, to the legionary behind him.

They left the doorkeeper with a purple, swollen eye. The doorkeeper fed their violence with his fear. Kallias refused to beg, even when he was struck. The doorkeeper kept pleading. At length the guards left. The doorkeeper swore that their torture session had only begun.

Kallias had no fear anymore. In the place where there used to be so much regard for his physical safety, there was emptiness. He wasn't afraid to die anymore. He thought he became a man when he took someone else, but he was a man when he wasn't afraid of dying.

The next day, a Praetorian peered in. Kallias recognized him as someone Dion used to sleep with a few years ago. "That's enough, Statius," said the Praetorian crisply. He held up a hand. "Agrippina's already confessed, and Caesar's not torturing the slaves this time."

"They always torture them though," said Statius, who had just stepped into the cellar.

"But not this time, that's his orders. You better fix them up in case he wants to sell them too. What's up with his eye?"

In the end, the soldiers came and threw open the cellar door and Ahenobarbus was there, standing on the top step that led back up to the house. He looked as if he aged by twenty years and his old bluster was missing. He said, "They were both mine, yes."

He didn't want them. The doorkeeper was irrelevant. The young one, the steward, was a little too close to his wife. "Give him to that bitch," said Ahenobarbus. "Since they like each other so much. Let them rot together."

The guards were at the house today for two reasons. To take him and the doorkeeper and move Ahenobarbus out. He had been ordered back to Anzio. Caligula confiscated everything his sisters owned and resold all their slaves except Kallias and that doorkeeper. They walked through the empty house. Kallias wondered why it was always him who was losing it all, always swept along by the vicious tide of life.

But he told himself he would keep rising again, like his father the Phoenix. He thought of that suddenly, out of nowhere. The Phoenix.

The guards walked them out.

With the charge of conspiracy over their heads, Agrippina and her sister would never be welcome in Rome again. They were already lucky to live, as Lepidus had been executed. But they would be here in this exile forever, until they died, and Kallias would die here too, having accomplished nothing in his life. He still refused to believe it.

Agrippina cried the whole journey to the island where they would be exiled. She wanted to hold on to him for comfort.

He saw her out the corner of his eye, bedraggled, harried, but he refused to speak to her. She did it, she dragged them all down together and now their lives were over.

For the entire voyage to the Pontine Islands they were distanced.

The house of their imprisonment was small and severe. Kallias claimed a seat on the edge of a tiny garden where no grass grew. He liked to sit there and stare at and think about nothing. Agrippina soon found where he spent most of his time brooding—and came out of the house one day and knelt beside him, not caring about getting her dress dirty. There was a guard only ten feet away, watching them.

"Kallias," she whispered, "you know it wasn't meant to go this way. But I don't know how it happened."

He sighed. Her breath broke into weeping and she cried while he sat rooted.

On the third day of their exile on the island, he lowered himself onto the dirt next to her and looked into her face. Her cheeks were swollen and her nose was red.

"We're where we are," he said.

She gasped. "You're talking to me. I thought you hated me."

His freedom should have come from the deal. He did hate her. But they were together for now. He put his arm around her.

"I want Lucius," she said.

"Just try not to think about it."

"Is that what you do?"

"He'll be too small to be sad."

There was nothing to do on the island. No reason to rise in the mornings or sleep at night. Agrippina wore plain tunics and plain sandals and let her hair hang to her shoulders. She sat up for long hours. There were no outsiders but the guards, who did not permit any visitors. Everybody ate at the same table, even Agrippina.

"We would have had everything," she said. "I don't know how it failed. Why do we always fail?"

Chapter 30

Kallias found ways to irritate their captors. They had to be in the house by evening, but he'd wander down to the end of the street when the curfew was already underway. He was never doing anything but sitting by an old abandoned well.

He had nothing to do by leaving. But that was fun because it meant one of the guards had to go through the trouble of finding him to remind him that he should be returning to the house. The guards were lazy, hated walking, and that was why he had to make them do the extra traveling.

Agrippina also played her part to make their guards miserable. Every other day, just around breakfast, she would ask if they would be free today. The answer, of course, was always no. She would plop down on her chair with a long face, and say, "I'm going to die here. Fuck, I'm going to die here."

The first time she did it, which was about two months into their captivity, the soldier had said, "Well, there is a consequence to treason." And looked at her sturdily.

The second time she did it, she got him to exhaust himself on a lengthy spiel about how lucky she was to have her life and not turn out like her lover Lepidus. The guard was incredulous that she could think she would leave any time soon. After all she'd done. He asked her if she understood what she had truly done. She threw back her head then and laughed in his face. His face went stormy.

Now, when Agrippina asked the same question, as if she would ever get any other response, none of the guards would answer her.

She asked them too if she could have a loom—she hadn't been a good wife, if she had, she wouldn't be here—but somewhere through the past few years she had gotten very accomplished at weaving, and had genuinely come to enjoy it. But the guards always shook their heads, or were silent.

The days dragged on and on. Agrippina played with her nails and Kallias paced the room. That was generally the height of their physical activity. But there was no chance that they would ever grow overweight or out of shape. They were never fed enough for that. The guards brought them the same alternating meals of bread and lentils and sometimes a slither of meat. They drank water and cheap, disgusting wine. Sometimes there was no wine, or meat.

Somehow though, there were always grapes. Agrippina made a joke that there must be a lesson in that. She said they'd have to be like that fox in that famous fable. If political power was what they wanted, they'd failed to reach the vine by just a few feet, and they'd have to content themselves now by telling themselves that they never really wanted it in the first place.

"Because we're never leaving here," said Kallias.

She gazed at the wall behind him.

It was a very bleak prospect. But it was their future. They had better try to be like that fox.

When she wasn't antagonizing her guards, or staring into space, Agrippina was crying. She couldn't believe that her son would have to grow up without her. She hadn't been allowed to contact him since the night she was arrested. She had begged the guards to let her send the letters she had written. She wrote these letters herself, and she wrote one every week. Every week too, she went to the head guard and asked him if he would send it, and every time he shook his head. The last time she asked him, he took it from her and threw it to the ground.

Agrippina just stared at it while the man stared at her.

Then she went to her seat, and buried her face in her sleeve while she cried and her shoulders shook.

There were days when Kallias wanted to cry too. He never did—he hadn't cried in a long time now and he doubted he was physically capable of doing so anymore. But occasionally he wanted to, and it was always when he thought of Gaius Calvinus. And Kallias had thought about him everyday since being here. He sat around and dully remembered everything from the moment he met him until the last time he saw him that evening at Ahenobarbus's house.

His recurring memories were of the first time he walked into the dining room to pour the wine—he had been given a long talk on manners by the steward before he went in, and when he did, there was Calvinus, sitting and waiting. When Calvinus looked up his face was only a neutral expression, and the pitcher Kallias carried suddenly felt heavier.

The other memory was from the time Calvinus stood on the steps of the Senate House talking with two other men, and the brights of their togas were very white. Then another senator walked out, and down past them, and they all put up their hands in a greeting to him. That was the second time Kallias had gone to the Senate House with Calvinus's entourage, and that random scene was somehow unforgettable.

The scene that returned to him in the most detail was the summer when he was sixteen, at a villa of one of his master's friends. The man had purchased a new horse and invited Calvinus to see it. Calvinus brought Kallias—he used to take him everywhere. The animal was massive and had a shiny dark coat. The friend said it was an excellent Spanish breed. They were going on and on about this horse, and then Calvinus turned to Kallias and said that the friend had a treat for him.

Kallias had been all too happy to sit on the horse. The groom and the friend and the rest had stood in the background watching. As he sat there he had suddenly began to laugh.

Calvinus had grinned at him and said, "This is fun isn't it?"

And the setting sun was right behind his head and Kallias thought this was how it should have been all the time. Why couldn't Calvinus treat him this way all the time. Smiling genuinely with a summer glow behind his head.

That was only a month after that time Kallias impulsively kissed him on the lips and got an odd stare in return. Calvinus hadn't liked affection he didn't initiate.

Kallias could still envision exactly the way the man tilted his head when someone said something he disagreed with, the way he walked, and his frame—everything about him that was so reminiscent of ease, and confidence and power. When he was mean and cruel, it was easy to forgive him because he seemed like he was right even when he was wrong. It was so much simpler to take the anger out on someone else, to blame anyone but him.

And see, even now, it was Calvinus who Kallias thought of and not Malika. Because he should have been thinking about his mother, the one person who was worth remembering. And Kallias hated Calvinus now, even if he was dead.

But still Kallias thought of him and his mind ran through scenes of things that didn't matter and should have never happened. That was the worst part of all of it, being years removed from it, and seeing so plainly and clearly how wrong and bad it all had been.

Agrippina told Kallias that he loved Calvinus, and maybe she was right. Maybe he had, in the very beginning. He was very young, hopelessly seduced, he was in awe of a man who showed him everything for the first time.

It was very hard not to love someone like that.

Now all that love, turned to hate. Too bad he was dead, too bad he would never see Kallias matching him, and too bad Kallias and Agrippina were never leaving this damned island.

Chapter 31

Agrippina freed Kallias anyway.

He stood before her in the bare white vestibule of their little house, and the guards, eight of them, lined against the wall watching with amusement. They thought it was funny that she was freeing a man from slavery while she was in a prison herself.

Agrippina needed only seven witnesses, but eight were here, and the magistrate at the table with the lictors. Agrippina pronounced Kallias a free man and tapped him on the shoulder with a stick one of the servants had brought from the yard.

"You will not leave me, Kallias?" she asked suddenly, after she had spoken the formal words. He smiled because he couldn't leave anyway. She gave him the manumission roll, and they shook hands.

The magistrate clapped twice, bored. Two years ago Agrippina had lost everything. The public probably thought that her family would never have a break from dishonor. And now here was, trying to establish herself even while in exile.

The guards thought they were lovers. They never were. Agrippina was tall and classically beautiful, but nothing good could ever come of a physical fling with her. She had a higher status than him, and Kallias had sworn to himself to never again get in bed with someone outranking him. He also didn't want to think about what happened when things were emotional instead of physical.

A freedman of Agrippina. He attached a form of her name to the end of his, after the added 'Libertus,' as it was common for freedmen to do. He was released from his obligation to call her mistress, although calling her by her name was still awkward for him.

He went outside that day, and stood under the doorway, leaning his head against the post. It was a perfect world of gold and white and blue and birds. He suddenly remembered that when he was a boy he said he wouldn't be a slave all his life like his mother, not when he was her age. And he was the age now that she was then, and that wish had come true. He began to laugh to himself.

He rubbed his eyes. He thought he might be dreaming. One of the guards walked by, and glanced at him.

But after that, everything went exactly back to dragging. He had his freedom, but now what? Nothing. He was sitting there, in the same spot in the grass that he sat in every day, and he would never see Rome again. All that trouble he went through to gain his freedom, and now he hardly needed it because he wasn't in the world.

At least it felt good to know that legally, no one owned him. Even if it was in exile. He looked at his hands and said out loud, "I belong to me."

Then he stretched his legs out in front of him, lay back against the cool damp grass, and fell into a light slumber.

Then one afternoon, the guards came and told them to pack up, they were leaving, and the centurion waved a scroll. Agrippina sat at breakfast, nibbling on grapes.

"What, what?" She stood. The grape fell and rolled across the floor. "What did I do wrong?"

"Nothing," the centurion said. "I regret to inform you that your brother is dead, and you have been recalled to Rome by the new Caesar."

"What? What do you mean? Gods. Well, we'll pack. Then. Alright." Not fully composed, she touched her nose, her face.

Kallias said, not moving, "Who is the new Caesar?"

"Caligula's uncle." And as if Kallias, who once worked on an unfinished biography of the imperials, might not understand, the centurion added, "Claudius Drusus Nero."

"Wait." Agrippina caught her breath. "My brother is really dead? Really dead? But I wanted to see him!"

She sat again and broke into tears. Kallias and the soldiers respectfully turned away. But she wanted to kill him anyway, he thought, while they listened to her wail.

When they arrived in Rome, they learned that Caligula had not died of natural causes. He had been murdered by the Praetorians. No news reached Agrippina on the island so there were so many things she would have to learn. Caligula had been leaving the Circus when the Praetorians struck him. They butchered his wife and month-old daughter, too.

Caligula had gone insane. Agrippina had been right after all to think that he would not be capable. He tried to declare himself a god and had his horse made a senator. He infuriated the Jews by putting up graven images. He depleted the treasury. And then Agrippina learned she was a widow. Ahenobarbus died last year. She bowed her head when she heard this.

She was even more stunned to find out that her mother had not been dead when she married Ahenobarbus, but had actually died in her imprisonment while Agrippina was on the island.

Chapter 32

Claudius, stuttering, drooling, seemingly inept Claudius, was the new emperor of Rome. Somehow the news had reached common ears, and now the whole city talked about it. The Praetorians had found him cowering in the folds of a curtain in the palace after Caligula's assassination in fear of his life. They saluted him right there, as he stood quaking, and named him emperor.

Kallias went with Agrippina to the palace when she was summoned. The Praetorians swarmed the place. Two of them searched Agrippina roughly, cocked their heads at Kallias, and the first said: "Who is he?"

"My secretary," Agrippina said, after an irritated pause.

"He'll have to wait here," said the Praetorian. "Caesar's only seeing people who were directly summoned."

"He can't," she said. "He's with me. And don't touch me like that! You can't grope me like some little bed slave."

"What's it, Agrippina? Back from exile only less than a week and already acting like you rule the place?"

"Let us in already, thank you, please? I said he's with me."

They stared each other down.

A freedman, stocky and grim-faced, walked out just then and surveyed them. "What is going on here?"

"Sorry, Narcissus," said the guard. "Caesar's orders."

"Please respect the secretaries," said Narcissus. "They work hard."

This caught Kallias's attention. He was going to say something, but Narcissus said to him first, "It is only because Claudius is very wary. His Excellency did watch his own nephew die, after all. So he is very cautious. But it is not to be offensive. I appreciate your understanding."

And then he turned and disappeared back into the room. Agrippina cursed and the guard raised an eyebrow. He was about twenty and there was an insolent look on his face. "Go on, will you?" he said. "Other people are waiting to see the emperor, too, Agrippina."

"This is ridiculous," she said. "I take my secretary everywhere. And I told you, don't talk to me like that, I'm not some servant girl."

Then she swished past him with such a violence that he had to step aside and look at her. Kallias laughed, looking the Praetorian straight in the eye. It was always funny when Agrippina caused a scene.

Kallias sat on a bench and stared at the ceiling. It was so high and wide it gave the impression of a sky. And there were paintings of the sky too, and meadows and streams. In his peripheral vision he could see the Praetorians eyeing him. A secretary with no supplies.

When they left the island, they packed up so fast they left half of the few things they had. The guards rushed them. Kallias still regretted losing the biography of Agrippina the Elder in that hustle. He had worked so hard on it, writing till his fingers cramped. That biography taught him shorthand.

The two magistrates standing a few feet from him laughed at something one of them said. A senator arranged his striped bordered toga and murmured a question to one of his attendants. The fountains poured and Kallias watched them without really seeing them. He could sense the feeling of life beginning again, a palpable energy that sped his heartbeat: he was excited for something. He flexed his fingers.

He was back in the world again, in Rome.

Little Lucius was returned to his mother on an afternoon when Agrippina was directing the placement of furniture in the house. Claudius restored her wealth and her husband's property. Everything had been sold after Ahenobarbus died, and the house locked and deserted. No servants, furniture, nothing was left. Agrippina said, "Dreadful," and her words echoed through the room.

Domitia Lepida had sent a nurse and two servants with the child. He stood leaning back and forth on his legs before Agrippina swept him up in her arms, crooning and suddenly vibrant. Claudius called her to the palace three days later to tell her he would restore her son's inheritance as well.

Suddenly, Lucius Domitius Ahenobarbus was a rich little boy. Of course, he understood none of this. He barely reacted to his own mother. He was an unremarkable child, quiet to the point of being odd. When Agrippina held him in her lap and asked him questions he stuttered, and when she kissed him his blue eyes opened wide.

"That old cow Domitia never kissed the poor baby," Agrippina said. She was tiring herself with trying to win over her son. She thought he should remember her. He was two when she was taken away.

Lucius was just shy in a child's way of being shy. He was fragile, she said, when Lucius couldn't hear her. He needed extra love. He was too quiet and he always cried at the smallest of things. Bread too hard, one of his marbles rolling under the desk. Always looking for someone to pick him up. And pick him up they did, and pampered him. If it wasn't Agrippina, it was Kallias or one of the few servants.

His mother did it out of love, Kallias did it out of a desire to stop the weeping. That was their first tactic, to hold him, and rock him. Then they started to tell him that big boys don't cry, and the child changed so fast.

He would always be sensitive, they knew, but everyone had decided he needed to be strong too. And Agrippina brought him a wind-up toy, which so delighted him it seemed to cure all his melancholy.

"You can't make your mother cry," said Kallias to the child, as he jiggled him in his arms. "Good boys don't make their mothers cry, you understand?"

Agrippina was summoned to speak with Claudius again.

"He wants me to remarry," she said. "Well, he ordered it."

"Who, this time?" Kallias said.

"It's crazy, you'll say, when you hear it. " She leaned across the desk. "Gaius Sallustius Passienus Crispus."

"Well, you and Domitia are really going to like each other," Kallias said, and they laughed because the truth was too ironic.

Claudius had asked Crispus to divorce Domitia Lepida to marry Agrippina. Brother-in-law and sister-in-law to wed. No wonder it was so hard to write a family profile of the Caesars.

The wedding was nothing like Agrippina's first. It was a hasty affair thrown together before wellwishers could gather their clothes. Kallias, who had overseen the details and feast, was wary at first of Crispus. But he had an open, witty face, and when he clapped Kallias on the shoulder and honestly thanked him for his service, Kallias thought he was likable.

They moved to his house, and Kallias didn't need to buy a steward after all because Crispus already had one.

Agrippina, deciding to launch out and make money of her own, brought an amphorae warehouse, and as her personal secretary Kallias had more wax tablets to fill with sums. He was excited. He told her he would make her warehouse successful.

"Crispus is rich," he said. "But you won't have to wait for his money. I'll make sure you never have to wait on him."

Agrippina said that was an excellent idea.

"Oh, darling," said Crispus to his new wife, "why tire yourself out with business? It's not good for a woman with a child. You need to focus on Lucius."

"I have things to do, and I have to do them," she replied firmly.

She never listened to him. He was a sweet man, which made him easy to override. His wife had her own mind, and she would go where she wished and come in when she pleased.

The joke among the servants was that if Crispus thought he was being freed when he had divorced the ornery old Domitia Lepida, he had simply exchanged his bonds when he married clever and wicked Julia Agrippina.

Agrippina suddenly had her life again, and it was really time for Kallias to build his. He would not be stuck in her household no matter what. He was thirty, he was free, and he had the whole wide world to do something in it. He sat figuring the numbers, and he calculated exactly what he wanted.

He came to Agrippina with a bill, an income statement, and his own wish.

"Remember," he said. "We help each other. I'd like that position in the palace, as you promised me."

"I know," said Agrippina.

CHAPTER 33

He twirled the pen in his hand. Things had turned so quickly. Only months ago he'd been in exile with a disgraced prisoner thinking they would never leave. Now at this very moment he sat in an alcove of an office in the palace with the pen he twirled and two sheets of papyrus before him.

The bureaucracy was expanding, and Kallias wanted to be a part of it. He thought it would be a perfect job. Cushy, useful, and an opportunity to make money and be at the center of the world's happening. Claudius had appointed all his freedmen to the top ministry posts in the new government, and it was a good time for merit.

The jobs in the bureaucracy were not pennies to be handed to beggars. There was no way to directly ask for a position. To be considered a man needed patrons, good connections, or at least a good birth. He had the first two things.

Kallias stopped twirling the pen and focused. He needed to think clearly. His success on this exam determined whether or not he was hired as a civil servant for the Roman government. He could not foul this up like the plot, the thing with the old house and all those other times he had failed. He began to write.

After he finished, he spent the rest of the day at various places of entertainment in the city, where he won a small bet on a gladiator match. He was glad that after all he had learned shorthand. At a tavern he brought himself a drink.

Crispus called him into his office a week later, to show him the letter from the palace. Kallias passed the test with all questions correct except two. "You're not perfect," Crispus said with a wink, "but you were close to it this time."

Kallias returned to the palace and spoke this time to a man named Albinus. They sat at a table in a humming office of bureaucrats, magistrates, and slaves. Albinus was a typical equestrian, but he did not sniff condescendingly at Kallias. "Your patrons recommended you," he said. "Very good compliments, I heard. Agrippina told me you were once working with her on a biography of her mother."

"Yes, that was years ago. We never finished it. I think she's getting someone else to write another, though."

"The First Family in Rome, " Albinus said. He sat back in his seat. "I was interested in meeting you. Agrippina seems so extraordinarily fond of you."

Kallias began as a very junior correspondent on the staff of the secretary Narcissus. The same man who walked out that day when Kallias and Agrippina were at the palace for the first time again in years. Narcissus was Caesar's most important secretary.

Kallias was on the first rung of the ladder. Dozens of men ranked higher than him, and amongst his peers, he frequently rubbed elbows with equestrians irritated that four freedmen were running the empire and too many more freedmen were finding places in other positions in the government.

The capital was one complex power struggle. Claudius was wary of the senators, so he made sure that different ranks of men had important positions. The patricians had always been ill about sharing powers with the equestrians, and now it was the equestrians' turn to be indignant too, having to make room for the freedmen. And everyone resented everyone.

Kallias vowed to do everything to make their lives as difficult and frustrating as could be. He would do it just because he had the opportunity. Why not?

One day, his associates admitted a broad-shouldered equestrian with a deep scowl. He wanted to speak to Claudius about his family's land and some dispute tied to it. Kallias didn't even know what the issue was, because no one was going to listen to the man without him paying the right amount of money.

"There are thousands of letters ahead of yours," said the man who worked with Kallias. They sat at a desk, while the man stood staring at them angrily. "There is no way we could find yours just by looking."

"You must have some easier way of going through them," said the man. "This is Rome. Everything is in order in Rome."

"Sorry, no way," said the official again. "They have to be read one by one and yours could take years to come up. Sorry, we can't find yours today."

They could have, really. Kallias spent a lot of time organizing. That was his whole job, making sure that everything was in the right place and could be easily found. They could have helped this man too. They just wouldn't. Kallias and the man laughed when the equestrian slammed the door and left.

For the other part of his job, Kallias wrote a lot—mostly about mundane happenings in the empire, and read a lot, mostly letters that would be discarded long before they were anywhere near Narcissus's desk. It was interesting to see who wrote the emperor. Cult leaders and Jewish rabbis, whining about something or another that affected their worship. Businessmen seeking direct intervention on some commercial issues. There were countless letters bearing seals from equestrians, letters that were generally dispensed as soon as they came to the desk, or sent over to the petition bureau under Callistus.

"They'd better learn to pay something to speed it up," Narcissus said, "if they want a word with him. We can't waste time with somebody who can't give us a good reason to stop and look."

Narcissus ran the department that way. The bureaucrats were paid salaries from the treasury, but there were other ways, Kallias soon learned, to make money. One of them was to ask for payment before sending a letter to the higher tiers of the correspondence. A letter might reach Narcissus, but if the appropriate payment did not accompany it, all that work to be heard might be in vain.

Kallias began to tell people, when they came to him, that he simply could not hear them.

"This is the emperor." That was his favorite line, usually delivered as he folded his arms. "You think this man can listen to your petty issues—and yours may not be petty—but still, when he has to run an empire?"

Usually then, the petitioner would offer a payment.

Money was everywhere, like low hanging fruit. Besides his salary, and the bribes, he was also being paid from managing Agrippina's business on the side. Eventually he'd be too busy with his own life to do that, but for now, it was good. And it was even better to have money coming from all those places. He might have stumbled upon a mine of gold.

Feeling very elevated, he changed his personal style. He bought new clothes and got a Roman haircut: close cropped at the forehead and edges. After that, he moved out from Crispus and Agrippina's and into an apartment. He did not haggle about the top floor, which everybody knew was the worst. He stayed nearer to the bottom, in the better, bigger rooms and where he could easily go downstairs to a shop for breakfast.

Agrippina was immersed with her own life and did not talk to him as much those days, but she came by once and sat with him and said, "I see you are really where you belong, in the palace. So it's working out."

"It could not be better," he said.

"Oh, it could be," she said. "And it will be."

If Sejanus hadn't come along and tried to knock her family off the block, her father would've been emperor. Her son should've been next in line to the throne. She couldn't help but want more. She was the daughter of Rome's most beloved general. She sat in the capital now, important by her very birth, and wondering how she might leverage all that to matter.

Of course she wanted more.

Kallias felt the same. He'd always believed he deserved more even when he was a slave. For him it had certainly started when he was a child and everyone fawned over him. He remembered them saying how sweet he was and pinching his cheeks and his feeling afterward thinking, with a sense of wonder, I am? I'm really all that? Good looks was its own stake of royalty.

Something at the heart of him always longed for more, too.

Chapter 34

Kallias had an advantage being so close to Agrippina, the emperor's niece. The second point to put him in a good position was working under the emperor's best man, Narcissus. Narcissus was very rich, wrote all of Claudius's letters, and knew everyone important. Agrippina thought she needed to bring him very close to her.

She invited him to her house, with Kallias.

"This man talks to the emperor everyday," she said, before Narcissus came in. "We'll have to make the very best of friends with him!"

"I know," said Kallias. "He's very professional, though. It'll be hard to make him slip up. He won't reveal things."

"We don't need him to, Kallias, not just yet. We just need to get him comfortable with us."

There were voices then. It sounded like he'd come in.

They went silent.

"Kallias has been with me through everything," Agrippina told Narcissus later in the meal, as they sat in a circle.

Narcissus nodded. He was the typical Greek freedman, and he had that quick look in his eyes. Kallias knew he was taking in everything and had summed up their relationship already.

She said, "I'm sure you know about absolute devotion to a master."

He nodded again. "Everything I do is for Claudius."

"Yes," she said. "So, what you are to Claudius, Kallias is to me. Treat him well in your department."

Just like that Kallias was promoted past all the others who he worked with. He had come in for a few months, and now he was above them. He had more work than what he was accustomed to and he barely knew what he was doing. He didn't understand the priority of certain petitions, and was absolutely castigated by Lucius Melius for discarding a response that Narcissus had promised an answer to by the next day.

"I'm sorry," said Kallias, sincerely this time. "I simply didn't know."

"Are you too stupid to do your job right?" scolded Melius, all while his secretary glared at Kallias. "Why would you throw away papers you don't understand? Tell Narcissus I can take him to court for his slackness if he takes my money but doesn't do the deed he promises."

Narcissus settled it in the end by getting Claudius to rewrite another statement. Kallias felt stupid, but he had been so used to discarding citizens' requests and storing records as a routine. Throw out one, keep the other to give to the freedman Polybius for cataloging if relevant.

Crisis settled, Narcissus took him aside.

"I know," he said, "that your patroness favors you very well. That is good news, great news. But this cannot happen again."

He had an odd way of enunciating every word. But it didn't sound snobby. It made him sound patient and diplomatic. He informed Kallias that in this new place, working more closely to the emperor than before, he would have to learn the rules very quickly.

Kallias apologized again. He needed to prove himself, and he swore to himself to try harder. He had a lot of power now, and he would learn how to handle it all.

Those whom he had pushed by might have resented this newcomer for establishing himself so quickly above him. But they didn't bristle, at least as far as he could discern. There was no talk about how he had only recently come in and was now in the trail of Narcissus.

No one could complain about it because he was so tight with the emperor's very own niece. She may as well have been Caesar, the way she wielded her power. And no one with good sense was going to make an enemy of her.

Except the empress herself, Valeria Messalina.

Valeria Messalina wasn't as pretty as she thought she was. The emperor's wife floated down the path in a green silk gown and stood before him. She had mischievous eyes and her mouth was too small. But still when Kallias was introduced to her, he played a gracious part and was all smiles. He was learning from Caesar's favorite secretary.

"So you are Narcissus's mentee, then," she said, as they stood in the gardens that day. "Narcissus will take the best care of you, that's for sure!"

"There's much to navigate," said Kallias, glancing at a beaming Narcissus. "He's patient with my efforts. I appreciate that."

"Served the family for years." Messalina gave a raspy laugh. "It's all he knows. Narcissus couldn't live any other way."

"Well, things have to be done," said Narcissus.

"So very true," said Messalina, still looking at Kallias. "Which, brings me to the question, do you know Julia Agrippina?"

Kallias, carefully blank faced, said that she was his patroness.

"That's marvelous!" Messalina smiled. But Kallias could see right through her. And he was right, because then she said, "She has been asking to see Caesar quite a bit, hasn't she?"

"I think it was stuff about her little son," said Kallias dismissively.

"He already gave them back their money, no?"

"I think there were other things. Related to it."

"Oh, maybe so. Well, I was just thinking that since you were so close to her, you could tell her that Narcissus can handle all her requests. Instead of her asking to see the big man himself, you know? I hope that makes sense?"

When Kallias said nothing, her smile tightened. "I'm not saying it's a bad thing, I know she has her needs and all to get herself together again. But Claudius is fragile and we like to leave the important and stressful things to Narcissus."

She touched the freedman's arm, and he nodded.

Kallias said then, "Yes, that makes sense."

"She might feel a little cut down if Narcissus says it," said Messalina. "He's got this... professional tone that stings, you know. That's all. I wouldn't want her to think that he's whipping her. So it's better for you to say it."

Kallias sat on Agrippina's couch and told her everything. His lips had practically burned all day with the news.

Agrippina didn't appreciate this at all.

"How can that bitch dictate who I speak to?" she said, and tilted her head. She was standing by the window. "I have things that matter, unlike her. Messalina is a sex-crazed drunk. She should stick to that. Why does she care how much I speak to Narcissus or my uncle?"

"She's annoying."

"He's my uncle, you know. I can talk to my own uncle as much as I want."

"The very first time I met her," said Kallias. "And she goes trying to tell me what to tell you. I just thought it was unwise."

Agrippina closed the shutter, and paused with her hand up near it. The light fell and darkened across her well-sculpted face. "You know why she's doing this," she said.

"Why?"

But he knew the answer, and then as if to confirm, it came and stood in the doorway in the form of little Lucius Domitius Ahenobarbus.

"Mama," the little boy said, rubbing his eyes. "I'm hungry."

"I made millions last year," said Narcissus. He sat at his desk. Kallias sat next to him.

"So I hear," said Kallias.

"I make millions every year," said Narcissus.

Kallias felt hungry. He shifted in his seat.

"It really pays to be here," said Narcissus. "Get the most of it."

"I could make that," said Kallias then. "With just some time."

"You can. You certainly can. I take whatever I want and at the same time I do everything Claudius wants. Come to my house and we will have more time to discuss it."

Every time Kallias visited, Narcissus talked to him about business. He was all about work, and thought he needed to always seem as if he were the most devoted freedman. He wanted Kallias to really understand how he could always make the best decisions if he understood how the government worked, and that he would never have to answer to anyone but the emperor if he stood above reproach.

"The key," he said to Kallias, "Is to always do your main job well if you never want to be questioned. Then you can do whatever else you want."

Kallias saw Messalina often, more than what he would have liked. But she was the emperor's wife, and he dared not show that dislike in his expression. When he saw her, he was friendly. He pretended her snide insinuation about Agrippina was forgotten. Messalina, careless in her position, soon began to warm to him.

She stopped him once in the hall, while he was rushing to meet Narcissus. She was clearly drunk and overexcited. He hid his impatience and smiled. Her entourage parted as he drew near.

"You remind me of someone," she said, gesturing with a hand that clutched a cluster of white flowers. He asked who.

"Growing up, there was this boy in our household named Ajax. He was so nice, would help out with anything, never stole. He died young, about fifteen, he'd had a fever or something. But I was so upset. I think if he were grown he'd somewhat resemble you. Maybe a little."

"What a story," Kallias lied. "Remarkable."

"It really is! I got a fancy grave for him because he really did deserve it. Ajax was a nice boy, that really hurt me. I hope you're as nice as him."

Maybe she thought that because he was close to Narcissus, who was close to her, that she could trust him.

Messalina's first invitation to her party came late one night, when a palace slave stood in Kallias' doorway and said that his mistress would like for him to attend her dinner event tomorrow. Kallias was surprised. The empress wanted to party with him, the freedman of a woman she clearly considered her rival.

"She understands," said the slave, thinking his hesitation came from fear of his life if he denied the call, "that you may be too busy. But she invites you because she thinks you'll have a lot of fun and love the entertainment."

Chapter 35

"How could you be so stupid? You should've gone!"

Kallias turned down the invitation because he thought parties were a waste of time. And he didn't want to party with Messalina or her crew. But Agrippina didn't like that.

"No," she said. "You have to go, this isn't how it works. You should let her think you like her. If she knows we don't—"

"You've never greeted her in public yourself."

"But I'm different. She's friendly with you and we need to find out what she's up to regardless. What if she gets upset anyway? That you didn't go?"

He went the next time. It was a typical party, with all the usual party-going kind of people and sex. Messalina was obsessed with an actor named Mnestor, who sat near her the entire time and caressed her back. They drank as usual until the music got louder, and then Messalina vomited on the floor and on the feet of the slave girl standing near her couch.

Kallias told Agrippina all this later, and she just frowned.

He declined the subsequent invitations. But he was on the list to attend whenever he wanted.

"You know what's strange," said Agrippina to him and her husband's doctor, as they stood in her bedroom. She was not pregnant again after all, and she was grateful she wasn't. Lucius was all she cared about and all the trouble she needed. "I'm always sitting just at a distance. Remember, the one we don't like to talk about? My mad brother."

The two men nodded.

"Now it's my uncle, and his wife thinks she can belittle me."

"These things could wear your health down," said the doctor, shaking his head. "Better to leave it to the gods."

"Shut up, Xander. I'm not pregnant. And even if I were, I wouldn't have the luxury of leaving things to gods. I'm trying to make a point here. I'm saying that this makes me feel like it was the year Lucius was born all over again."

"I can see that," said Xander, stroking his chin. "But you're married, Lady Agrippina, at least for now. To someone who cares so much for you."

"You've said it right. For now I'm married. To Crispus."

"Messalina won't leave you alone," Kallias said. "She'll keep going. You'll have to strike."

"Oh I know, I know. And good, the best woman wins."

Xander shrugged, but Kallias and Agrippina met each other's gazes.

If Agrippina was interested in Narcissus because he was close to Claudius, Narcissus was interested in Kallias because he was close to the very formidable Agrippina. The emperor's own wife, Messalina, spent her days partying. Agrippina spent her days plotting. The freedman knew he needed to befriend her, and he could do that through Kallias.

Narcissus was careful never to be seen by the one woman when he was with the other woman, but he talked to them both frequently. He said that if Agrippina needed anything as she resettled in Rome, she could rely on him to provide it for her. Kallias wouldn't have to carry the burden all alone of being her secretary and confidant.

"Your friendship with her is so admirable," Narcissus told Kallias once. "I think everyone should have someone to trust."

"No doubt," said Kallias.

Narcissus was not the only one establishing a connection to Agrippina. Pallas, the good-looking freedman who headed the treasury, had more than enough reason to take an interest in the emperor's niece. Kallias saw them flirting once in the doorway of his office, and his hand resting too low on her back.

"Pallas," she was saying, "you are so clever!"

"Well, you don't get this little job without being clever," Pallas replied. "Just tell me what you need and…" He said something else, but Kallias had passed by at that point.

Agrippina told Kallias later after he dined at her house once, "Can you believe it? He was the one who literally took the letter about Sejanus that day to the Senate!"

"Really?"

"He was the messenger boy!"

One day, when they were walking the halls together, Kallias asked Pallas himself.

"Agrippina told me it was you who made it happen. That was a big concern for us back in the day, about Sejanus."

Pallas had his bag on his shoulder. He shifted it, and looked at Kallias with a small, crooked grin as they walked. "That was me. I was proud of myself for getting to bring the message on something that turned Rome upside down for weeks."

They paused to go separate ways. Kallias said, "You've always been involved."

"Couldn't get a break from the greats if I wanted to," said Pallas, and grinned again.

"Sometimes it's a good place to be," said Kallias, and waved goodbye to him.

Agrippina was so skilled at forming alliances. She always found those who liked her or needed her or related to her and then she offered them what they wanted. She made sure that Claudius's main freedmen were on her side. It was wise to court the men who ran the emperor's government. Now, she could ignore the senators who looked down on her for being a woman.

She made friends with Narcissus, Pallas, and his brother Felix. But she couldn't sway Polybius. The research secretary was close to Messalina and clearly had nothing for the woman who had once been on trial for plotting to kill her own brother. Polybius had encountered Agrippina several times, and not once had he spoken more than three sentences to her.

"One of these days, he'll regret making me his enemy," she said. That was all she said of him. She was safe enough with her connections to the other two freedmen who controlled such important departments.

Everyone was using someone else. Basic politics. Kallias, too, found himself constantly collaborating with other bureaucrats who would support him whenever he asked. He could tell by the way they looked at him that they didn't quite know what to think of him. Was he arrogant, kind, brutal, or smart? But that didn't matter, he had professional manners and he could smile winningly whenever he needed to.

And he decided he would play his own game to stay around. He could not go back now, he could not lose now. He would have to seal himself into this position.

Chapter 36

Kallias' game was Narcissus's daughter Thalia. Narcissus introduced them. He wanted them to be friends. He practically shoved them in each other's faces, with a hand on both their backs. It was just too perfect.

"This is the brilliant fellow who is good with the money," said Narcissus to Thalia, who had come out into the peristyle of her father's house to speak to them. Every time Kallias looked around the house, he was reminded of what Narcissus said about the millions. In just some time, he thought. It would be him. Just some time.

"It's really Narcissus who's so good with it," he said, and both men laughed. Thalia smiled and flashed a dimple.

Thalia was very pretty but had no manners. During dinner she fell asleep, laid on her back with her arm resting on her face, and when one of the servants poked her awake with a ladle handle, she sat up and said, "This conversation bored me, honestly."

But aside from that, she was interested in Kallias. Her gaze when she regarded him was full of fascination. She thought he was so smart and serious. She was so excited that he wanted her. It wouldn't be hard to play her as the game.

Every time he saw her there was a question about him and his life.

"Did she really try to overthrow Caligula or was he just insane like they say and paranoid?" Her eyes shone wide.

"Let's not entertain nasty rumors. People love to hate her when they've never even met her. Don't more interesting things happen at the palace with you?"

Thalia smiled. She was one of Messalina's hangers-on.

For weeks, Kallias dined almost nightly with Narcissus and his daughter Thalia. Then it was down to Kallias and Thalia alone. Their conversations were never beyond the superficial. It was either about her, or gossip about enemies, or whatever new habit Messalina was adopting. Thalia was obsessed with the empress, and seemed to have no other dreams beyond being her friend.

Her entire personality revolved around her socialization with the empress and her senator friends, entertainers, and lovers. Thalia was a tablet to be inscribed upon, not at all clever and thoughtful and purposeful like her father. Her one distinguishing feature was green eyes that sometimes looked honey brown.

After she met him she would always leave to go to the palace. She liked to be there at night, when he was not there. It was for the parties Messalina threw.

"You're not afraid of venturing out late?" he asked her once. She was going to get into the litter that her servants brought around to the front door for her.

"That makes it more fun!" she said. "You really should come to the parties. Try to be fun sometimes!"

Thalia was an Epicurean. According to her beliefs, Kallias' ambitions would not bring him peace. He laughed and said he wasn't looking for peace. She shook her head in wonder.

"I've never had pain," she told him later. "Not like my mother. Did you know one time her mistress beat her just because she didn't like the way she framed her hair?"

"How is that related to your philosophy?"

"Well, her mistress was going to meet the emperor and some other important men that day, and she was worried about the style. That's why. But she got to the event and Tiberius didn't even notice her. I think it was Tiberius, I'll have to ask my mother the story again."

"Oh, well. I still don't see your point."

"You have to think about it, Kallias. Eventually, it'll make perfect sense."

"I need to talk to you," Agrippina said one evening when he came to report to her about the business. They set all the work aside. "It's Messalina."

He nodded.

"You would think she would at least try to hide it. All the stuff she does. I heard she had a threesome, right under his nose."

"He's so weak, he doesn't mind."

"I know. I wish I had something on her that was so bad that she would have to leave. Sleeping around isn't that interesting."

Everybody did that, so it wasn't interesting.

"That's where you come in."

"You want me to spy on her."

"Yes, please. Something has to be her real downfall."

"I'll try," he said, thinking of Thalia and her connection to the empress. He would actually enjoy this. "Thalia's always with her."

"Don't tell Thalia though, she loves her. Don't tell Narcissus either."

Of course he wouldn't tell Narcissus that he was spying on Messalina. Because Narcissus was still supporting her, and Narcissus thought that Kallias was watching Agrippina for him, when it was really the other way around.

It was really Agrippina who was running everything in her personal circle. Even Pallas reported to her now, and last week he had personally forgiven the interest on her business loan. Agrippina had never intended to pay it, Kallias had advised her not to, and now she never had to. And Pallas, kind and funny, didn't mind getting entangled with the beautiful Agrippina.

Kallias would rather keep it business, and if it wasn't business, he would rather keep it with someone young and stupid and who wouldn't interfere with his plans.

He had two missions: spy on Messalina and marry Thalia. One would deliver him the other. By the time he was done, the circle would feed itself.

He went to the next party, and this time, he sat with Thalia. Messalina came over during the middle, hugged her, and they put their heads together and spoke for some time. "So, you and Kallias have this thing!" she said, and reached across Thalia and tweaked his arm.

"You both are so good-looking," she said sincerely. "I almost feel envious of you two. Can you imagine if my Claudius didn't stutter?"

Thalia giggled while Kallias only smiled.

Everyone made fun of Caesar's stutter when he was not around.

Messalina's gaggle of friends were young, rich and obnoxious. They were the sons and daughters of aristocrats and popular ex-slave entertainers. They threw food and laughed too loud and interrupted the poet who had stood to recite. Messalina had her arms around two men. She let them kiss her hair and her neck in front of everyone.

When it was over people began to rise from their couches and stagger away and soon there was only Thalia, diligent follower that she was, with Mnestor and three of his friends, two women and a young man who had played a flute. They sat in a circle while the man read his love poems that he wanted to give to the girl he loved, who was not here at the moment but visiting friends in Corinth.

Messalina left with the men.

"She'll have to make Claudius mad enough by doing that," he told Agrippina about the party later. But they both knew it was not enough.

Thalia was perfect. Extremely pretty, not involved in any political games, and couldn't handle him. He convinced her to marry him. There wasn't much convincing to do, however. They were kissing in his bed and he said, "What do you think? We'd be good together."

Thalia was excited, and so it was settled easily.

Both Narcissus and Agrippina had thought this was a good idea and urged him into it. A man had to marry at some point in his life, and Kallias had to get Thalia before anyone else realized she was in a good position because of her father and did it instead.

Kallias announced the engagement, in the dining room of Narcissus's house, while Thalia held his arm and grinned. She was so pretty and there was a shame that nothing ever went through her head, but that was alright. That was for the better.

"It's going to be amazing," Thalia gushed.

Claudia, her mother, who had also once been a slave, stifled a groan and ran out the room in tears. She wanted Thalia to aim as high as possible and try to marry a citizen, an equestrian. But Kallias and Claudia were of the same rank, and he was not just any man off the street. He worked for the emperor.

"Ignore her," said Thalia to the company, rolling her eyes. "Nothing's ever that serious as she makes it."

Agrippina and Crispus paid for everything. Crispus said he shouldn't have to spend a penny on his own celebrations. Not after all he had done for Agrippina and the many ways he had supported them with his good service.

"This man," said Agrippina, during the wedding dinner, "would give anything for me. He was one of the first people I ever trusted. It was a good decision. When I met Kallias, it was the beginning of the turnaround of my life for good."

Agrippina made the speech about her, and poor Thalia was just a member at her own wedding. None of it was ever about her though. She never got the chance to speak or show off after the vows were said. When Agrippina sat, Claudius shuffled in at exactly that moment, with a trail of servants, and congratulated them.

That was the only word he managed to say without stuttering. He struggled through the rest of his three sentences, while there were some snickers. When he was done they applauded like none of them sitting in the circle had made fun of him. But he wasn't offended, or maybe he didn't even notice it.

When he sat, Kallias offered a toast of his own.

He immediately faced Agrippina. "I owe everything to this person here," he said, raising his cup, "and she brought me everything as well. She was also the turnaround of my life. We really have grown great together. Here is to the future and only more greatness for us."

Thalia lay on her couch staring into the cup ahead of her.

Chapter 37

When Narcissus went to Britain, Kallias stayed in Rome with the other bureaucrats, taking care of the empire's correspondence. Their job was still mostly to take care of these state matters, while Narcissus was acting now as Claudius's personal agent and more often away from the palace.

There was a lot of excitement about this new undertaking. Julius Caesar had attempted this invasion over a hundred years ago and had withdrawn from the island after taking only a small tribute. Britain was difficult to subdue. If the conquest was a success, Claudius would finally be able to say he had achieved something outstanding.

He was not so dumb after all, the courtiers said of him. He simply had a speech impediment. But he had a mind and goals and dreams like other men. He wanted to be like his predecessors, notable figures the world would remember forever.

Thalia wasn't thinking about any of that. She was imagining having a child. Her idol, Messalina, had given the emperor a son only a few months ago. Although the birth was private and not heavily publicized, an imperial heir was a big deal. This devastated Agrippina and delighted Thalia. They had very opposite reactions to the same news. Agrippina cried, and Thalia celebrated.

"I want a baby," she said now. "Wouldn't that be nice?"

He told her simply, "Have one then."

She got pregnant, and Kallias got an angry letter from Narcissus. When a mutiny broke out and he tried to settle it, the soldiers booed him and shouted "Io, Saturnalia!"

"Simpletons!" wrote Narcissus. "I could buy them all and sell them again with my money. But I just laughed, we all laughed together."

Kallias wrote back, "You're Caesar's best representative, they can take it or leave it!"

Some people were stuck on their blood, the patricians on their old wealth, their ancient families.

Kallias' money was new, his family was random, and sometimes the contemplation of this still galled him. Thalia, in a way uncharacteristically discerning of her, hinted at it. That was after the baby was born, and they named him Marcus and were so lucky to have everything during the birth go right.

Kallias said, "Look at him, Thalia. Our little citizen."

And Thalia said, "Isn't it so wonderful?" And sat up to kiss him. "I wonder if you ever imagined all this."

"No," he said, and went silent.

There was a nurse, from Narcissus's house, already taking the sleeping child away. Thalia had looked at it for the first hours after its birth and then decided she was too tired to give it any more attention. She'd play with it later when it was more fun.

As soon as she was up and walking again, she began to examine herself.

"I almost ruined my figure trying to have him," she said, and took to exercising at the baths. She had a slim, perfect figure, perfect like a lovely Venus statue. She was extremely proud of it.

Kallias started to throw discus and train. He'd always been slender but now he turned lean. They looked at themselves, at their bodies, at their baby, their money, and loved who they were. He bought a house. Thalia bought a cook. She played at being a matron, although her ignorance about all household matters astounded Kallias.

This was the beginning of their frequent fights. But he excused her at first. She had never really done anything useful, important, or stressful. He'd once been the steward of a very large household.

"You just have to give it time and pay attention and then you'll understand everything, you see?" he told her. "Just try to figure it out with time."

But she wasn't interested in that. She'd been honest when she said that she only wanted to party. Her casual attitude grated his nerves. He thought after some months she'd soon become interested in running the day-to-day functions of a household.

"Your problem," he told her, "is that you think life's a joke."

They didn't speak to each other for an entire week after he said that.

The Britain conquest went on. Narcissus was coming home, and was thrilled to be doing so, since the island was no place for him. "The natives here are absolutely incorrigible," he wrote. "And they are ruthless in their attacks. We have all the advantages, except they know the land and like to ambush us. Which is a serious problem. But I have done my work here."

In another letter he wrote, "The question amongst the officers is whether they or the Germans generally are worse. I can't say about Germania, as I've never been there. Vespasian seems to think nothing can compare to the Britons. The army has had to go against marshes, cold weather, and men streaked in blue paint yelling and running headlong at them in battle. But Vespasian is determined to help make this mission successful."

Kallias knew Vespasian from all the way back in Moesia. Vespasian was a tribune then. And he had been sturdy and cool headed. He and Kallias were nearly the same age. He used to come to the parties there and sit and drink watered-down wine. The only reason Kallias remembered him was for his perpetual scowl. That had been years ago, though, and Vespasian couldn't have remembered him now.

Kallias and Thalia prospered. Finally she was out the shadow of her father's protection and falling into place in her new life. When they argued, she always threatened to go home with the baby in her arms, until Narcissus finally made it clear she could not backtrack. He was not in Rome, and he would not take her back when he was there again.

She had married Kallias, Narcissus thought he was wonderful, and she would be with him. And so she was. The baby was thriving with the nurse and would soon be crawling. Already he could say "no", which his family thought was funny.

That year Kallias did make his million. And then he made another and another, and each time he felt his heart swell, and finally they decided that the house they lived in just wasn't good enough for them, and they were better than that place, so he bought another bigger and grander home and sold the first.

Chapter 38

The new house was fashionable and on Aventine Hill. Thalia insisted on having pretty gardens. They had baths and a gym and the structure had been designed by one of the best architects in Rome. This was wonderful, but Kallias knew they were only at the beginning of how far up they could go.

His sudden realization: this was only the beginning.

"I'm so pleased with us!" said Thalia on the first night they slept there. "Look what we did!"

He rolled over in the dark and thought, We? It was all my work.

But he didn't say it at first.

As he made more money, he became less tolerant of everything, including her. For years he'd trained himself to be obedient and polite and private with his thoughts. Now he had the urge to say whatever he wanted.

He didn't want to argue with her all the time, but he began to believe more and more that she was not only stupid, but useless.

In his first house, he hadn't lectured her too hard on running things, but now he had an investment that he was adamant about protecting. He thought of the new place as his, not theirs. She hadn't contributed anyway. She was not the one who made all that money to afford all those nice things. She had not contributed at all.

Their worst argument yet came about the steward. Thalia stood before him and said she didn't like the way the man managed things, and Kallias said it was only because the man didn't take her orders. She said she hated that he would never listen to her, only Kallias. She'd told him to order new benches for their gardens and he refused.

"Spending my money without asking me. So thoughtful, Thalia. But you never were."

"You're rich, you wouldn't have even noticed."

He was fumbling with the pin on his cloak. Now he looked up.

She stared at him with open anger in her face. "It can't be that hard for you," she said, spreading her hands. "You work at the palace and I know you take bribes. Who knows what you do. You and my father. I should be able to order anything in the world I want."

"That is none of your business," he snapped. "My work has nothing to do with you."

And so very quickly into the marriage, more of their conversations were fights instead of friendly. It was so tiresome and annoying and over and over he asked himself why she hadn't matured in the normal way and learned to finally pay attention to business.

Besides the conflict about running the house, there was still Messalina's behavior that made things worse. Recently, the empress had turned on two very important friends and had them killed as easily as flies. The freedmen looked the other way when it was Valerius Asiaticus, who was unlikable to them. Messalina acquired his gardens that she wanted so badly and laughed about his murder.

Agrippina had laughed too, when she heard that poor Polybius had lost his job and his life. After all, she'd been certain that her enemy would regret not aligning with her and now she was right again. That laugh turned to an intense stare when Kallias told her the next part: Narcissus and the other freedmen were furious.

They put their heads together and walked through the trails of her garden.

Messalina had walked straight into their trap, and she couldn't see her own feet.

"He despises her," said Kallias. And Agrippina began to smile again as it all sank in. It was not a petty issue, and Messalina would not win her husband's secretary again after killing one of his friends.

"I want to see what Narcissus does when he doesn't like someone," said Agrippina.

"Our dirty work," said Kallias.

Narcissus was still playing the perfect courtier. Polybius had only been gone for a month, and Narcissus was communicating with the empress as if nothing had happened. When she stood on her tiptoes and put her arm around his neck as a parting greeting, he smiled and patted her back.

But later to Pallas he said, in his clear perfect voice, "This bitch kills one of us without blinking, who do you think will be next? Me, Pallas, or you? Maybe one of the others. Or maybe Kallias. I assume she no longer likes Kallias, since he stopped going to her very ridiculous parties. She might send the Praetorians on him."

He tweaked Kallias's sleeve. Pallas, who was reading a scroll, sighed and got up from his bench and walked away. The easy going and amiable Pallas was not for plots and rage, although clearly what Messalina had done was stressing him out. The easy smile had faded over the past weeks.

While Messalina could not be removed because she was Caesar's wife and obviously it would be overstepping to even put forward such an idea, her downfall was certain. Kallias was waiting for her to condemn herself, which she inevitably would because of her own carelessness. When she did, Narcissus would kick her to the ground and Kallias would make sure to tell Agrippina to pop up to the palace at just the right time.

A promotion for him, and for Agrippina.

All he had to do was wait a bit, and Messalina would fall.

But Thalia still followed her.

"She's going to go down eventually," Kallias said, the first time he admonished her. "Cut her company if you want to look good."

Thalia said she would not. "You and Father just don't like her because Agrippina doesn't. You think you have to side with her."

"Are you blind? Agrippina has nothing to do with this. Do you understand how these things work? She killed two important people."

"Of course I know how it works. And I'm friends with an empress, who can do what she wants. Do you think I'm going to give that up?"

With the birth of their second son, he thought finally that Thalia would slow down. But she didn't, and Marcus and Titus were handed to caring servant women while Thalia kept up with her old friend every time the other woman made a move. Thalia couldn't help herself, and she said the children would be alright anyway. She always saw them every night.

"You don't know how much work it is," she said. "Caring for them every moment of the day. Just because I don't want to do that, doesn't mean I don't love them!"

Kallias said she was crazy and intellectually devoid. She said that he was too obsessed with control.

He couldn't even divorce her, because the marriage was not made of that kind of freedom. When he complained about her to Agrippina, she said, "You fund her whole lifestyle, I don't know how you could let one woman trouble you."

Kallias had an idea then. He said Agrippina was so wonderful, and she kissed him on the cheek (she was in a really good mood) and then Kallias went to his wife.

"Thalia," he said. There was a chest sitting at his feet. The servants she brought when they moved to the house stood around watching them. He pointed to it.

"You ever been out of Rome?"

"What are you talking about?"

"I'm sending you on holiday."

"Holiday?" She looked from them all, confused. A slave came in just then, and said that Marcus was awake. Before Thalia could reply, Kallias held up his hand. He pointed to the things on the floor. He told her she was going to Greece indefinitely and that it was already settled.

"I'd rather go on holiday from you, forever," said Thalia. "That's what I'd thank you for."

"You can do that," he said coolly. "But you won't take them."

The room was so quiet and the servants so still. Thalia opened her mouth. She closed it again. Her face was soft and young. She pulled a bangle on her arm and sighed. All of the money she spent was his, and Narcissus didn't give her an allowance anymore, which she blew through when she had it. She had no choice.

Tears of frustration welled up in her eyes and she made her small hands into fists. She called him a name. He heard it, but he chose not to reply. He got up from the bed where he was sitting and strode out.

There was peace in his house when she left. There were only the servants, with whom he did not interact, and his sons. They were the things, he knew, that would bring Thalia back, like an invisible string connected to her heart and body. So she was normal and she loved them after all. She laughed at everything before, but now he knew one thing to make her cry. And his mother and Agrippina too.

If he and Thalia divorced, law meant the children would automatically stay with Kallias. But Thalia wouldn't do that. Nor would she write any letters to Narcissus from Greece to say that Kallias was mistreating her. One of the slaves he sent with her would see to that.

None of this would really hurt her. She'd be physically fine. Maybe she'd even come to her senses. He couldn't let her ruin his career because of her own bad choices.

Months went by. Narcissus asked about her, and Kallias said, "She's relaxing in Athens. Tells me she loves it."

"I am very surprised she detached from Messalina," said Narcissus. "But that's good."

Kallias told Agrippina about it when she came to his house.

She laughed. "When will you let her come back? "

"When she wants to in her heart," he said, which made Agrippina grin. She said she knew he'd figure it out.

"So she hasn't written to you? What if she's really dead because of an accident, and all the servants are too, and it's all just out of hand?"

"Do you ever think about her dead?" she asked, when he didn't say anything.

"I don't need to do that."

"Sometimes it can be necessary."

He saw where this conversation became about her, which was more and more inexplicable of their conversations these days. Every time he talked to Agrippina now, she hardly listened before launching into discussions of her own devices.

She said, "Your marriage is very much like mine with Crispus, except that you're the husband and I'm the wife."

"He still tries to control you? You? Agrippina?"

"He's a wonderful man, a rarity these days, the gods know. But delusional."

Crispus was a good man, but he could never manage someone like his wife.

Chapter 39

Passienus Crispus sat at the desk in his office and studied the paper in front of him. He didn't scratch his head in hesitation, but he looked like he wanted to. To his right, stood four of his equestrian friends, Agrippina, and Xander. On the left, Kallias stood beside the doctor's slim African wife, Zelia. Zelia, an astrologer, had said the omens were a good time for a man naming his heir.

Agrippina, being as superstitious as she was, always liked to know that her plans were auspicious. Zelia had convinced Crispus that it was the right day, Xander would bring the poison later, and Kallias would take the will to the Temple of Vesta after Crispus signed it. They were all very good at keeping secrets and none of them acted as if they understood the role the others were playing in this tense moment.

"You're like his father anyway," said Agrippina, as Crispus sat rereading what he had written. Crispus had already done all of this with his lawyer and one of his own secretaries. His previous will was very elaborate, and now he was changing it to make it very simplistic. It clearly made him nervous.

All he had written was:

Lucius Domitius Ahenobarbus, my adopted son, will inherit the entirety of my estate upon my death.

"Well, I don't have other sons, so it does make sense," said Crispus finally. But he was still rereading.

Zelia, dark arm lined with gold bangles, moved just the barest and they made a sound. Zelia said, "Every man has to have an heir! And it's a good day, so I'm seeing only the good for you, Passienus. Only the good."

He picked up his signet ring and stamped it.

Seven witnesses, a will signed and sealed. His own fate.

After the funeral, Agrippina refused to see anyone. It was not so much that she was grieving, but because she didn't want anyone peering into her face and trying to ask the questions that would answer why when Crispus had named her son his heir, he died only a few months later from a strange illness.

It looked very suspicious, and very obvious. Xander, who had administered the poison, decided to avoid interrogation by leaving the city for a while with Zelia. His excuse was that he would return when she healed over the grief of her patron. After all, Crispus had been very good to Zelia when she was a girl. Her father was a glassmaker who traded with Crispus, and Zelia made friends with her father's business partner. Crispus had allowed her to read the fortunes of senators and lawyers, and then when she was popular in their circles, he helped her establish her a shop to practice on the common people.

"I can't believe I thanked him this way," said Zelia before they left the funeral. They were standing in the street in a huddle. She kept wiping her eyes with a pinky finger from each hand. Agrippina snapped at her to get over herself. They'd all done something good for Lucius.

"You have to keep focus of the plan," said Agrippina. "You can't act like I did it out of spite. This is for all our good. And my son is one step closer to the throne."

She'd given Xander, Kallias, and Zelia ten thousand sesterces each for helping her.

When Kallias visited her again, she mentioned the busts of Crispus that were still in the front of the house, and how she'd never moved his cloak from his bedroom table. Kallias didn't want to talk about it, so he said something instead about servants being too lazy to do thorough cleanings. He added that when he was a steward, he always made sure things got put in their proper places. He walked himself right into the topic she wanted to discuss.

"Remember Polycarp?" she asked.

Of course Kallias remembered him. At the time he thought he'd escaped guilt, but over the years, he'd thought about the old steward more often than he would have liked.

Nothing to do but keep on stamping it out, drowning it out.

The man had been useless anyway.

"Polycarp was nice, when you could overlook that he liked to sit on his sorry ass all day," said Agrippina. "Remember?"

"He was lazy."

"And he didn't serve a purpose, so that's why we got rid of him. It was nothing personal. Just like my husband."

"It's all over now."

"I miss Crispus, a little, honestly. He was so nice and so funny. "

Kallias didn't say anything. He ran his finger around the rim of the cup and stopped a drop of wine from falling onto the table. His arm had gone dead from the pressure on it. He sat up and shook it.

Agrippina was very still. "Zelia told me that my son would be both emperor of Rome, and my ruin. I never told anyone. I'm only telling you now."

"Zelia says a lot of bullshit," said Kallias. "She told your dead husband it was a good day to make his will."

"I don't care," said Agrippina. "As long as Lucius is emperor."

Lucius was a long way from being emperor, but he was richer than ever now at only ten years old. All that money would come in handy and give him a chance at the best life and the most important men by his side when he needed their friendship. He was growing up steadily, and watched with an unmoving gaze by his mother who had only the grandest of plans for him.

On the morning of the first day of the Saecular Games, he was surrounded by servants and guards his mother had hired. Agrippina couldn't stop herself from ruffling his hair. Everyone was excited, but her movements buzzed with an anxious energy, as if she were afraid something would go wrong. Lucius would be riding his horse in the Trojan Games play battle, and Agrippina was always extremely wary of him coming to any physical hurt.

"I'm excited," he said, bouncing up and down. "I'm so excited."

"You just don't fall off, alright? Don't fall and you'll be fine," she said. And smoothed his hair and ruffled it again.

When he pulled his head away, she frowned at him.

Kallias had accompanied them with some of Agrippina's other group, but now he made his way down the sidewalk to see what Messalina was up to. Her entourage was easy to spot—it was an even larger group than Agrippina's and some members of her household liked to wear white and green. Obviously, purple was only for senators, but her entourage felt equally significant, and wanted a common shade to say so.

And green was Messalina's favorite color.

He weaved his way into the circle easily, hoping no one had noticed that he was only just with Agrippina and her group. Something very different was going on here. Little Britannicus, the boy who stood in the way of Lucius inheriting the throne, sobbed and rubbed his eyes with balled fists. Messalina squatted before him, whispering something to him in a hushed voice. Kallias strained to hear, but some freedmen were blocking the way. Then someone bumped into him—it was noticeable even in the throng of talking and moving people, and it was a young man in the clothing of a senator. He squeezed past everyone else, and Messalina glanced up just then.

"Gaius!" she shouted, and straightened.

He greeted her warmly and then turned to Britannicus. The three of them looked like a small perfect family for that one moment. Britannicus stopped crying, and someone else came up behind Gaius, carrying a helmet small enough for a child, and gave it to Messalina. It was an interesting scene, but Kallias couldn't hear anything much. One of her friends spoke to him and said, "Oh, it's you, what are you doing here? We haven't seen you in a long time."

He smiled, and disappeared into the crowd. Agrippina and her entourage were already moving through the rest of the people. She would never speak to Messalina in public.

Messalina had to walk right by her once, and she spit near her. Agrippina pretended not to see how Messalina's entourage had parted so Agrippina could clearly see her rival perform the disgusting act in front of her.

"What's with her, really?" said Agrippina, without turning her head. "Beastly behavior."

That day, though, Agrippina came home delighted, and Lucius's cheeks were bright. The crowds had clapped for him, sitting astride his horse, for one full minute. When the applause began, it was stunning. Through the din, Kallias heard someone shout, "That's Germanicus's grandson!" The clapping only picked up and carried across the stands until everyone was on their feet. Kallias counted the seconds all the way until a minute. It was a very good public day for Agrippina and her son.

"They don't even know me," she said. "And they remember my father! You see, you see? I'm so happy. Fuck Messalina, and not in the way she likes, either."

On the other hand, Britannicus hadn't received nearly so much applause. They clapped for him just like all the other boys who performed. No one shouted anything about him being the son of anyone. Britannicus was six, and probably didn't care. But his mother did, and she was fuming.

"I just don't like it," she said. "It just wasn't right. Her boy is bigger. Of course he could ride the stupid horse faster and control it better. Do they know my son's going to rule Rome and that he's the one they should be going hoarse cheering for?"

Kallias told Agrippina all this. This time Narcissus was there. He said Messalina deserved to be humiliated. She was a bully. She didn't deserve a sweet child like Britannicus.

"I never realized you hated her so much," Narcissus told Agrippina. "I wish you had told me years ago!"

Keeping up with those two women was exhausting. But Kallias could deal with it. He was very patient when he needed to be. And he waited for it to play out, for Messalina to do herself in.

"She will," said Narcissus. "And if she does not do it fast enough, I will help her. I have been thinking of what I can do."

Narcissus was sending his own spies to keep up with what Messalina's many lovers were doing. The good-looking man at the Games who came and spoke to Britannicus was Gaius Silius, a senator. Messalina had been seeing him for a few weeks now.

"I bet he is the one who does it for her," said Narcissus, "because it appears to be a real thing this time. She gave him so many gifts."

Narcissus knew through his spies, and his own visits to Silius's house that some Claudius items were now in the other man's home. He had recognized a portrait from Claudius's vestibule, and two slaves who were very popular in the emperor's Ostia home. There must have been other things too, but Narcissus had been in a hurry to leave when he sneaked there himself.

That's what Narcissus told Kallias and Pallas. They were sharing stories as usual, and Pallas never had as much to say as the other two men. He was so passive, Kallias thought suddenly. Easygoing, good natured. That was why Agrippina liked him so much and could go to bed with him over and over. He knew how to be whatever she wanted him to be at any time, and he didn't want to plot.

Pallas wanted to let Messalina fuck herself over on her own.

But Narcissus said he was going to help her get there. As they stood in that circle that day, just outside Claudius's audience room, Kallias felt an irritation rising in him about Narcissus. Kallias liked it when his plan was known only to Agrippina. That way there was more opportunity to adjust the outcome of the empress's certain failure to their own desires.

Here comes Narcissus, with additions to the plan, and a chance to steal the glory when things went to shit. Kallias didn't like that. It was not his plot anymore. He saw very clearly that he would not be the first messenger to bring the news. And he began to resent his mentor.

Not too long after all this, Thalia came back.
He said, "I'm sure your holiday calmed you down, Thalia," and she murmured that it did.
Titus could run now and speak in full sentences. Kallias, who had been so busy following up with the schemes he and his patroness and her associates were crafting, hadn't even realized this himself. He never kept up with his children, and sometimes forgot that they were there until he walked into the house and heard them. Then he would stoop to kiss them on the forehead before rushing to something else.
But his youngest was three and the eldest, nowhere to be seen now, was nearly the same age as Britannicus. Titus ran up to his mother now, and stared at her. Kallias watched, leaning against a pillar. Thalia looked like she might cry. She looked like she might curse him. But she didn't.
He had all the money, and therefore all the power.

Chapter 40

Agrippina was getting impatient. She wasn't like Kallias, able to count to a hundred before striking for something. But that was why he was good at investing, and money, because he knew how to wait. He had learned that after years of drudging slavery.

The plan was still the same: to remove the next person in the way of complete power. The next person now, being the empress Messalina.

"What if we tried the poison on her?" she said. But they had no ties to her household and certainly knew no servants who handled her food. It was not that easy anyway, they concluded. Because if it were, the empress would have been dead long ago. So no, they had to wait.

In the meantime, Lucius was growing up nicely. He read impeccably and pleased his mother with his good manners. He could be sullen, but that was normal for an eleven year old. Agrippina tried to indulge his requests in things that didn't matter, but never let him win when he tried to resist her on something that did matter.

Once, she had a messenger call for Kallias when she and her son were having one of their worst disagreements. Kallias rushed to the house, muttering to himself that she must think he never had anything important to do. He had been looking at her accounts when the servant summoned him. When he walked inside her office, Kallias found Agrippina seated at a desk and shaking her head. She had her legs crossed and her arms folded.

Lucius stood on the opposite side of the room, frowning like he had chewed on a bitter grape. Standing together were Zelia and the steward of the household. Kallias could tell as soon as he walked in that they had been trying to convince Lucius of something.

"Tell him," said Agrippina. "Tell him that playing the kithara is not as important as learning solid, flawless vocabulary and letters."

"Yes it is," said Lucius hotly. "I already read like I should. And I like my kithara."

"I'm sure you do, but playing music doesn't win you wars or make people think of you as a leader."

"I don't want to be a leader, I just want Orion back."

She had fired his dance tutor, who had been with him since he was a year old and his mother was in exile. Orion had been his only consolation for a long time, when his mean, old aunt would never hug him or bother to even look at him. Orion's dismissal must have hurt Lucius a lot.

Then Agrippina told Lucius he would only have music lessons once a month, instead of twice like before. She didn't like that he was more interested in that than his Greek and Latin and arithmetic.

Kallias felt sorry for the child, but sighed and agreed with Agrippina.

"No one cares about music, honestly," he said. "It shows talent and cultural taste, but someone important like you, Lucius. Like you'll grow up to be. You'll need more."

"See," said Agrippina. "Kallias knows stuff. He can tell you about what everybody cares about and he's never wrong."

Lucius looked at him with resentful eyes. Kallias held his stare and soon Lucius looked away.

The steward scratched his nose, and said, "We could have twice a month, mistress, but maybe shorten the time. Thirty minutes instead of an hour."

Agrippina glared at him.

"A suggestion," he added hastily. "Since Lucius misses Orion so much, and then the kithara —"

"He can play that in his own time." Zelia put out her ringed hands. "He can play it in his own time, Agrippina can tell him when he's allowed and everything is settled."

"Zelia knows too," said Agrippina to her son. She ignored the steward. Kallias was surprised the man had the audacity to offer a small disagreement even in the form of revision. It was bold. He was lucky that instead of reproaching him, Agrippina only ignored him.

"See," she said. "Everybody your mother trusts can tell you that what she's saying is the best thing for you. You know I care for you, don't you, my baby?"

There were clear tears in his eyes. But he didn't cry, because he was too old for that, and would have been sharply reprimanded for it by the woman who sat before him now holding his beloved kithara captive on her desk. She held out her arms in command, and he walked to her and embraced her dutifully and put his head on her shoulder.

Calling Kallias to the house for this was stupid. He said so to Zelia as they walked out, but she only laughed that high, fake laugh she always did, and said that children had to be brought up a certain way. Kallias thought, despite everything, that part was true. Everything had to be in order, and a boy whose mother wanted him to one day rule an empire had to be strict about what he was allowed to do and learn.

But still, Lucius would probably one day resent that control.

For no apparent reason, that scenario brought to memory a time when Kallias was the same age as Lucius, eleven years old. It was the year he had begun to realize with sharper and heavier understanding that he could not do what he wanted. One day in his lessons with Rufus, the tutor chided him for some minor infraction and sent him to stand in the hallway.

Pouting, Kallias had decided not to go back inside. He sat out there so long, he went to sleep, sitting on the ground. And then the trusted servant who used to walk him and Rufus around the city saw him, and kicked him in the side where he slumped. He woke up and asked indignantly why he did it.

"You're not even the tutor," Kallias had said.

"Preparation for when you're older," the servant had said. "And Spinther beats the shit out of you for upsetting him. You shouldn't be sleeping, go back inside."

"He doesn't beat people," Kallias had said, thinking of the master who always ruffled his hair and gave him sweets.

"Oh yes he does," the servant had replied. "Just wait until you're older and he's having a bad day."

Kallias hadn't thought the kick was necessary any more so than before the conversation, and Spinther had never actually hit him. But he had ended up resold, and gods yes, he had learned a lot about beatings, and in the present he decided that people must be prepared for the situations they were meant to experience.

Chapter 41

Claudius was away in Ostia touring building projects. His wife Messalina was in Rome partying. Thalia was in an awful mood because she could not be with her, and Narcissus was bringing a report to Agrippina every ten minutes about what the empress was doing. This irritated Kallias, who felt he was being made redundant. The spying was his job, and the reward for the empress falling was supposed to be for him and Agrippina. There was never enough space in the world for too many people to benefit from one thing at the same time.

Recently, everything about Narcissus had begun to annoy him. The lead secretary had been indulging himself more often lately and had gained some weight around his waist and wrists. Kallias, who always judged people for being physically unappealing, couldn't help but look at him in disgust. He could feel himself sneering every time he looked at Narcissus.

Kallias also despised his tone. The perfectly enunciated words with the emphasis on every syllable was an oratory pretense. He heard Narcissus speaking to his wife Claudia once, and he had sounded so very normal and not overly sophisticated. The palace voice was fake. But of course it was, Narcissus was a courtier. And now he walked around with this self-satisfied smirk because he was going to take down Messalina.

"Did you know Narcissus doesn't really talk like that?" Kallias told Pallas. Kallias was hoping to stir up just the smallest distrust, to sow a little seed of discomfort. "Ask the others if they know he speaks very normally when he's with his wife."

"I'm not sure I understand," said Pallas. "I've only known him one way all his life. Why do you say that?"

"No reason, I just thought it was interesting."

He'd hoped Narcissus would be ignorant to what Messalina was doing, or even supportive of it. Then when she slipped up badly enough, Kallias could report her to Claudius and say that Narcissus was also suspect. Maybe then Narcissus would be banned, or fined. Or maybe even executed. But Narcissus would certainly lose his job. Then Kallias could have his spot, and maybe or maybe not he would do away with Thalia. Messalina just had to go and kill the man's friend. So, things would go as they were, and at least at the end of it, Agrippina would be wife to an emperor. Kallias was going to win anyway.

Hell, he thought, let Narcissus do the bulk of the dirty work, I put my finger on a few things and push, and then I find a way to get him dismissed afterward.

Kallias stood in his study counting coins in a box on his desk when Narcissus came over to tell him and Thalia the empress was throwing a huge party tonight.

"I can't believe I wasn't invited," said Thalia, following her father into the room.

"You don't want to go to this." Kallias kept counting without looking up.

"Thalia, you did not write to her for a long time, she has forgotten you. And Kallias is right, you do not want to go."

"Why, why?" she said.

"Use your head, Thalia." Kallias glanced at her. "Didn't your father ever teach you to be clever like him?"

Narcissus looked a little taken aback, but then his face cleared and he just smiled. "My Thalia just sees the good side of things," he said. He pointed to the doorway.

A servant came in, carrying a folded, green fabric in his arms. His head was bowed.

"What's that?" asked Kallias, and stopped counting. He picked up his stylus and wrote down quickly, six hundred sesterces. He looked up again.

Narcissus nodded, and the servant shook the fabric out. It was a very exquisite dress, all in Messalina's favorite color. The servant was one of the empress's wardrobe keepers and wore a linen belt of the same color.

"So?"

"She is having a play wedding this evening."

Kallias grinned. "It's the Gaius Silius man?"

"How did you guess?"

"Play weddings are so fun," said Thalia. "I did one once, with my friend Basilius. We were seventeen."

Her father and her husband glanced at her the way people look at small children who say silly things.

"Does Agrippina know?" Kallias asked then.

"No," said Narcissus. "But she is not in Rome at this very moment, no?"

"She went to see a friend, she'll be back soon."

"I see. She stays so busy, for a woman! Well, we have a big day for us, I will be going."

"Agrippina has things to do, she can't waste time."

"No, no, you can not afford it with certain things. Is she still not talking to Pallas?"

Agrippina was in Portus to meet a wealthy businessman. She had taken a liking to him since Kallias introduced him to her. It was going to come to nothing, because Agrippina never let little things distract her. But she and Pallas had met privately in a while, mainly because Agrippina said she was tired of his docility. This man she went to see would excite her until he inevitably annoyed her.

Kallias smiled. "Pallas gets nervous when she's in a bad mood. You know how he is with her."

"They get along so well, though," said Narcissus. "I am sure that she will speak to him soon."

"Most likely."

Narcissus nodded, and then he and the servant easily disappeared out the study. The door was left ajar, and Thalia stood in front of it frowning.

"What was that all about?" she said. "You and Father plotting."

"I didn't tell him to make her hold a mock wedding. Nobody told her to make a mock wedding. Nobody told her to do something that stupid."

"But why, why do you care?"

"Just think about it, Thalia. Gods, it's like your brain doesn't reside in your head, isn't it?"

"You don't have to always talk to me like that, it's getting old now."

"Well it's true, so there's that. Timon! Come here quickly."

The steward came in. He was always nearby.

"I need you to find a servant, anyone who doesn't dally and will get back on time, but find someone to run and tell Agrippina that she needs to get back here to Rome as soon as possible. I don't know why she even left, knowing we've got all this going on."

He said the part mostly to himself, but the steward was still nodding with understanding. Thalia left, and Timon followed right behind her, calling for a slave.

Kallias counted his coins and comforted himself. It was finally happening. A mock wedding would be a bad look regardless of intention, and Messalina would finally see that even something as silly as having too many partners could ruin a person. That was good, and he knew exactly what Narcissus would do.

He hoped Agrippina would hurry back.

Chapter 42

Narcissus wrote to the emperor at the same time and advised him to rush back to Rome because his beloved wife was marrying another man in his house and attempting to overthrow him from his position. That was as plain as treason could get.

Everyone in the circle knew it was a mock wedding. That had been an odd little trend going around at some parties, although it never really quite took off enough to be popular. Regardless, it was plainly a joke. A woman would never divorce the ruler of an empire to marry a man any lesser, even if that man was a handsome, rich senator. The desire was where the power lay. Everything else was a good diversion.

Gaius Silius might be the empress's favorite lover, and she could fake marry him all she wanted, but it didn't mean she meant it.

Kallias caught the scene as it happened. Messalina was in the street, in that very beautiful green linen, sobbing her eyes out because two Praetorians held her by both arms. Her man had his hands up as the Praetorians herded the rest of them out of the house.

Narcissus was right beside an officer, a man he was often seen speaking to.

"Come on, Narcissus," said Messalina. Snot rolled down her lip. "Be serious, you know it's just a party."

"Shh, shh." Narcissus waved a paper. "This is serious, and you are not aware of how much trouble you are in."

They waited for Claudius to return while Messalina was under arrest. Her favorite senator had to kill himself, just like that. He was simply a casualty of politics. Narcissus told Messalina that she would have do the same, but Messalina, more composed since last night, said she would not. She said she couldn't wait to see her husband, and then he would know what a big misunderstanding this was.

"And you're dead," she told Narcissus.

Her mother sat on the bench in the corner of the room where they were held, and cried softly into a white handkerchief. Messalina rocked her with one hand tightly on her shoulder, and made a derogatory symbol with her other hand.

Narcissus only smiled, before turning to leave. He didn't even slam the door.

Pallas was standing behind Kallias.

"Can't you freedmen do something?" said Messalina. "Narcissus is being unreasonable. Everybody knows you can have a fake wedding."

"You're really not taking this seriously," said Kallias. "Are you?"

Messalina started crying again.

Her children Britannicus and Octavia were in the house, but ignored. Narcissus said under no circumstances should they leave their rooms. The emperor would get home tomorrow morning, first thing, to order her execution for marrying a man right under his nose. What did she think she was doing?

Chapter 43

They waited for Claudius and his entourage to appear on the road. It was chilly outside and there were no leaves on the trees. Kallias sat beside Narcissus on a hired cart that the driver had pulled off to the side, as to not block traffic. The only traveler Narcissus wanted to block was not here yet. He would see to it that she never reached the destination she sought.

Narcissus hadn't been able to hold her in her prison after all. Some of the Praetorians said she had to be released because she was still the empress, and so any time now, Messalina would make her way here to try to shout down Narcissus and explain to her husband what had really happened at her party. But so far, Narcissus and Kallias beat her to the main road.

Narcissus was tense, drumming his fingers on his lap. Kallias didn't realize he was doing the same thing until he looked down at himself. He stood, walked around the cart, and pulled his cloak closer around him.

"I hope he believes me," said Narcissus from where he sat. "He will, I know. I never lie to him. She did try to marry him and we all saw it."

The Praetorians accompanying them laughed, and one of them said that no one would miss Messalina. "Personally, Narcissus," he said. "I'd take you for a drink."

The freedman smiled tightly.

Kallias hoped things would hurry up. He needed the climax of this to happen very quickly and fall into place for him. The best plots had a buildup—rigorous and clever planning until the final day, and then everything falling into place. He blew into his hands. It was really cold for October.

One of the Praetorians stood beside him and began a conversation about Rome being in trouble because of that traitorous empress, but Kallias barely heard a word as he nodded along. He rubbed his face, glanced at Narcissus, at the road, and blew out his breath.

Then the emperor's procession approached in the distance.

Narcissus leapt off the cart. As he did so, Kallias turned and saw that none other than the empress was coming up in the opposite direction. He was certain it was her because of the color of the carriage. It was the most ridiculous timing. What are the odds, he thought. He looked back to Narcissus, who now jogged down the middle of the road to stop the emperor.

The emperor and Narcissus both stopped. They were talking to each other. Claudius was probably asking where Messalina was, and Kallias already knew what Narcissus was saying about that. Narcissus was saying there was no point in looking into a traitor's face and that it would only break the emperor's heart for him to see his wife after she had tried to dethrone him. She had bad intentions for him and there was no need for him to grieve by even having to see her. She was a wicked, wicked woman.

And of course, because her carriage was riding fast, Kallias and the Praetorians rushed to promptly block them. Everything slammed to a halt. Kallias ran up and told the guards to turn around, drive back.

"Let me talk, let me talk!" Messalina was trying to climb out of her seat, but one of the Praetorians pushed her back.

"Stop it!" she hissed.

There was a little struggle with her and the guard.

"Sit down before you fall," Kallias ordered. "You can't block this imperial procession —"

"This imperial procession is my husband!"

They had an angry back and forth where he told her over and over she could not progress. She was nearly shouting, but he could talk faster than her and the Praetorian held her fast. In the background, Britannicus and Octavia watched with wide eyes.

Kallias gestured again for them to move. The guard pushed her back and she fell and then the driver pulled the reins to turn around.

Kallias was in a hurry not only because Narcissus had told him to do everything in his power to prevent her from speaking to Claudius, but also because right along now, Agrippina should have been arriving from Portus and he had to tell her everything.

Chapter 44

That was the end of Messalina. A soldier cut her throat and all her statues were taken down. She died for something silly, all because she offended the wrong people at the right time.

In her sitting room, Agrippina lay flat on her couch while Kallias sat opposite her.

"Good! Good, excellent!" she said, and clapped her hands. "So you and Narcissus will speak for me?"

"That, yes. And…You'll have to make Claudius see that it's you."

"That part I dread. He's deformed, and my uncle."

"Well, you want to be empress."

Claudius had been in a bad mood in the weeks following Messalina's execution. Only Narcissus was seeing him, and he said that the emperor had been drinking a lot. Claudius missed his wife, wished he hadn't been so quick to have her killed over something he wasn't even sure about, and most of all, was afraid of dying alone.

"I tell him everyday," said Narcissus later, "that he cannot keep going like this."

"He'll get over it," said Kallias.

If only Narcissus could access Claudius in his most private moments, only Kallias could speak to Agrippina in hers. He told her to go to Pallas again, and that he had already told Pallas she was not dismissive of him anymore and wanted to speak to him.

What Agrippina didn't know, and didn't need to find out, was that Pallas had been sulking and had suggested that Narcissus put forward another woman to be the empress instead of Agrippina. Pallas only said it because the other woman had a heritage rivaling Agrippina's, and Agrippina had not showed up yet to the palace. It was probably not out of malice. Pallas didn't have a bone like that in his body.

So Agrippina made up with Pallas, who then agreed to back Narcissus in speaking to Claudius for her. That was, when the emperor finally let someone other than his most trusted freedman speak to him. They agreed that they would put forward Agrippina and scratch off the other two irrelevant options.

After two more weeks, Narcissus said that Claudius would love to be comforted now in his grief and was open to visits. Agrippina should go before any of the other women rushed to beat her. Agrippina was right on time, never to miss an opportunity. She put on her best clothing, the kind of fabric that draped her body. She looked beautiful, determined, and smelled of spikenard. Kallias, who met her in the palace, said that she would be Claudius's dream when he saw her.

"You like what you see?" she said. "I see you looking."

He laughed. "Go make us both proud."

"I'll try not to throw up," she said.

He watched her until she was out of sight.

Chapter 45

Agrippina saw Claudius six more times. He was still swimming in grief over Messalina, but hungry, she said, for her body. Claudius was finally allowing visits from more than only Narcissus and Pallas, was in his study to work again, and had agreed that he would remarry one of the women they had picked for him.

"You won't go wrong, Excellency, marrying this one." Narcissus put a hand on the emperor's arm. "She's is the closest thing to a Caesar you can get, and she is far more discreet and loyal than that thing you had to execute."

Claudius said, "Questionable. She's m-my n-n-niece!"

And Narcissus said, squeezing just a little, "That is not a problem at all. Would you regard something as simple as that?"

The emperor said nothing, but they both knew that he had been enjoying that niece very much in the past two weeks.

"This is about Rome surviving, Caesar. Surely, you can see that. She is the best pick."

"Well, Rome surviving is what matters," said Claudius then, in a perfect sentence.

Narcissus straightened and patted him on the shoulder.

The men around Claudius all thought that he was a figurehead. They loved his faults and fears. He couldn't walk as fast as them, or talk quite as smoothly.

People had always degraded him for it. Since the Praetorians killed his nephew in broad daylight, he'd been afraid, and had never quite recovered from that anxiety. His freedmen loved these details. Making Claudius feel secure in his decisions was always key to gaining his submission.

This was how they spoke to him all the time. And when he agreed with them it was all they could do to hide their triumphant sneers.

Narcissus met eyes with Kallias, above the emperor's head, and they smiled. At just this moment, Pallas walked in. And Narcissus gave him the signal that the conversation was a success.

Agrippina, wife to Ahenobarbus and Crispus, daughter of Germanicus the famous general, niece to the emperor, sister to the emperor, niece again to the emperor, became wife of the emperor on New Year's Day.

Kallias turned forty. He didn't celebrate, as he was attending Agrippina's wedding. There had been no question of which he would do, celebrate himself or her. But he was already celebrating himself, since he'd gone so far up in the world.

Chapter 46

The wedding itself was the grandest event in Rome since the Saecular Games, and Agrippina was the most famous woman in the city. Scores of children led the procession, followed by music and dance and more attendants. Flowers lined the streets and cheers brightened the way. Agrippina was brilliant in her wedding gown and her smile was bright and confident as she waved at the crowds. Kallias remembered how subdued she was when she first married Ahenobarbus. Back then she was a frightened girl.

Now she was glorious.

Claudius beside her, was decent only when he was still. When he moved he was awkward, and after they said the vows, just briefly before they went to their couch, Agrippina put a hand on his lower back. It was as if, just for that second, she was the husband and he was the wife in need of gentle physical guidance. Her back, so elegant and straight, made his frame look bent and withered.

Kallias was placed between the people Agrippina had relied on the most the past years. Her former husband's doctor, Xander, his tricky wife Zelia, Pallas, Narcissus, and some other palace goers. All Kallias could think about through the din of everything, was that it was only the beginning. He couldn't stop smiling.

The guests greeted the couple, saying well wishes. When it was Kallias's turn, he kissed Agrippina on both cheeks and he said was so proud of them.

The years that followed saw Kallias prosperous beyond his dreams. Courtesy of Agrippina, he went from the job in the palace to working now as a stenographer in the Senate House. She wanted to know what happening in the sessions, and if he sat in, then he could report it all to her, since as a woman, she could never enter the building.

"Isn't that something?" she said. "If you think about it! You're my freedman, but because you're a man, you can go in, and no matter how high I am, I can't."

Kallias couldn't say one job was better than the other, except that working in the Senate House meant he got to hear the voice of Rome itself debating and deciding on laws. The group of toga-clad men with purple stripes on their clothing were always a little haughty. It was in the way they walked, and greeted men they thought were lesser. After all, they had this thing about dignity. They carried themselves with an air that said they would never disgrace themselves, even if one of them was a liar or another did not understand the laws being presented or another was going bankrupt. They had that dignity.

Kallias overlooked them. No one could say he was not as good as them now. It did not matter that they were Rome's honorable and wise fathers. He had made a lot of money and he was successful. And he was proud, so proud. He would walk in and take his place at the table to write the notes in the shorthand that he had learned so very well.

He was so good at it, that one day he went to Tiro's school and spoke to the students there on the techniques they could use to better themselves at learning.

"This is Kallias," said the instructor. "He knows all about this subject. You should ask him questions about other things as well."

Agrippina settled into her role with no stress. The freedmen at Claudius's court were wise to court her, but in those days, anyone was. Claudius was hesitant, alternating between anxious and too trusting. But nothing surprised Agrippina. She knew everything and her informers were everywhere.

Her handsome, clever lover Pallas was secretary of the treasury. Sometimes after the wedding, they had begun sleeping together again, while she neglected Claudius. She was pleased with Narcissus as the secretary of letters. Narcissus deferred to her, and tried to agree with her when she spoke to Claudius.

Britannicus, the little son of Claudius by Messalina, was properly ignored and shamed beside her noble Lucius, who was growing into a fine young man and always put ahead of his stepbrother. Britannicus was too young to see through Agrippina's game, and never said anything to his father about his treatment. Not that Agrippina would have allowed him to complain. She had spies watching his every move, even when he laid in bed and played with himself or when he threw away the food he didn't want.

Agrippina was going to get what she wanted. She was winning. One thing after another.

She would give Kallias, the man she had known since she was a young girl, any job he wanted. After years in the Senate House, he said that he wanted to do something different, and knew another man to replace him who could report to her. So she bestowed another honorable position on Kallias: quaestor.

"This is perfect for you," she said, with her hands on his shoulders. "It's all about money, and I know you'll love working with it."

The money represented power. Of course he loved it. And if he had ever thought he was important, all that was foolishness compared to this. Now he had climbed high enough to truly breathe the air on a mountaintop. And it was fresh, and here was a view to look down on the world.

The first day at his position as a quaestor, he laid his hands flat on the desk and he said to the people in his office, "If you can't understand what I want before I even open my mouth, then you should leave now, because you won't like me."

His voice changed as he gained more power. He still had the flawlessly professional courtier's tone, but he no longer bothered to be polite. He said exactly what he wanted and he didn't care who it bothered. He had an amazingly swift temper, too. He walked into his office one day where they gathered together the taxes for the city, and saw one of his assistants was busy looking at some papers. Kallias stopped beside the desk and scanned them.

"This is what we did last week," he said, tapping on it. "This is old. How aren't you caught up?"

"I didn't realize," said the man, looking up at him. "No one told me."

"This is not the place for slow people," said Kallias. He gestured to a door. "If you want to be slow, go and sweep streets."

Their harsh exchange culminated in Kallias telling him to leave.

There were stares as the man stood. But Kallias only felt irritation.

He hated when everything wasn't perfect and rapid. He wanted everything to be done exactly the way he thought it should be done, or else he was angry. He felt that no one else knew how to do anything as thoroughly as him. Everyone was floating in their own ignorance and inability. He was the only person who had good sense.

He knew behind his back those in the palace described him as a nasty man who was best to be avoided. Once he overheard one of the senators say, "Pallas and Kallias are the worst of the freedmen, one's too mean and one's too nice. At least Narcissus and Callistus are normal."

"They both love Agrippina too much," said the other man. "That's the problem."

He turned the corner just then, and looked them both straight in the eye. They jumped and nodded to him. Now would these same two ask him for something next week? People couldn't gossip about him and then expect his favor.

There was also this disconnect, of seeing him as this man with a good-looking face, and wanting to trust him because of that, only to find out he was cold. It was rather funny. People had always liked him because of his face, but that hadn't actually helped him and he didn't need it to now.

But Kallias had another expression for his two little sons.

He loved to spend money on Marcus and Titus. He spoiled his sons with sweets and toys and everything he thought they might want even if they didn't ask. Because they never asked for anything at all—that was how they were, well-spoken and well-mannered, and always obedient, and nobody ever complained about them.

He sent them things more than he even saw or spoke to them.

When he did see them, sometimes running around his house, they always hugged him and said how grateful they were for whatever new thing he gave them. That would make him genuinely happy.

"Do you really see the emperor all the time?" Marcus asked him one day when he ran into him in the atrium. He was a thick little boy, and maybe he got this from his grandfather. Narcissus was stocky.

"Yes," said Kallias. "It's not a big thing, though."

"What do you do?" asked Marcus.

"I help run an empire," he said.

Marcus, three years older than Titus, was the leader. Everything Marcus did, Titus copied. If Marcus went into the kitchen to thank the cooks, Titus blurted his gratitude too. And when the cooks laughed at them and Marcus frowned, Titus scowled too. When Marcus studied hard, Titus did too.

In their street games, Titus supported whomever Marcus supported. He couldn't run as fast as his older brother, but he always tried to keep up. The nurse told Kallias of finding Titus sleeping in the crook of his brother's arm, after a long day.

"That's really nice," Kallias said.

He hoped the gifts made up for the fact that he never took the time to walk to speak to them, or the fact that someone else was raising them.

But he had things to do.

He wanted more and more. No matter how rich he got, there was always something at the heart of him that just wanted more. He always thought that maybe if he made just more money, and had more power, more of everything, then he would be happy, then he would finally feel complete, achieve, satisfied.

He only needed to prove it himself.

Chapter 47

He was unsatisfied.

And like him, so was Agrippina. She rushed Lucius's manhood ceremony, and then on a night when Claudius was drunk and making a lot of silly promises, had him draw up papers to make her son his heir.

"You never relax, darling," Claudius told her. "W-w-why? J-j-just drink. Here, here."

But she pushed the cup aside and smiled at him and gestured to the lawyers.

Everybody in her circle understood what she was doing except Claudius. Or perhaps he was just too weak against her. He named Lucius Domitius Ahenobarbus his heir and excluded his own young son Britannicus.

Zelia had a new friend, a young woman named Locusta, and she had made a profession out of making poisons to kill people. A very lucrative business. After Claudius made his new will, Zelia introduced them all to Locusta.

Locusta had wiry brown hair, a nervous demeanor, and large eyes. She came in with Claudius's wine taster. He was a fat man, and breathless as he looked all around. Kallias had stayed up late writing up an entire plan. Everything must be meticulous.

Last time they did this trick, Xander was the one who put together the concoction. But he wasn't a poisoner. His profession was—or at least was supposed to be—the craft of saving lives, not taking them. Xander refused to make the poison now, but as the emperor's second doctor, he would be sure that Locusta's wasn't reversed by an antidote.

Agrippina sat tapping her fingers on the desk, not following any rhythm. The rest of them were stiff as they stood around or sat on chairs, not looking each other in the eye.

They kept Narcissus out of the plot, because after all he was so loyal to the emperor, and he might frustrate the plan. This wasn't the kind of plan that could fall apart with no consequence.

"Here's what happens," said Kallias. "Today at noon, Locusta puts the doses in two vials and gives it to Xander. He can have something on hand in case the first vial doesn't work. Tomorrow, he meets the wine taster at the front of the Temple of Saturn to give him one full vial."

"Why the Temple of Saturn?" asked the man.

"Xander lives nearby there and it's better if he gives it to you outside the palace. Don't interrupt me, you'll miss details."

Agrippina said to read on.

"Alright so. After that, a slave gives the menu for the emperor's meal. And that's planned days in advance. The taster tries it before Claudius, without the poison in it. Then he takes some of the food back to the kitchen and says it needs more salt, but stops in the hall and pours in the poison. He comes back with the same serving and takes the other, pretending to add more salt to them, too."

"That's good," said Agrippina. "What if it's not enough?"

"It'll be enough, when Locusta makes her dose."

Locusta nodded.

"Does everyone understand?" said Kallias.

Everything had to be perfect. Kallias had planned for it to be. Everyone would do their roles flawlessly. Locusta would make sure the dose was strong enough to kill the emperor that very night. No lingering. The doctor would not be implicated by being seen at the palace near the emperor's food. The wine taster would look as if he were doing his job as usual. And if things did go wrong, the doctor could make sure they went right.

Agrippina couldn't wait any longer to be the mother of the emperor. She would be the ruler of the empire.

All those years, and they were at the place they wanted to be.

"My son," she said, and he read the pride on her face. "The emperor of Rome. Doesn't that sound so good?"

"This is going to be interesting," Kallias said, thinking of the boy. Lucius had grown up, still pudgy around the edges, but now eager to try out the world. "You'll have to coach him," Kallias said.

"He listens to me," she said. "As long as that Seneca doesn't get in my way. He listens to him, too, you know."

"Maybe you should have fired him five years ago."

"But he was the best tutor in Rome," she said. "My son deserved the best."

There was no one on earth who didn't believe his son deserved the best.

There was always gain in standing on top of someone else, or in this case, laying someone down.

Chapter 48

Claudius Drusus Nero was only sixteen when he became emperor of Rome. His uncle was poisoned and lay dead for three days before Julia Agrippina secured power and announced his death to the world. And Nero was draped in purple, at last. His closest advisors were his mother Agrippina, the Praetorian prefect Burrus, and his tutor Seneca. They told him everything to do, and at first, he listened.

Kallias didn't think young Nero was particularly bright, although of course he kept that to himself and supported Agrippina. But the boy wanted to play music and perform plays, and how could he be a leader when he was fixated on entertainment—and not watching it—but performing it? Agrippina, having attained what she wanted, had relaxed her attitude toward his enjoyment of arts. He took full advantage of that and began to practice music with more passion than ever.

They had to go to his play one day, and everyone had to listen and pretend to enjoy it. The people in the front row, including Kallias, had been told to clap as hard as they could at three of the intervals and at the end. "If you don't," said Agrippina to them beforehand, "it hurts his feelings and it's really not good for him to be hurt."

So they clapped, at all the right times, and then Kallias put his arm around his shoulder afterwards and said, "You were excellent," and Nero brightened and hugged him tight.

Getting away with murdering an emperor made them all satisfied and reckless. Agrippina freed the wine taster and gave him a house on the Esquiline. Xander retired early, and Locusta's customers tripled. Zelia started a cult. Kallias made another ten million sesterces in a single year, and acted as personal secretary to the most powerful person in the world.

Agrippina ruled Rome, not the boy who was called emperor. That was clear from the beginning. She'd done all the hard work of getting him there, and all he needed to do was follow her guidance. It was her throne, the one she should have always had.

Nero wanted to do things his own way, but his mother would never allow that. So he played his music, and when he proposed silly political ideas, she laughed him off and said that a ruler was only as wise as his counselors, and that he should wait for them before trying to make any decisions.

Chapter 49

Narcissus was now one of the richest men in Rome. And Kallias, back at the palace to work with him, coveted his position as the secretary of letters. It felt like serving under Polycarp all over again. There was just always someone blocking his ambitions, which could never be satisfied.

Why would he stop? Success fed ambition. When he saw what he'd accomplished so far in his life, he knew he could still do more. And it gave him a sense of worth, purpose, and goodness. Maybe he'd done some bad things, but that was human. His drive was virtuous even when he wasn't.

"I can do his job better than him," he told Agrippina. "Tell him to retire."

Narcissus had aged overnight since the death of his patron. Besides gaining weight, he was balding and graying and always complaining about his feet hurting. He and Agrippina had always been cool toward one another, even though it was the freedman who proposed her marriage to Claudius. But they were never the best of friends and now Narcissus was fearing for his job and hoping that Agrippina didn'tt have it out for him the same way she had the former emperor. No one had confirmed it, but he strongly suspected that Claudius hadn't died a natural death.

"I can sense that she does not like me," Narcissus said, wiping sweat off his forehead. This was after a meeting with Nero and the rest of his advisors. The room was clearing out. During the session, Agrippina had been seated in a chair at the head of the table, a position she always took to demonstrate her power when speaking to her son's court. Now, as they walked through the doorway, she pressed a guiding hand to his shoulder.

Kallias glanced at them and looked back at Narcissus with a bland face.

"You cannot see it?" said Narcissus. "How she spoke over me the entire time? She waved her hand at me when I tried to make my point. I felt as though I were a slave again!"

Kallias started to pack papers in his bag but Narcissus waited for him to respond.

So Kallias said, "You know, I think it's because you don't look so well these days, Narcissus. If you really want me to tell you the truth."

Narcissus's normally smug face showed real torment, and Kallias thought, Yes he really is suffering. Great.

"I am in pain all the time, Kallias. That does not mean I cannot do my job. If anything, it shows my resilience, my determination."

"Maybe, but she probably thinks so. And you know, you have disagreed with her on occasions concerning Nero."

"I made her empress!"

"Why don't you talk to her about this, instead of me?"

The meeting itself had been about the taxes leveraged by the government. Pallas, being the head of the treasury, had the most to say about the main issue: how would they tax their subjects without putting too much of a strain on them? He had been joined by two quaestors and a tax collector and the other important bureaucrats who nodded along. But when Narcissus tried to talk about the letters he received from petitioners begging him to bring the tax issue before Nero, Agrippina waved her hand at him and said they would talk about the letter later.

"People complain about many things," she'd said to Narcissus. "It's understandable, but it's also your job to decide which of those complaints are worth your time. That's something that requires discretion, Narcissus. Use it, if you have it."

Then she'd gone back to speaking to Pallas, and Narcissus had cleared his throat.

Agrippina gave Nero advice for the economy, for foreign policy, domestic issues. All he had to do was listen, agree, and his bureaucrats would carry out her orders. One time as he sat in the curule chair, she took his hands in her face, and she said, "My baby, you have to listen to me because I've done this longer than you."

Her hands were locked around his cheeks. He looked like he couldn't breathe, and he dropped his gaze and nodded.

When Narcissus sighed long and hard at this, Agrippina took her hands from Nero and glared at him.

Kallias couldn't help but feel sorry for the young new emperor. Agrippina should show Nero a little more sympathy. Nero might start to feel as if he really couldn't breathe, and what about when he hit his streak of rebellion? That was inevitable, with youths.

Kallias saw that Nero's resentment of her began to develop. He remembered the incident with the kithara and countless other times. He told Nero, "You really do play well, and I think soon you'll learn how to rule without anyone's advice."

No one could rule with no counsel at all, and Nero certainly needed formidable Julia Agrippina, but Kallias said it to make him feel better.

"Thank you," said Nero. "It helps that someone believes in me."

"Of course I do. And when you know how to run things yourself, then you can do whatever you want and play as much music as you like."

The emperor smiled.

Chapter 50

Kallias's own sons grew, kind and mannerable. He was proud of them, but he also hadn't really raised them. They were raised by the tutor who taught them, and the woman who cared for them at all times. He couldn't even lie to himself and believe that they were the way they were because of him.

They were eleven and nine years old and they watched their parents fight all the time. He knew it scared them but they wouldn't understand. Thalia had been distant with him ever since he allowed her to come back from Greece, and at some point, they dropped all pretense of friendliness toward each other.

Kallias never regarded her wishes. For example, he once had the cooks make shrimp three nights in a row, knowing Thalia was allergic. But shrimp was what he wanted and Thalia could deal with it. She constantly complained about him, too, except when she wanted something. He would buy it, what she wanted—then take it away if he felt she didn't deserve it after all. She would cry, and then do petty, imperceptible things.

And back and forth they went. Once she came to an official event without Kallias, and sat on the opposite side of him with a group of people who were not friends of him or Agrippina. That looked very bad, and people talked about them.

Around this time, Kallias was having an affair with a senator's wife. Aemilia wore expensive perfumes and elaborate, fashionable hair. There was nothing more she loved than men and attention, and she had plenty of both. Her husband hated Kallias, since a few years ago he'd to pay him about fifteen thousand sesterces in bribes. The husband said that Kallias was arrogant and shady. It was very fun to fuck his wife, after all that.

Kallias enjoyed Aemilia for a while, and then when he was bored of her, he let her down hard and ignored her efforts to speak to him.

So she told her friends and the rumors started.

Thalia found out about it and screamed in his face and said she would get him back somehow. She hadn't screamed in his face in years. Everything was just silence and anger.

"You can't do anything," he said. "You won't do anything."

"Wait and see," she said.

She began by spending his money on a new litter and a new vineyard.

He paid a visit to her rooms. "What on earth made you do this?"

"I wanted my own wine," she said. She was perched on a seat, looking pointedly at him. "And I wanted to travel comfortably to get it and drink it. So?"

Their sons stood in the doorway watching the whole thing. Their eyes were very wide. He walked out past them. He ruffled the one's hair who was closest to him and said, "Tell the servants if you want something. Why don't you go play?"

He didn't want them to see him so angry.

He walked into Thalia's room one day and saw her naked in bed with a slave boy kissing her neck. They were a tangled mass of limbs. She was in the middle of sighing when Kallias walked right up to them and cleared his throat. Her eyes opened and the slave jumped up and cowered on the floor.

"Thalia," he said. She got her clothes and started putting her hair together. The boy, no older than nineteen, sat cowering. Kallias said, "Put some fucking clothes on."

And he scrambled.

He said, "You can't touch my slaves like this. They are not your toys."

She wouldn't look at him.

He cornered the boy later in the hallway. The slave said he didn't mean it, he just did what Thalia wanted. Kallias said he was lying, because Thalia was very physically desirable and didn't have to convince anyone to kiss her anywhere.

"You don't have to listen to her," said Kallias. "She's not the master of the house."

The slave kept his eyes down. Kallias flicked his arm, to make him look up at him. But the slave cowered even more. Kallias punched him in the stomach.

The boy doubled over, gagging, and sank to the floor.

Kallias hit him one more time as hard as he could. He heard something crunch, he drew back, looked at his fist in surprise and cursed. He felt like he had just gone out of his own body and suddenly come back.

He was getting beyond himself.

He strode away.

Thalia came sobbing to Kallias later, blocking the doorway of his room. She'd never cried this hard before. "You hurt him! You broke his nose!"

"You're ugly when you cry," he said. She was struggling with him, trying to hit him. He pushed her off. She stumbled. She kicked out at him. He caught her this time by the wrists. She was struggling, weeping. Then he put his hand around her throat, felt the soft flesh there, and gripped tight.

Her eyes went wide.

He told her very slowly to shut the fuck up.

He let her go. She backed up, slack with shock.

Marcus stood only a few feet behind her. He stared at Kallias and then he turned and ran down the hallway.

Their slaves gossiped about them. They were stunned at this freedman and his wife's cruelty to their slaves and each other. The freedman had once been a slave completely at the whim of a master. He must have understood the life of living in fear. Thalia had to have understood it too, being a woman and the daughter of an ex-slave. But they were determined to be as cruel as they could be whenever they had the chance.

They were richer than ever, and they wanted everyone to know that they were going to do whatever they wanted. In the meantime, he purchased a third house (last year he'd acquired a second) and Thalia began to throw lavish banquets. She was happy when she threw banquets, and she didn't bother him when she had something else to focus on, so he let her.

The parties that Thalia threw always began the same way: with their guests on their couches before the hosts entered, and the food laid out but everyone instructed not to eat. Then Kallias and Thalia would walk in and stand in the center of the room, and wave to everyone and thank them for coming and their guests would clap.

They dined on the most expensive meats, pheasants, whole pigs, fish eggs. They brought the best wines and ice from the mountains. Their guests were greedy, but Kallias and Thalia never ate much. Thalia nibbled more than anything else, while Kallias made sure that none of his food was wasted. If a guest tried to leave a plate with food on it, he would go and sit beside them and say, with a cold little smile, "What, it doesn't taste good?"

And then the person would dutifully slop it up, and a slave would pour them more wine.

Kallias was not like some other freedmen, who were desperate to prove with their new wealth that they also had class. He didn't like to over decorate, overindulge, or waste. Everything was always expensive, but nothing could be in excess.

Although they always entered together, he and Thalia hardly bothered to look at each other at these events. People said, "Those two people want everyone to know how beautiful and rich and cruel they are."

Rumors, he found, often held some truth that was glutted with lies. The things that he didn't want his family to hear or know. The wealthy good-looking freedman, twenty-five years ago, was once the pretty boy favorite of his master. His idolization of the man had been visible, and it seemed that he had followed in his footsteps, both in violence and the need for control, and in crushing his enemies. And he used to appear everywhere with Gaius Sulpicius Calvinus, even to an appointment with the emperor. What had happened before they were never seen together again and the boy landed in another household?

This dogging thing. Kallias thought it was a private situation he could keep close to himself. After all, the only person he had ever told the whole story to was Agrippina. But people always speculated, even when they didn't have all the details.

Kallias didn't have to be drunk to hit someone. He was usually sober anyway. He was at a party at Agrippina's house when some man named Gabinius repeated one of the rumors to him. They had only been introduced for five minutes and the man was already spewing shit. He said it as a joke, with a laugh, but he had already gone too far.

Kallias punched him, and Gabinius crumpled to the floor. Agrippina and Pallas rushed over, and Pallas pulled Kallias away and started talking him down.

"It's alright, it's alright," said Pallas, grasping him by the shoulders. "No more, before it gets worse."

Around them the music still played and the people still drank and dined. No one but Agrippina and Pallas and a few servants had seen the commotion.

"What did he say to you?" said Agrippina. She never broke her own calm these days.

Gabinius got to his feet, holding his face. A bruise was coloring already under his eye.

"Fuck you, man!" he spat.

"Say it again," said Kallias.

Pallas said, "No, no, Kallias. Stop, he's winding you up."

Pallas was still holding him back. Agrippina told Gabinius to not say rude things to her people, and to leave the party now before she had him run through with a sword.

"He hit me and I'm the bad one?" said Gabinius.

"Whatever you said, you insulted him."

"Unbelievable. No apology? Look at my face, look at my face."

"Get out, or I call a guard."

Gabinius stormed out and the party continued without any other incident. Agrippina went back to the other side of the room. Pallas tried to make a suggestion, and Kallias told him he could keep it.

But it turned out that Gabinius was a senator. He'd only recently been admitted to join the conscript fathers, was not extremely wealthy just yet, but his rank was a bad sign. And he was sore about that punch.

Kallias knew, when he sat in court and the judge ordered him to pay a fine of ten thousand sesterces, that he'd have to learn to temper his anger. If it hadn't been for who he was, he might've received a much harsher sentence.

Granted, ten thousand sesterces was nothing.

But next time he wouldn't be blinded by anger. He'd been striking other people for a long time, and that was immature of him, lashing out like that. He was not some hothead youth. And despite the small sum, his hand itched after having to pay the fine.

He also wondered if Gabinius would try to find him again. He didn't think so, but he would be ready.

The two burly hired servants who followed him weren't enough. They hadn't even been in the room during the incident. Kallias wanted someone trained for this—ex-gladiators.

He hired himself two new bodyguards. Their names were Decius and Platius, both German and recommended to him by a friend in the Praetorian Guard. A person could always count on a Praetorian to get something done, whether that was killing emperors, running schemes, or finding guards.

Kallias liked the look of these two very much. They never smiled, never spoke to him unless he spoke first. He also posted more guards at his houses, an addition to ones already there. Everything was doubly secured.

His newly-hired personal guards knew he had a long list of enemies and a tendency to find himself in things that led to violence, and they were more than willing to back him in any way. And that was perfect. Next time, they could do all the hitting for him.

Chapter 51

Narcissus, feeling unwell and barely able to walk some days because of his gout, requested a time to go away to his hot springs in Baeie to rest. Agrippina said it was an excellent idea, so he left.

Narcissus had hardly been able to focus the past weeks. Every time Agrippina came near him, he was jumpy and stammered more than usual. She eyed him with amusement, knowing that he was so afraid of her. His fear gave her joy.

He had no easier time talking to Kallias, who reminded him at every opportunity that he should be very careful because of his new physical weaknesses. Kallias reveled in the disheartened face that his father-in-law made whenever he tormented him. It was never in a way that Narcissus could outrightly say, This man doesn't like me. Kallias just kept him facing his faults, insecurities, and the idea that Agrippina was no doubt annoyed at him trying to advise her son to disagree with her.

So Narcissus left.

While he was gone, Kallias spent a week writing a report on the man who had once mentored him on how to be a successful bureaucrat. He sat and reread his intro over and over.

He had written:

As the closest assistant to Narcissus, I think it's my responsibility to report on his character. He consistently delegates work meant for himself specifically to those lower than him. When I returned to the palace to work again, I began to discover his disloyalty. I have elaborated on all the evidence I have carefully compiled. All of us in civil service know that every report must be accompanied with sound evidence. I've done my part. Narcissus has taken multiple bribes from the businessmen I've listed lower. He has also attempted to undermine Caesar on multiple occasions, which is unforgivable treachery to the state.

He sat with the report for another few days, and then he handed it in to Nero at their next meeting. Kallias spoke to Agrippina before and told her that he was going to help her get rid of Narcissus, and make it look legal.

"Legal," she said, laughing.

Agrippina already had a copy. As Nero read his, she said to the group, "Oh yes, this is a very important announcement. Narcissus won't be joining us after today."

Kallias took his seat last, and Agrippina paused so he could speak. Everyone was looking at him, but he was only focusing on the emperor and his mother.

He said, "I've seen how he creates disturbances between you, and I wouldn't do that, not if I held the position. I also have as much experience now and I'm fit for his place."

Pallas, across from him, went pale in the face.

Narcissus would have to be executed, because he was overstepping his power—that meant challenging Agrippina. Treason was not a crime that could be acquitted.

"Well, didn't we do treason too?" said Nero under his breath, laughing. Only his mother and Kallias could hear him.

"This is different, Lucius. What we did for you, was something good."

Nero said to the whole room then that they should talk about it later, and Pallas, still looking very nervous, agreed with him. Then the rest of the table also nodded, before Agrippina could say anything more.

But the time was up and the next day, Agrippina brought the charge that Narcissus had been corrupt and stolen money from the government for years.

"He is getting so very hard to control," she said. "And this isn't how things go here, everyone has to work together as one."

She signed his death warrant. Kallias stood behind her shoulder and read it while she did.

Nero finalized it with a press of his seal. He'd never had any attachment to Narcissus. He was clearly annoyed that his mother was pulling apart the court, but then he threw up his hands and said, "Well, we should make fresh changes. I think I'll make some of my own. I like this breath of new air!"

Agrippina looked at him wearily, but he ignored her. He had already signed her paper and done what she wanted.

They hadn't seen the freedman in weeks. He was trying to escape on his boat since he realized that he was never welcome in the palace again. Messengers brought the word some days later that he had committed suicide.

"Good," said Agrippina.

Chapter 52

Immediately after this news, Kallias was named secretary of the treasury of the Roman Empire. He thought he would be promoted to Narcissus's position as secretary of letters. But something else happened. That morning, Nero dismissed Pallas, his mother's lover. He said that she couldn't make all the decisions all the time, and he was getting tired of them all telling him what to do.

Nero said to Kallias as they sat side by side that evening, "Mother is not always right about things, you know. Someone like you is better for overseeing the money."

"I appreciate it," said Kallias. "And I agree."

"That Mother is not always right?"

"Absolutely. You are Caesar, after all."

"I know, I really am. I'm the emperor of this world!" Nero said it almost in wonder.

Kallias decided he wouldn't try to advise Nero anymore. He could see that very soon, the young emperor would be vindictive to anyone he thought was constraining him. And he must be paranoid because of his mother.

"I would like," said Kallias suddenly. "To change my patronage to you from her."

Nero looked at him, cheeks bright with satisfaction. "You really would?"

But they wouldn't have this conversation with her yet. She would go into a burning rage if Nero tried to shuffle not one but two of her favorite freedmen on the exact same day. Sending Pallas away had been his act to stop her from dominating him. All the men she loved were people who reminded him to listen to her.

Except Kallias.

He would be a part of this new court that he could already see would form after Narcissus, Pallas, and Polybius were gone with Claudius.

Soon, there really would be fresh things coming to the palace, just as Nero had mused. People who would smile and clap the emperor on the shoulder no matter what he did, people who had his youthful, delusional, and artistic view of life, and it would—no doubt—be a mess. Regardless, someone would have to run the government and the court. Kallias was not leaving, not now.

His appointment as secretary of the treasury was the first time that he'd won something major that had not been in tangent with some conspiracy with Agrippina, and he could see that he'd broken away from her.

To be more specific, he realized that he didn't need Agrippina anymore.

He had a new and complete sense of freedom. He had one of the highest positions in the empire that anyone could have. Nero gave him a gold ring of equestrian status.

The only people who were equal to him were Callistus and Epaphroditus, two freedmen still in their positions.

As the secretary of the treasury, Kallias had a massive office. He walked into the room, stopped and looked at the bureaucrats beneath him.

"I never liked speeches," he said. "But listen to this. My father was a gladiator and my mother was a slave girl he fucked. And now I'm your new head of the treasury. Do you believe in rising up like the Phoenix?"

They looked at him as if he were crazy, but he grinned.

Chapter 53

Kallias finally divorced Thalia. She would have to survive off the money from the vineyard, which he decided to allow her to keep. "I'm being generous," he told her. "If you really think about it, giving you this useful gift."

Thalia cried the entire time the servants packed her things and moved them out of her rooms. He left the house to avoid hearing her. She might have thought that all that noise would change his mind and make him feel pity, but the sound was driving him crazy.

He kept his sons and someone else kept raising them.

He had so much money that he really didn't know what to do with himself. He had three houses and hundreds of millions of sesterces. Every official in Rome needed his friendship because of his position in the government and his proximity to Caesar. He had an enormous job, being head of the treasury, but that was good because he loved responsibility.

He should have been happy. Maybe he was. But he still felt there was something missing that kept him from being satisfied. There was still so much upheaval in the capital, and he was always trying to predict to himself the next thing that would happen—and how that might affect the position he was so determined to keep.

He did his best to avoid Nero and Agrippina. They kept trying to drag him into their fights. Agrippina said Nero was humiliating her. Kallias said that it was a good thing to let Nero be himself. He made sure he said this in front of Nero, who beamed.

Afterwards, Agrippina followed him down the palace steps as he was leaving. He could hear her calling him but he pretended not to, until she caught up with him and grabbed his arm. There was a Praetorian standing right behind her, watching it all. Her beautiful face was bitter. "That was very wrong what you did there, not supporting me."

"He's growing up," Kallias told her, spreading his hands. "You have to understand that."

"He can't run it without me and you know that!"

"He'll learn it, he'll learn it on his own."

"You have never, ever, not sided with me! What the hell has gotten into you?"

"Honestly, Agrippina. You are not really helping him the way you're doing it."

She stopped. He said, "You know it's the truth."

"Get out."

But he was going anyway. He traveled to his house in Pompeii. Let Agrippina and Nero struggle by themselves. He needed to fulfill was what was missing. He was still empty. One afternoon during the siesta, he lay on his back and gazed at one of the frescoes in his sitting room when he had the idea.

He got up and wrote to one of his friends in Rome, Murano, and told the man that he wanted to buy a plot of land and build a gladiator school. He said the faster he could have it done, the better. He would leave all the details up to Murano and then when he got back to Rome, he would pay the man a lot of money if he had the project well underway.

This was obviously illegal, since it was really only the state who was allowed to train and house gladiators. But he was going to do it anyway. "I really am the state," he wrote to Murano. "Or at least, a part of it. So who would really stop me? And we'll figure things out. Make it look like a regular house."

When he got back to Rome, Murano was there to greet him with open arms. He was also Greek, and one of the people whose business Kallias supported through legal and illegal means. He helped the man pay less taxes every year, and whatever else he wanted. Murano owned many apartments, and he always knew about properties. He took Kallias to see the half-finished gladiator school.

The servants stopped the litter and they climbed out and looked at the half of it, gone up. He could play out all his fantasies now. When he was a small child he wanted to meet a gladiator, be a gladiator, and now he owned them.

That was even before he wanted his freedom, before he and that other boy he followed began to hate and compete with each other.

And that was what he told them, when the building was finished and the men he bought, a dozen of them, stood in the courtyard of the ludus and watched him while he spoke. He was standing on a stool, looking down at them. He was so proud of himself. He wore a brand new signet ring, which glinted in the sun as he raised his hand.

"How would you like to fight for me and for glory?" he said to the men assembled before him. "You can get rich too, like me."

There were some laughs at that. These gladiators were the hardest-looking men he and Murano could find. They would fascinate the crowds with just an appearance on the sands.

"Listen to this," he said. "My father was a gladiator and his nickname was the Phoenix. None of us knows who that is now, and that's alright. It was a long time ago. But my mother told me that he always rose again and again when he fell, and he always won in the arena. He took a lot of wounds, but that's how it is when you're a gladiator. You're going to get a lot of wounds, get it into your head now."

The manager of his school, who was also a former gladiator, and very bald and very rough-looking, nodded from where he stood down beside him.

Kallias said, "You're a good bunch. The crowds will love you. Make me proud, too. Things can change for you. I was a little slave boy once upon a time, and my master laid me on a couch and fucked me while I bled and cried. Do you think I liked that? No. But I had to take it. And now I'm here, and I'm one of the most powerful men in Rome."

Murano and the manager stared up at him in disgust. He didn't really care. Life wasn't easy. There was no need for them pretend otherwise. And they wouldn't go repeating what he'd said regardless.

His gladiators looked great. He was having fun. This was good for him, maybe he could even feel less angry about everything all the time, because he was doing something that made him happy.

"I give it to Murano," he said. "He will tell you what to do next, about the oath." He was going to jump down from the stool, but then he paused.

"Think about it now," he said. "One moment, you could be on the sands fighting for your life, and then the next, you're rich in your own house and you have all the money and things you want."

Agrippina and her son were more at odds than ever.

"She is your mother, you must listen to her," said Seneca always.

Kallias stopped speaking to her. Since their argument, he'd always had a pretext for not answering her. He was too busy, he wasn't in Rome, he'd missed her messages.

Meanwhile, Thalia kept messaging asking to see the boys. Kallias declined her request every time. Soon her letters to him were tossed away unopened.

He spent more and more time at his gladiator school, watching the developments.

The men at the school were tattooed with a brand that symbolized the house they were from, which he named the House of Fire. The house appeared like a regular dwelling on the outside, but it was heavily guarded and no one could walk from the street and enter.

He loved to watch them spar. He couldn't wait to present them to the private games to his friends, and then he would debut them in the Circus Maximus. It would take time, but he was willing to wait. He wanted to have them provide the best entertainment, and the bloodthirsty crowds would love it. Many of them would have to die, but that was a part of being a gladiator.

He bought more and more. He spent a lot of money building up this school, and supplying it with weapons and doctors and cooks for the gladiators. And for his house in Rome, he also arranged a space for them to come when he wanted them to fight immediately.

All during this time, Nero was growing into a man and naturally turning on his mother. He took it a bit too far during the visit with the Parthian ambassadors when he made Agrippina sit in a lower seat, but no one could really advise Nero these days.

On top of it, Nero was in love. The girl's name was Acte, and she was a slave. Nero thought he was living out a forbidden love story, but Agrippina just saw it as foolish.

When he became emperor, Agrippina had arranged for him to marry her old rival's daughter, Octavia. But that was just an arrangement, and they barely acted as husband and wife. It was all his doing as Octavia liked Nero well enough, but he was not so carried away with her. Now Octavia was on the sidelines, while Acte received the love.

Octavia kept her head down. Agrippina had killed her brother, Britannicus, and treated him horribly before she did by orchestrating his rape, so Octavia was very in awe and fear of Agrippina and certainly would not complain about the woman's son. But she didn't have to, because Agrippina said all that silly shit with Nero and Acte had to be stopped right away.

She arranged to have the girl sent away, but Nero thwarted it.

Then the issue of taxes came up again. Nero wanted to stop imposing them entirely, and when he said that, Agrippina laughed in his face.

"You're not ready." She shook her head. "I shouldn't have put you on this throne."

The room was silent. He stared at her, clearly dumbfounded. Agrippina got up, shoved her chair to the side, and strode out.

She left Rome on vacation, and did not return for weeks. Kallias did not reach out to her. He ignored both of them, and proposed a tax rate of his own judgment.

After a month, Nero said that if she ever came back, the guards should hound her until she gave up. They should harass her so much even, that she would be uncomfortable even in her house. This seemed like a joke, but his face was serious.

But in any case, Agrippina hadn't spoken to her son for a month and some days.

Chapter 54

Their relationship, strained impossibly by years of her heavy-handed control, couldn't be reconciled. Nero didn't want to speak to his mother and beg her to come back. He said if he made up with her, she would go right back to bullying and dominating him when she was back in Rome again. Because her actions were patterns. She would degrade him, comfort him, and do it all over again.

"She's your mother," said Seneca. "You have to talk to her and respect her even if you don't always agree."

"No, no I don't," said Nero.

Agrippina didn't want to talk to him, either. She'd been sending the word through courtiers that she thought Nero was a stubborn, oversized boy who would ruin himself without her. She said he had to learn to respect her and appreciate her, for all she had done for him, and that she would hold out on him until she saw he needed her. His empire would collapse without her. Soon he would see. He had better apologize to her before it was too late.

She must have underestimated his anger, because she kept sending these kinds of messages, and maybe all the while, he really hoped that she would reach out first with an olive branch. Just one last time to show that she loved him more than the grand plans she had for him, more than her own ego. Now it wasn't just a child who misunderstood his mother, who'd had the kind of petty fight with her that could be made up with a hug and tears. The tide of the feud turned and revealed something deeper. Nero was bitter against her, and had been for a long time.

He wanted her dead, and he said so.

Kallias was in Pompeii when heard that Agrippina was out of favor and running from her own son. He came back to Rome to a bunch of letters from her stacked on his desk.

All the letters were written with the same lines of desperation. She wrote, "My own son is trying to kill me. This is fucking ridiculous. Do something. Remember what you said to me when my mad brother was the emperor."

Another time, she wrote, "He has it out for me and soon he will for you. You need to come to me. Talk to someone. I can't even leave the house without someone following me."

"Do something, Kallias! Will you ever write back? These letters get delivered in two days! Say something!"

He thought to reply to them, then thought better.

He gave her letter to Nero instead.

She wrote again demanding that he help her. Nero had set a trap in her house, so that the roof collapsed on one of her rooms. She knew it was his doing, because after the investigation of the collapse she found that it was clearly engineered. In her letter, she asked if she and her retinue could stay at one of Kallias's houses. They would no doubt be safe there. She admitted that she was frightened, but more than that, she was angry. Everyone had forgotten how much she helped them before Nero went mad on her.

"You see," Kallias said, "she really has lost it now."

"Thank you," said Nero, after he read the fifth letter. "Thank you for not protecting that bitch."

"It's all about your safety and wishes," said Kallias simply. "It's all I pray for."

Kallias made a quick switch. Agrippina had supported him for all their lives, but he still remembered how she hadn't hesitated to include him in a plot that could have had him tortured and killed—and this after all he had been through months before he was sold to her household—and he had never really forgiven her for this.

Nevermind that he had taken part in that plot for his own gain. That he had inserted himself into the murky business of it. She was the one who thought of doing it in the first place. That was what he told himself.

The truth was that he just was tired of Agrippina. He had lived through years of her. The woman never stopped. She never stopped, and now she was fleeing, trying to escape her son's displeasure. And Kallias would not go to her.

Why would he align himself with someone who had been declared an enemy of the emperor? That was what Nero did—issued a warrant for her arrest on the grounds of treason.

It was her turn to go down, but Kallias would not go with her.

He read the rest of the letters, drank, and read them again, and then discarded them. Nero was the emperor. If he was crazy enough to want to kill his own mother, then let him. He would certainly regret it, and everyone would have to wipe his tears after he realized what he'd done.

Agrippina wrote to Kallias again. She said, "You are my freedman and my client. You are obligated to support me. Come to me at once and escort me to your house."

He ignored that too. He had already, without her knowledge, switched his patronage to Nero. When he heard the news that she was under arrest, he knew he'd made the right choice.

"She has to go," he told Nero. Because that was the only thing Nero wanted to hear. Nero's advisors said the same. They were closer to Nero than he was, and whatever he said they usually had already said. But that was alright, as long as he was part of the new court.

He wouldn't lose his place for Agrippina. He wouldn't lose his place for anyone.

Chapter 55

They told him later about the death of the greatest woman he had ever known.

Julia Agrippina ran through the house and the soldiers chased her out to the gardens. Then she suddenly stopped and faced them as they approached her. It was a sunny day and she was radiant in the light. There was no more running to do. And she looked them in the eye, and did not disgrace herself by crying and begging for mercy. She was a patrician through and through. Her voice was clear and resigned. She put her hand over her middle, pressed it and said, "Hit me here, where I carried Nero."

A Praetorian stabbed her in the belly. She crumpled to the ground.

The blood flowed out from underneath her dress and stained the concrete beneath her, and then Julia Agrippina was dead.

A long time ago, Ahenobarbus said nothing good could come of him and Agrippina. That was certainly accurate. A man had to be a certain kind of twisted and angry to have his own mother killed. Already, the news was spreading, and people were shaking their heads. But that man was the ruler of the greatest empire in the world, and so his will be done.

Julia Agrippina, the little girl who jumped down from the litter without a servant to hold her hand. The girl with enough fear, hatred, and ambition to win back the throne she certainly deserved. She had been just as interesting as

Kallias thought she would be, the first moment he laid eyes on her. There were not many people who could be as compelling and driven as her. Stopping at nothing.

He missed that woman. She was the only person he allowed to know all his mind and motivations. She was so brutal and so determined to have everything her own way, and that was really the only way to be in life. She had lived a good one. She really made the most of it.

He poured himself a cup of wine as he sat alone in his dining room that night.

"Agrippina, you terror," he said out loud. "This is for you."

Chapter 56

Kallias was at the peak of his power.

He was free of Agrippina and he needed no one anymore. Sometimes he thought of her and wished just for a moment that he had been loyal to her till the end, but the relationship had never been made of that anyway. His thoughts always ended with a sigh. They went on a journey together, and she happened to end it at the sharp tip of a gladius. That was all.

Soon after that he met Ofonius Tigellinus, the prefect of the city's vigiles. This was around the same time that Nero increased his performances. Tigellinus sat right beside Kallias at one of the shows. He was the kind of man who looked brutal right on the outside, and Kallias liked him just for that. Tigellinus was so funny and easy to talk to.

"Make sure you tell him it was an honor to attend," said Tigellinus, imitating Agrippina's higher voice. Kallias laughed.

"No more her," he said. "But she was really something."

Vespasian was on the other side of them, and when they laughed loudly at the pantomime that was just before Nero's performance, he leaned over and said, "You are grown men, how do you find this funny?"

Tigellinus leaned past Kallias, glared at Vespasian and said, "You always look like you're dying to take a shit, that's what's really funny."

For a moment they looked like they would go outside. Kallias sat staring straight ahead, unmoving. He was taking deep breaths. He wished he could tell his guards to beat up Vespasian. There was something about the man that always irritated him.

Nero came onto the stage. He wore a simple gray tunic and carried a lyre. He looked ridiculous.

"I am so grateful I get to express my soul with you," he said. "It is very important to express yourself. And art makes the world better and livelier."

Vespasian nodded in sleep, and Kallias slapped him on the arm. Vespasian jerked awake. The people behind him tittered.

Kallias whispered, "It'll be really funny when he signs your death warrant because you slept during his performance."

Beside him, Tigellinus chuckled.

Tigellinus liked racehorses in the same way that Kallias liked gladiators. This made him and Kallias warm to each other instantly, and Kallias liked that Tigellinus was brutal and reckless and said whatever he thought. They soon became best friends. They would go to Tigellinus' stables and look at his horses.

"The power behind these things," said Tigellinus, stroking one of the horse's flanks. "Do you know how much just one of them cost?"

And he told him. The horse snorted and stamped up dust while Tigellinus stroked it and talked to it.

Kallias said, "I pay as much for every gladiator."

Tigellinus began to visit everyday and drink with him.

Tigellinus betted on a horse one day that got into a bad accident. They saw the rider laid out on the track in the sand with both legs broken and twisted obscenely. He was making a noise for help. Two servants rushed him to him with a stretcher and began to load him on. Kallias and Tigellinus got up from their seats and went down into the tracks, but it was not the rider they were interested in.

"This would have been a good game," said Tigellinus. "Shit, shit."

Tigellinus told him to kill the horse. They stood in the yard and the groom was struggling with the animal. He had it tethered and his clothes were dirty. The horse whinnied and reared as he tried to calm it. It had been abused before Tigellinus bought it and attempted to train it.

"That's a waste of money." Kallias looked at him. "There must be a better way."

"I already lost a lot," said Tigellinus gloomily.

"So you will lose more."

"No, I need to soothe the rage."

Kallias said, "Fair."

Now he had the gladiators, and the money, and the houses, and the friends, but he was hurt that his sons weren't close to him. They were nearly grown now, and someone else had raised them. But they grew up in his house and they knew what he was like. His eldest left to join the legions, and never replied when Kallias wrote to him. Kallias said to himself, Give it time, and he will speak to me.

Marcus had seen too much, and hated the way he treated Thalia. But he would understand, with time.

Kallias wrote to the legate of the legion and the governor, and arranged for his son to serve instead as a tribune. He would not have him working through the ranks. Why should he? Marcus was a citizen and his father was one of the richest men in the empire. There was no reason for him not to start at the top.

At the same time, he discovered that his youngest was sneaking around the city, so he hired people to watch him. He was leaving the city to visit the catacombs, and always on certain days.

"Not sure what he does," his spy said. "But it is suspicious."

But then his son came to him in his dining room one day and said, "I know you're watching me."

His voice was shaky. He had a good reputation. All anyone ever said about him was that he minded his own business. He certainly did not want to be associated with the violence and politics of his father.

"Of course I watched you," said Kallias. "I have spies in this city who tell me everything, even things about the emperor. Is it wrong to watch your own son?"

"No, but I guess you hate me now."

"Don't say silly things like that. Just tell me what you do when you leave the house at these odd times."

Titus sat across from him and searched his face.

"Just tell me," Kallias said. "It really won't matter."

Titus said that he was visiting the catacombs because he was a Christian and they held their services there.

"Oh," said Kallias, "is that all?"

Chapter 57

But then he said, "Why them? You know they're freaks, don't you?"

"I thought the same," said Titus, nodding. "I thought that too until I actually began to hear them out. And it changed my life in the best way."

"Right," said Kallias.

"This is really different from anything that you will find in this world, though."

"What do they believe then?"

Titus began to explain, while Kallias nodded as if he understood. He hadn't realized he was fully asleep until Titus shook him by the arm.

"It's not you," he said, when his eyes came open. "Philosophy is so boring."

"It's not philosophy," said Titus, looking disappointed. He wore every emotion he had on his face. He was certainly no courtier.

Kallias sat up and said, "Well, good on you, finding something that feels good. As long as they're harmless."

They were harmless. But they were also unpopular. They refuse to say that Caesar was god, which was a problem because Nero believed he was a god now. But that would be overlooked for a while. So Kallias didn't debate it. He let Titus tell him all about his new faith and its strange practices.

Titus wanted to convert him. Now when they saw each other in the house—"Would you ever like to see how the Christians really are?"

"Well, I have things to do. Maybe another time?"

And then it was the reverse. He couldn't help himself from encouraging Titus to go into civil service.

"You should just look into it, " he said. "You could get very rich and I will help you every step of the way. I know everything to help you."

"I never liked the palace," said Titus simply.

He was still young and finishing lessons. He wasn't sure what he wanted to do. But he would figure it out. In the meantime, he wanted Kallias to come with him to see the Christians, just to understand that they were good people.

He asked so much that Kallias decided to go. One day he said, "You know, I will see what this is all about," and got off his couch and put on a nondescript tunic. He took off his ring and put on his heaviest cloak. It was cold during that time. He and his guards all wore dark, plain clothes in an attempt to be insignificant. When they emerged from his private rooms, with Titus in the hall waiting, he looked at them.

"Why are you dressing like that?" asked Titus.

"When they ask what I do, we'll say I am a merchant! I am, in a way."

Titus agreed. He hadn't told them that his father was a top official in the government. He didn't want to make people uncomfortable.

"With the Christians," he said. "Rank doesn't matter. Nobody cares if you're free or a slave or rich or poor. Everyone is equal."

Kallias just laughed at this. They headed down the lantern-lit hall.

Titus said to him as they walked, "I figured out what I want to do. And you have to meet the man who helped me realize it. "

"Oh, ha."

"Yes, he's a doctor. I want to study medicine like him. He's the wisest, kindest person I've ever met."

Kallias stopped him right there. "People aren't wise and kind, come on. You're too old to think like this."

"I know they aren't," said Titus. "But he is, and that's rare. At least it seems so."

"Is he fucking you?"

"What?" said Titus, making a face.

"Be honest," said Kallias. "Your mentor, your pretend pedagogue."

He looked horrified. "That's…no! Love is between two equal people. Luke is a healer. He's not like that, what you say."

"He better not be like that. Let me tell you now. If I find out this is the kind of man he is, I'll kill him myself. My guards will hold him down and I will gut him clean like a fish."

"Maybe you shouldn't assume everyone is like your friends," said Titus. He looked away. "I'm sorry if it sounds rude but I do mean it."

Kallias went quiet. They walked on.

They crossed through the alleys and back streets and they went out of the city in the catacombs. They entered through a tiny door and went down a passageway. Now they were in the mazes. And other people were following them through the cramped spaces. One woman even spoke to Titus. They group entered a large room where some people sat and others milled around. Servants brought out more seats.

Kallias's eyes darted all around. Would he recognize anyone?

He did not.

He sat beside Titus. His guards sat in different places to not attract attention. Merchants from the same guild if anyone asked too much. But people paid them no mind.

They began singing. Some of them had tears streaming from their faces. Kallias looked at his son, singing with his hands over his heart. It was interesting that cults were so powerful. The Christ cult clearly made people feel intense emotions. They were probably all a little crazy.

But he struggled not to appear bored. Their rituals weren't as exciting as he thought they would be.

They sat in rows, while their leaders sat to the side in their rows. Then the man who led the group stood up, and he began to talk about Jesus Christ. Kallias was listening now. He remembered the rebel leader of the Jews crucified some years ago. That was a good point, to start off talking about a crucified man to get an audience's attention.

Titus told him in a whisper that this was Peter and he had seen Jesus Christ himself. Peter said that Jesus's words had been for them to love one another, the greatest gift.

Peter said a lot of things, but what stood out was his statement that the bread and wine they were about to consume was a part of Christ's body. Kallias looked at Titus. Titus was staring straight ahead, listening.

The servants walked around with trays, passing out cups of wine and bits of bread. Titus ate some. Kallias didn't take any. But so far, that was the weirdest thing about the innocent little cult. And then it was over and everyone began to leave.

Titus caught the man—clean-looking, and certainly a doctor just by the look of him—and introduced him to Kallias. The guards joined them. They all tried to act normal. Kallias said, "These are friends," and gestured to them. Luke looked as if he were waiting for him to say their names, but Kallias didn't. He asked Luke if he was from Rome.

"No," said Luke. "My accent gives it away?"

Kallias said nothing.

"I came here a few years ago to help the church," Luke explained. "And doctor my Christian friends. But my practice is for anyone."

"Good," said Kallias. "Do no harm." He smiled blandly. Luke was sizing him up, he could tell, and he was sizing up Luke. He had an honest face. Kallias wouldn't bother him.

"Your son wants to study medicine, and then work with me."

"Maybe he can."

"I hope he does! But it's a lot. Will take some commitment. So, what do you do?"

"I'm a cloth merchant."

"Really?" said Luke. "I would have said secretary, because you have the look and your thumb is stained with ink."

Kallias looked at the hand, and then at the man. He grinned. "I was joking with you," he said. "I'm the secretary of the treasurer for Caesar and I deal in gladiators in my free time." He laughed at the man's face.

Titus said something under his breath. Luke was rigid.

"I don't know if this is the place for you," said Luke.

"No," Kallias. "I'm not a Christian. But your service was interesting, at some moments. I liked the bread and wine! You should use that as a point to bring in more converts. People love bread and wine. If you want your cult to grow."

He looked around. Some women were staring at them.

"Anyways," he said, "You should be careful of the things you say. I can tell you personally Caesar wouldn't like it."

"He is not God," said Luke firmly.

"Exactly that," said Kallias. "He wouldn't like that, and it's not good when Caesar doesn't like things." He made a sign of instability with his hand.

Titus said, "I think it's time to go." They looked at him. Luke took up his bag and then stopped again.

"Please understand this," he said, holding up a hand. "Our only mission is to help the broken-hearted, women, children, and the poor. I just hope that's clear, Kallias. We don't want to do anything against your government."

"No," said Kallias. "I didn't think that."

"Caesar doesn't have to know everything all the time, does he?"

"He doesn't know everything, in fact."

"Thank you," said Luke.

"Remember," said Kallias, and looked at him with another smile that made him feel clever. "Do no harm."

Chapter 58

The Christians weren't interesting. They were a petty group with a message that could only appeal to people who had no agency or power and needed the promise of an afterlife. That was just the kind of thing that women, poor people, and slaves would enjoy.

There were far more interesting things happening than religious ceremonies. Kallias let them be and he knew that in time when they became too much of an itch to Nero, he would scratch them.

Kallias also assumed that Titus would grow disinterested with the cult. He was not their target for its gospel and if he let go of this idea of saving people, he might see how he was wasting his time mingling with the Christians. Certainly if he saw what happened to them when Nero was irritated enough with them, he would cut his ties.

But Kallias wouldn't be a tyrant to his son. He loved his children even when they did things that he disliked or refused to speak to him. He'd never force them into abandoning their interests when there was no reason to. Titus spent the time studying medicine, and Kallias paid attention to what was happening at the palace. There were more interesting things happening there.

Nero had a new wife, who had convinced him to divorce the shy and pitiful Octavia. The new woman Poppaea Sabina was lovely, rich, and cruel. She was not political like Julia Agrippina, or messy like Messalina, but she was a social star and fit the court better than anyone else Nero could have chosen. Poppaea Sabina had the most winning smile. Her smile was a glimpse of the sun. She didn't have to fake happiness when she hosted a dinner party.

Seneca, the near opposite of Poppaea beside the wealth, was retiring. He threw a party that no one could drink at, which everyone found remarkably dull. He also said no taking liberties with the slaves, or being rude. He wanted to have a party that was free of bad distractions. The party was meant to be a representation of himself. When Seneca made his speech, Kallias nodded along to everything. Nero needed to see how he did.

Seneca cleverly left out any references to Agrippina and anyone else Nero had fallen out with over the years. "From the moment he was born, the world knew Nero was a hero," he said. "And he will continue to triumph. My greatest achievement has been to serve him. And now I retire full of rest, knowing I did my work."

They all clapped for him. "Seneca," Nero exclaimed, "you are the most wonderful man alive. I love you, teacher friend!"

Everyone clapped again. Some of the attendants threw flowers.

Unfulfilled when the party was over, they all went to Otho's house, where the real fun began. They drank and someone bought some strange leaves for them to chew on. The leaves were supposed to give them visions.

Kallias passed them up, just for drink. He wasn't interested in seeing visions. But everyone else was wild and excited. There were a lot of people there, including equestrians and freedmen. Then Tigellinus brought out two gladiators trained at Kallias' House of Fire. That was what Kallias was alight for.

They were two of the biggest men anyone had ever seen. Kallias began clapping as soon as they walked out. He went around telling people that his father was a gladiator named the Phoenix and just as Phoenix rises from the ashes, so had he and he wanted his gladiators to be just as iconic and legendary. He had new ones performing in the Circus in the next summer games. He was excited.

He finally sat with Tigellinus and some Praetorians, and a senator. Nero left Poppaea and their couch to come to them and say that he was so pleased with the amazing evening.

"It's a gorgeous show," said Otho, laughing.

Otho wore makeup and Kallias couldn't stand him just for that. But he was Nero's best friend. And he had once been married to Poppaea Sabina, who swished over then, and said, "I think Nero wants to tell you something, Tigellinus." She knelt for a second before him, and her mouth turned up in a smile. He grinned and made space for her.

They all packed on a single couch, Nero beside Tigellinus and Kallias on the other side and Otho squeezing too close to Kallias.

Poppaea settled on the other side of Otho, kissing his neck. Nero kissed his hand. The three of them were always kissing each other. It wouldn't last long, give it about a few months, because the story was still the same: Nero took his friend's wife.

Nero said, "Tigellinus gets his big promotion to prefect of the Praetorian Guard."

Tigellinus whooped, and Kallias put his arm around him and congratulated him.

The party streamed out into the gardens to watch the fight.

Kallias leaned over to the emperor. "Want to see something fun?" he said. They had lined up in the same way outside, on another couch. "I could make them fight to death."

"Oh, yes!" said Nero. "Yes! It will make things interesting. We must have that!"

Kallias stood and said this. Everyone clapped and Tigellinus whistled.

So the gladiators fought until one pinned the other to the ground, and when he cut his opponent's throat and the blood spurted out, the party cheered. The winner was a muscled German purchased only a few months ago. He knelt upright, sword hand raised, rivulets of sweat shining on his pale face.

Kallias strode across the center to him, and stood before him and grinned down at him. The German stank of sweat and blood and something else, something like desperation. Kallias threw a bag of money at his chest, and told him to go fuck his prettiest slave girl.

Kallias was silent all the way home as he rode in his litter. He thought deeply about his early life for the first time in years, and of Malika. It was just a random thought, come out of nowhere. She stood on the steps, and he clung to her dress, and then his old master back then walked up to them and said something to her and she bowed her head.

Kallias wondered if Nero felt guilty about killing his mother. Kallias hadn't gone that far! At least he was better than that.

But still, he remembered the sadness in her eyes and the pain he knew he caused her.

The poor thing, he should have treated her better.

He was too consumed with a man he worshiped to care about anyone else. A man he never had the chance to have his revenge on.

Which would always be a pity.

Chapter 59

The fire burned for a week and ravaged Rome. The damage left thousands homeless and the vigiles were outmatched. There was nothing to do but let it burn out. Kallias went through the streets on his litter afterwards and saw the charred ruins and people rushing about and panicking in confusion.

A dirty child ran up to the litter begging for food. The guard shouted at them. Kallias took a look out, sighed, and then threw some coins on the ground and yanked the curtain closed.

He returned to his house. The damage was disgusting. He'd have to help in the cleanup.

A palace slave came running into his sitting room. He had been shown in by the doorkeeper. All Kallias wanted was to drink and play with the monkey he'd purchased a week before the fire began. He was trying to see if the monkey could hold a tray and set it down politely.

"The emperor summons you to appear immediately," said the slave, breathless.

Kallias shouted for another slave to come and put up the monkey, which he had named Aristocrat. That was his way of making fun of the patricians. Then he got himself together and hurried to the palace and the Praetorians let him into Nero's personal audience chamber.

"This fire," Nero said, as soon as he walked into the room. "I'm crushed. Half my city is burned to the ground!"

One of his advisors tried to console him by reminding him that he had Palatine Hill.

"Shut up!" Nero spun on him. Everyone flinched at the shout.

Callistus looked him in the face and said, "Remember when you are angry, breathe."

"Don't tell me to breathe, you fucking freedman. I'll rip your throat out."

Callistus inched back and folded his hands.

"We'll have relief efforts. Callistus and Epaphroditus can work on that. I won't see my city and my people destroyed by this tragedy."

They nodded.

"And Kallias, you'll help them, won't you? And we'll have to raise the taxes. You know what we need to do."

Kallias assented.

"I was giving out money from my own purse," said Nero. "I went down in the ruins with my entourage and we gave out money to those poor souls, didn't we?"

The members of his entourage all nodded.

"You must know we're working as fast as we can, Caesar," said Ephraphroditus, the new secretary of letters. He propped himself up against a table. His crutch lay on the floor. "There's so much damage. I've had all the reports and we'll have to rebuild half the city! And no one knows how it started, because I did ask!"

At that, Nero's face turned down. "We have to blame someone," he said. "No one's going to believe that the city just burned down."

"I don't understand it," said Epaphroditus, and the others murmured agreement.

"What about the Christians?" Nero said.

They all looked at him.

"They're a bunch of strange people. Nobody likes them. We could blame them."

"The fucking Christians," said Tigellinus. The few Praetorians in the room laughed.

"Tigellinus," said Nero. "I want them rounded up immediately. Every single one of them, but especially their leaders. And you had better have it done by the end of the week."

Kallias had been quiet all this time. When he heard that, he frowned.

"You will assist in rounding up the Christians too," said Nero. "I want your best gladiators on them for the arena. I let you get away with illegal things just for this. And start figuring out the new taxes. You know what to do. Do your job. Do it!"

"It'll be taken care of," Kallias assured him. But his racing mind was on something else.

As they discussed their plans, Kallias didn't wait to hear more. He left quickly.

As soon as he was out of the palace and in the street, he said to one of the slaves, "Find Titus and bring him to me as fast as possible. If you're not back in two hours, I'm sending you to the arena with the Christians."

The man broke into a run.

Titus had left home early today, as he always did. He was still studying medicine. It would take him years to learn, and he was going to go to Alexandria eventually, to get more into it. Kallias wanted him to have the best teachers and the best knowledge.

He was probably out now, helping people who were wounded.

Kallias paced the room and held the monkey and let it run around and break the cups and the plates on the table because the chaos was a wonderful distraction. Then Titus walked in.

"Good," Kallias said, and stopped pacing immediately. "You have to leave Rome."

Titus looked at him.

"Nero."

"What, why?"

"I don't have time to explain. I have some things to do. But you have to leave because Nero's going to round up Christians and send them to the Circus. So if you don't leave, you're in danger."

"Oh," said Titus. He put his hand over his mouth. His bag slid off his shoulder and he caught it absentmindedly with his hand.

"I already have servants packing you. I'll give you plenty of money, whatever you want."

"So, just leave? What about the others?"

"And what about them?"

"My friends."

Kallias hit him on the face. He said, "Use your head, Titus. You'll be ready to leave for Alexandria in five minutes, when that slave pops around this door. You have your whole life ahead of you, you're not a martyr."

Titus said rubbed his cheek. He looked at his father. "I guess it's God's will."

"It's Nero's will."

The slave came five minutes later, and said that he had two bags for Titus and another slave to go with him. Kallias gave Titus gold and a guard and said that everything would be taken care of when he was there. He should never say the word 'Christian' again, and never associate with them.

Kallias put his hands on his shoulders and he said, "You didn't have a bad life, Titus, besides this. When you let this Christianity go, you can be as normal as you want to be. That is all you have to do. That's all you have to do."

Titus nodded. Then Kallias hugged him tight, something he rarely did.

Kallias spent the next two days finding names. He suggested they look for someone named Luke, but the man had to have not been in the city for a very long time, because there wasn't a trace of him. Kallias' plan was to find him and then easily find all the rest. Luke must know a lot of people.

Some members of Nero's group really did believe the Christians had started the fire.

Kallias never believed they did. Likely no one had started it.

Some of his associates were burning for revenge. Kallias had his own motive.

He was going to make his cut of money off confiscated possessions. Some of these people were very rich, although they liked to appear plain.

He sat up late one night at the palace, reading through lists of people who had been noted or arrested. He wanted to be sure he never saw his son's name. He was also looking to see whose money would be his after this was all over.

Sure, the emperor would have most of it. But what else was Kallias here for? He'd be a fool not to help himself to the spoils of criminals. His back was hunched, he sat at his desk unmoving for hours. A slave came in and cleared his throat. Kallias said, without looking up, "Get out."

Tigellinus walked in. Kallias did look up for him. Tigellinus said, "There's going to be a lot of killing, and you look dead, too."

He said, "Not in the morning, Tigellinus, not in the morning."

Tigellinus laughed and walked on to wherever he was going. And Kallias read names and took notes of who had the most money. He'd come out of this even richer. Nero wouldn't be the only person who benefitted from this. Kallias read on.

Then one name in particular caught his eye.

He sat up straight, rubbing his eyes, and looked at it again. He said out loud, "No. I'm dreaming? I'm dreaming."

He had to be seeing things from lack of sleep.

But he thought, Who else would have that name? And if it were someone else, then that would still be interesting. But regardless of whoever it was, he had to know. He shouted for someone. A guard came in.

He showed him the paper. "I want to see that woman."

Chapter 60

Kallias went down to the prison at the Circus Maximus. The guard let him down in its depths. At the intersection of one hall he heard screaming. Probably some poor idiot being tortured. "Can't you shut them up?" he said to the guard. "What a racket."

Kallias had requested to see her alone. The whole time that he was walking he thought, It is just someone who happens to have this name. But that was not how these names went. The patricians had a set of names and everybody knew exactly who was who by those names. He was almost too sure that what he was thinking was true.

The guard reached the door and started to unlock it.

"This is fun stuff," said Kallias.

The other man swung the heavy wooden door open. Kallias didn't walk closer to the cell. He stood in the tight hallway. He said, "Bring her into the light."

The guard brought her into the light, and she stood before Kallias. He was expecting someone haggard, but she still had pins in her hair, and her clothes were nice. She squinted and looked up.

He looked into her face, for the first time, and he knew. He had the breath sucked out of him. She had the same dark eyes and nose. She looked so much like him, exactly like him. Kallias couldn't say anything for a second.

But when she saw him, she thought that he was her savior. Her eyes widened. The chains on her wrists clinked.

"It's good they haven't been bad to you," he said then, and smiled.

"I can't say good," she said, voice almost a whisper. "But I'm whole...and you're here."

"Why do you think I'm here?"

"I can only assume you know me?"

"But you don't know me."

She said that no she did not, not directly, although she knew that he worked for Caesar. Kallias was a little taken aback by that. But she gazed at him expectantly. This was fun.

"Do you know Titus?" said Kallias. "He's a boy who went to your services, he's close with a doctor named Luke."

"He studies medicine! Yes, I know him. Nice young man!"

It was getting too good. He couldn't believe it. It was pure luck. "He's my son."

"Really?" Her eyes fixed on him were even wider now. The chains clinked again.

"He told me all the names he could remember," said Kallias, looking at her very solemnly. "And I think for his sake, I have to help you."

She sank to her knees and put her hands together. Tears streamed down her face as she thanked him profusely. He resisted the urge to have the guards beat her. He'd have ordered it if he didn't want to wait to see the look on her face when he was done with her. Nothing could rob him of that.

"You don't have to cry like that," he said, after a moment. "I'm not a good man but I wouldn't let my son's friends be killed."

"Oh thank you, thank you," she said, rising with some difficulty in the chains. She dried her tears with palms of her hands, the chains clinking at every movement.

"So, how will you do it then?" she asked suddenly, and this question would've caught him off guard if he hadn't already planned it all.

He glanced at the soldier, who was trying not to laugh. All of them were in on it and had been paid very well to go along.

"Now," Kallias said. "I can't help all of you. Nero would kill me then, you understand."

She nodded. "I definitely understand that."

"Yes. But you and two others, I have them so that Nero will release you. I wrote for you and the evidence will say that you weren't in Rome and you aren't a Christian. I know how you all are about denying your God, so you don't ever have to say the words. Just know that in the arena on Nero's orders you will be released."

They held each other's gaze. He saw that she was as proud as him, and that the desperation was only because of her situation. She'd taken good care of herself too, and the bags under her eyes were clearly fresh.

This woman lived a good life, thinking she'd escaped the sins of her father. No doubt she never wanted to be associated with him. Kallias imagined that after Calvinus committed suicide, someone nice and wealthy took the little girl and raised her—maybe her mother did, even—and the rest of her life had been fine. He knew that look, and she had it, of someone who had been rich all their life.

"Thank you," she said, "truly." And in her eyes was a look of shining hope that he would be good on his word and get her out of here alive. She put her hands together and thanked him again, saying his name. He nodded as seriously as he could. Then the guard sent her back in, and locked the door.

"Amusing," said Kallias. "Did you see that?"

"Your former master's daughter?" said the man, chuckling.

"No less. And this is the first time I've ever met her."

Chapter 61

The gladiators lined up in front of Kallias in the courtyard. Their guards flanked them, ready if anyone made a move. They brought them out in lines and sent them back in, as Kallias examined them.

"They all look so good," he said, "With my brand. I love them, I made them so brilliant! You know, I would throw many people to the lions if I could. And to them."

"Well, Nero will be doing a lot of that soon," said the manager.

"Not fast enough. Did you know, I saw my former master's daughter in the group of Christians? He'd be ashamed of her for collaborating with people like that."

"Bet that's funny to you," said Banapho.

"I thought it was the best thing I ever had happen in my whole life."

The man grunted. Then the next selection walked out, and Kallias said, "I like these two. They look like you would just shit yourself if you had to see them just before you died."

He wanted to them look as ferocious and frightening as possible. He was so excited.

He couldn't sleep or even eat for the rest of the day. He imagined his blood was pure euphoria surging through him.

He was able to find, through some documents that his assistant discovered, that the daughter had indeed lived well. When her father had to kill himself after collaborating in a plot to overthrow the emperor, she had gone to live with her mother again. It was Caligula who restored her inheritance that was from her father's immense wealth.

Sulpicia was married twice, had divorced both men, but never had any children. She'd given money to orphans through the years, and even given up one of her inherited houses for women who left the streets. She had finally donated a second house to church elders, and focused on her weaving business where she employed low-class women.

She had sold that too, two years ago. She had always been able to make these easy decisions to help other people, because of her money, and she had stayed away from trouble until now. She had been so much luckier than Sejanus's daughter. The Praetorians raped the little girl on a public platform before they killed her. But not the daughter of Kallias's former master. The girl had grown into a woman and escaped her father's corruption and violence.

Kallias almost went to visit her again, but Tigellinus said she'd find it strange if he did. An official like him couldn't be that interested in her.

"True," he said. They were in Kallias's dining room, not eating, not drinking, just reclining. The monkey leapt up and knocked over a vase just then, crashing it to pieces.

Tigellinus laughed. "You should handle that idiot beast."

"Maybe, but I like it for now."

The steward ushered the slave in to stand before Tigellinus and Kallias. He was young, and mischievous, just like the monkey. He always twitched when he had to stand still too long. He was giggling now.

"You know what to do," said Kallias, and the boy bobbed his head.

"Say it," said Kallias. "Repeat it all back to me just as you are supposed to say it."

"I will tell her," said the slave, bouncing from one foot to the other. "I will tell her, The man in the box beside the emperor's was once the favorite slave of your father. And he was never going to free you because he has to get even with his former master who was very cruel to him."

"Good," said Kallias. "Perfect."

Tigellinus clapped twice. "You should give the boy something for it," he said. And the slave came and stood close beside him.

Chapter 62

Later the same night, more Praetorians crowded the house, bringing more slaves and wine. They stayed up through the hours. The excitement about tomorrow was palpable, and Kallias kept them all entertained. Only the messenger boy fell asleep, slumped beside Tigellinus. Kallias changed his clothing in the morning, after he dozed on the couch himself, but only for a few minutes.

Today, she'd be thinking she would walk free. Maybe she would and maybe she wouldn't. He couldn't say, just yet. But the slave would scare her regardless, and then Kallias would decide her fate from sitting in his box.

Either way, the chance for revenge was at last in his hand.

The crowd was massive in the Circus. Kallias was grateful he didn't have to mix with them. He went up the steps to the first rows with all the senators and other important people. Behind him, a slave carried Aristocrat. Another slave carried his tablets, in case he needed them. He still had a lot to do today, too, but there was only one thing on his mind. The crowd was loud and he couldn't hear himself if he wanted to.

As he sat, Tigellinus passed him and shouted, "This is brilliant today, Kallias."

Praetorians came by slapping him on the back because his gladiators from the House of Fire were no doubt assembling just now underneath the grounds of the Circus to prepare to do their slaughter today. And no one knew—but them—that he was running an illegal fighting house, and that was brilliant, too.

His new Egyptian slave poured him some wine. Senators filed in and took their places. Otho appeared, and then came the emperor and his long retinue. Poppaea Sabina leaned over and smiled at Kallias. He waved his fingers at her. That was a woman unmatched in beauty. It was not fair she had to lay under Nero. It was not fair that any of them had to tolerate Nero.

Then the gladiators came out, some of them from his house, and Kallias stood and clapped and whistled for them with the rest of the crowd. He was hoarse when he sat. He started coughing.

His gladiators turned to Nero and stretched their hands out and chanted, "We who are about to die salute you, Caesar," although none of them would probably die today.

Kallias clapped again. His slave offered him a cup but Kallias waved his hand. He wanted to be sober. He wanted to be as sober as the nights he was all those times he felt all the pain. Now he would feel all the joy.

The gladiators turned in procession and exited the sands. Now came the moment he was waiting for. He leaned forward, holding his breath.

"Bring them out!" Nero shouted.

The evening before, Kallias spoke to Nero briefly, and told him that one of them was not a Christian, and described exactly who.

"But she was close in association," he said. "And I think she should be punished just for that. Or maybe she should not."

"If you know it's true that she wasn't," said Nero. "Do what you will with it when the time comes. I know you'll take care of everything."

The Christians came out. Some of them were crying and praying. The guards prodded them into order. There she was, in the same silver gown she was wearing when he visited her, now clearly dirtied. But the pins were still in her hair.

She was never going to let that dignity go, just like a patrician.

But he saw her gaze searching through the emperor's box. Everyone was quiet staring at the Christians. So these were the people who wanted a god to come and destroy Rome. They didn't want that, Kallias knew. They were just a cult of freaks.

He stood.

They looked right at each other, and he smiled at her and waved. The sun caught and glinted on his ring.

All she could manage was a little nod. She was shaking now. It was very fun to be on the other end. She was shaking. Then the jeers started. She dropped her eyes. Her lips moved in a prayer.

The people had been instructed not to throw things, as to not disturb the show. Nero considered every game in the Circus to be a part of his personal list of shows. His personal tour. It was rude to disrupt.

But otherwise, the crowd went crazy with chants. Nero held up his hand and they quieted some, although there were still whistles. The slave boy ran out onto the sands just then, running wild. He ran up right to her, and tapped her on the shoulder. She jumped back.

The boy was telling her the words Kallias recited to him last night, and giggling and bouncing. She stared at him, with her mouth halfway open.

Then she looked up at Kallias again, as if to confirm if what she had heard was true.

He was waiting for this moment. He had been waiting for something like this for all his life.

When she looked at him, he smiled at her.

It was the broadest smile he had ever smiled.

Then he held up his thumb, just for her.

The person beside him said, "Yes, right, it is their unlucky day," and laughed.

Sulpicia stared at him with wide, wide eyes. He grinned at her. He whistled. She just looked at him. One passing guard kicked her in the shin then and she went down. The boy ran off the scene. The last of the guards cleared off as she got back to her feet. She kept shaking her head at Kallias, panicking now. He just smiled at her.

At that moment, the lions trotted out towards their prey. She closed her eyes. The first batch of the Christians, and she was standing near the edge. Some of them crowded in together for protection. Some of them broke into a run. Their screams were clear even from the sand. The lion caught a man first, sank its teeth in his leg.

A bony lioness mauled Sulpicia. Every time that lion jerked her, Kallias thought about everything Calvinus had done to him. He hadn't thought about it for a long time, because it was so hard to think about. And he had to focus while he tried to remember it all, because it was so long ago.

He sat very, very still and tried to remember it all. He started from the beginning.

He didn't take his gaze off the scene as he watched the lions tear her from limb to limb.

Chapter 63

The guards lit fires on the second batch of Christians. Kallias took a drink and hardly saw the rest of it, sitting with his eyes on the bar in front of him. The servant standing beside him may have been saying something to him, but he didn't hear any of it. He sat and thought over and over of her face—and that look in her eye when she realized that he was not for her.

Then absentmindedly. "Pour me more wine." And the servant did.

Drinking more. When he was a boy, and Calvinus told him that he would educate him, and dangled in front of him the hope that he was something other than just a sex slave, until it dawned on him in those very hurtful days that he would never be taken seriously or used for anything other than pleasure. And hanging him by his hands, and marking him up in so many ways.

And how hard he cried! Swinging from that ceiling. Thinking he was going to die.

It was exhilarating. He drank some more.

He came to Ahenobarbus's house in a daze. Knowing that he had to keep his head down and working so hard to forget. Meeting Agrippina and feeling for the first time that he had a grip on himself. Finding out that his mother was dead. With that haircut he realized everything could be different for him. Learning how to handle money, and power. When he put two numbers together and it all clicked, and it all made sense.

He drank some more.

It was so wonderful. It felt so good. When they dragged her bloodied carcass away—her crumpled body was still on the sands with the next batch, he stepped over to Nero and said, "You know what would make this even better?"

"What?" said Nero. "It's already fantastic!"

Poppaea Sabina smiled at them. Beautiful, winsome self. Cruel and beautiful.

"Have them fight each other next time."

"I love that idea," said Nero. "But can we get them to even fight each other? They don't like to fight, I hear."

He looked across the sands. "Probably not. Well, the gladiators will do it regardless."

"Yes, just enjoy the show."

"I think it may be the best day of my life," he said.

Chapter 64

The sudden comedown. The next day, sober and hungover, he sat in his office at the palace, and he thought to himself, that it really hadn't been all that exciting.

He had to sit there and try his best to remember everything that happened, just so he could feel he was having revenge. Those things had happened so long ago that he'd forgotten many details. All he knew now was that back then, it had all made him very distressed and frightened. But he hadn't had those emotions in so long.

He realized now how he had never really confronted it in himself, in the way a person does in the aftermath of something horrible. All he did was go from day to day, refusing to think of how it made him.

It was sickening trying to remember it. He'd rather walk through a gauntlet of spikes and thorns, the pain felt the same. It was so long ago, and he'd achieved so much, and had everything he wanted since then.

His messenger boy leaned against the doorway and said, "Was she really the daughter of your former master?"

"I told you not to follow me to the palace," said Kallias.

"The Praetorians know I'm with you," said the boy. "They let me come in anywhere."

Kallias looked at him. He reminded him vaguely of someone. He was staring at him for a very long time. And then he realized that someone was himself. The flawless dark hair and the brilliant wicked eyes and the little glow of excitement. He'd had the same demeanor years ago. He didn't think he'd moved and laughed so much, though.

"That was her," said Kallias.

"Did it feel good?"

"What?"

"To get revenge."

Chapter 65

A Praetorian came into his office with a box under his arm.

"Here's the things you wanted." He set the box on the desk, nodded to Kallias and walked out.

Kallias popped the box open, and there it was, sitting on top of the papers that gave him the deed to a fourth house. His former master's main house. There would have been more, but the daughter had sold all the rest, when she was busy being charitable and helping the poor disadvantaged women who had nowhere to go.

He picked up the ring, hardly believing his eyes. He rolled it between his thumb and forefinger. It was no less gold and sturdy than it had been thirty-five years ago, when the man who wore it could have anything in the world he wanted by pressing it to a piece of paper.

Kallias turned it over and stared at the inscription. SATURN. Men put different pithy phrases on their signet rings. Sometimes they just put their names, or a symbol of something they loved or valued.

There was no symbol on Calvinus's signet ring. Just that word. SATURN.

Kallias had been close enough to Calvinus more than enough times to read what was on the ring, but he never had until now. Strange how that was.

He put the ring back into the box and shut it. He would never know what Calvinus meant by that inscription.

And he didn't care.

Chapter 66

"Keep an emperor happy with vices," Tigellinus always said. He and Kallias had occasionally visited the slave dealers, searching for beautiful children to buy for Nero. There was a single intent—to keep Nero distracted by debauchery, and his guests entertained.

Kallias himself was uninterested in using frightened young slaves and preferred his partners to be willing. But he might be in the minority on that opinion. So he kept that concern to himself. His personal preferences aside, he didn't care anyway.

Tears and fear—and even feigned eagerness—didn't move him. He was paying a lot of money and the merchandise had better be exactly as demanded. They were slaves after all, and they must accept their lot.

Nero had to be appeased by many gifts and toys, and in many ways he still behaved like a child himself. He was capricious and petulant. He might caress a toy one day, and then kick it the next. But Tigellinus knew everything that he liked, and kept him supplied with it at the snap of his fingers—wine, women, boys, and art. Exotic animals. Dead senators.

Political enemies, obviously. It was very easy to offend Nero.

Which circled back to why Tigellinus kept him gorged on violence and sex. Why Kallias urged him to enjoy all the new ways constructed for him to sate himself. Nero's advisors encouraged him to indulge. They had to keep him happy.

Since Kallias was so good at planning things, and Tigellinus would force it all to work, they would put together the party for the Saturnalia.

Kallias wanted as much excitement as possible.

Nothing could top that day in the arena and what he had done to Sulpicia.

In the many years since his youth, time had taken the sting from his old hurts. Somewhere during all the changes in his life he had transformed into someone seeking power all because of his own ambition, and at some point, his desire to have control was no longer about the fact that once upon a time he had none. And he hadn't even noticed when it happened.

At fifteen, all he wanted was to be exactly like Calvinus. At twenty-two, he wanted nothing more than to one day defeat him. Calvinus was always his standard to reach. And look how it all played out. If Calvinus hadn't brutalized him, if Kallias hadn't rebelled, he would've never been resold to a new house where he had the chance to grow up and become his own man. The way it was, was the only way it could've been.

He told himself he wished he could have had revenge, but he hadn't realized until after he had it that he already had everything he wanted. And what he wanted was what he had all along.

Power—and the things that came with it, violence, money, sex—had always thrilled him. Maybe that was why he was so attracted to Calvinus in the first place. He had loved him so much, to his shame and his frustration, and then hated him so much, in just the same way, for years and years, and now he felt nothing towards him.

That was truly something: that he felt nothing toward him.

The one big moment in his life, when he finally got equal and killed his former master's only child. They'd said, years ago, that Calvinus loved her even though he wanted a son, and gave her everything and tried to keep her from knowing all of the things he did. That same man had harmed Kallias so much, and now Kallias had killed his daughter. What could match that?

So in the aftermath of all this, it was strange for Kallias to find that he didn't care about it anymore. It was so strange to look up and see that the feeling was gone.

That was why the Saturnalia ought to be as brutal and exciting as he could make it. He needed to feel something as intense again, as that one moment in the arena.

Nero was all for the creative cruelty. Poppaea Sabina too, who smiled and gleamed at the idea of vicious entertainment.

"I want something new," said Nero as they stood in his audience room. "Something really exciting. You know I get bored easily."

Ephraphroditus kept different descriptions of past shows from the aediles. Kallias, who liked to document whatever happened in the arena, also had extensive pieces.

"These are more in detail than yours," he said squarely, clearly offending Epaphroditus.

But Kallias didn't care. He never cared about anyone anymore.

Kallias was at the House of Fire everyday, preparing for his gladiators to perform for the party. They had to be in top shape. He ordered his managers to push them regardless of how they felt. Their glory would come after the pain. Kallias also bought a tiger from an African merchant, to walk through while the monkey Aristocrat stood on his back.

The Saturnalia was the wildest he had ever seen. And he had been to his share of wild parties. But this was on another level of excitement. Hundreds of people crowded into Tigellinus's house for the first day of the event, wearing their best and most expensive clothing. The couches were laid out with flowers on them and the food was wheeled in on carts.

Kallias entered with Tigellinus, Otho, Poppaea, and some other Praetorians and important senators. Slaves walked and threw more flowers through the duration of the meal. As soon as the second course began, Kallias and Tigellinus stepped out into the hall.

The man overseeing their new slaves waited there with his pudgy hands clasped in front of him.

If he didn't do his best at controlling the young slaves they bought for guests, they would torture him, and he knew it. He was especially afraid of them, even more than he was of Nero, sometimes.

They lined up six of the best-looking boys and girls, hand picked by Kallias and Tigellinus. None of them were a day older than twenty-one—the guests wouldn't have liked that. Kallias was not so much interested in their looks as he was the excitement of the guests when they saw them. He liked when he brought items to present and everyone said, "Oh!"

"They better be perfect tonight," he told the man, and tapped him on the side of the head. The man said they were. He was extremely overweight, and always breathing heavily from nervousness and exhaustion.

Tigellinus told him to escort them in.

Kallias had finally trained the monkey to carry a tray. "Look," he said to the guests. The room was silent, all eyes on him.

He put the tray on the floor, and went to his couch where the monkey sat. "Go get it." He pointed.

The animal looked at him, got up and waddled over to the tray and picked it up. Kallias winked at it. That was its signal. Aristocrat stopped, made a noise, and then ran over to the other end of the room and stopped in front of a gray-haired senator and slammed the tray down hard on the man's head.

The man howled and everyone in the room burst out laughing.

"Aristocrat!" said Kallias, smiling. The man lay on the couch, cradling his head. The monkey made noises and ran back to Kallias. He picked it up, patted it, and the crowd laughed and laughed.

The music had stopped, but it resumed again. The steward stood in the middle of the room and shouted, "Esteemed guests, here is the best part! Please be prepared."

At that, Doryphorus, a freedman, flung open a cage in the corner. Nero emerged dressed like a bear and began to run and attack the slaves tied to the stakes. The guests burst into screams and cheers. Slaves sprinkling flowers walked round and round while Nero ran and attacked the others.

Then Doryphorus escorted Nero away while everybody clapped again. Kallias started on his next drink of wine. As he was drinking he was thinking to himself that he had done it all, everything he wanted to do, and there was really nothing left. He had all the money and power he wanted, he'd fucked whoever he wanted to, and best of all, he was the one to send his former master's daughter to the arena.

And he didn't even care about all the things that man had done to him. Not anymore, and he hadn't for a long time, for years now, long before he realized he had gotten over it and was living the life he had always wanted.

While the others cheered for Nero, Kallias poured himself another cup.

Chapter 67

The Golden House, financed by the treasury, was built after the fire. Kallias was always at the parties that lasted through the nights. The new palace was a world unto itself, so beautiful it seemed immortal. He knew this all wouldn't last—how could it, when the emperor was young, foolish, and cruel, and the plots being spun in the capital were more dangerous than ever? And Kallias, himself, knowing he had as many enemies as he did friends?

But he was determined to not resign his position.

Titus became a physician, and did no harm to people. Marcus came from Germany and saw him only once. Kallias didn't even care if his son liked him. Sometimes children didn't love or like their parents, and it couldn't be reconciled.

"Good luck in Spain," he said to him, just before Marcus left.

Marcus, strong and stocky like his grandfather, only looked at him before he went to the door. They didn't embrace.

Kallias had believed that seeing his former master's daughter in that way would make him feel better deep down in himself for all those long years, but it really did nothing for him. Nothing had changed, not the past, and he had everything he wanted anyway.

He had been the steward of a great household, a secretary, an aedile and a quaestor, and finally the treasurer of the empire. He had made millions. His friends were crazy for his gladiators, and the fame of those gladiators won him more friends.

Now he understood what it was like for a man to have everything he wanted. It was being at the top of everything, surpassing everything, and feeling untouchable. This was probably how Calvinus felt too and why he was how he was. And people like them didn't worry about other people, other things, anything, as long as they had their way, their money, and their power.

Kallias understood him now. Now, at last, he knew what it was like to be like Calvinus.

As long as he had the power and the money and more and more of it, Kallias simply did not care about anything else. He didn't care what his enemies said behind his back, or if his servants thought he was cruel, or if his ex-wife had been stirring up rumors about him and complaining about his preventing her from seeing their children for years. He simply didn't care about anyone else, as long as he had what he wanted.

And everything bored him, inevitably. Even the entertainment. He had been going to the Golden House day after day, drinking himself to a point of easy and excitable cruelty. In its first days of opening, he never missed a party there. He drank more than he ever had in those years than his whole life. He slept with whoever he wanted, including his messenger boy who was now nineteen, a stunning youth, and who laid down willingly on his couch. Kallias thought it was like fucking his younger self, and that made it so thrilling and intense.

After the boy annoyed him, he gave him back to Tigellinus.

Kallias was surprised when he saw his own self in a mirror one day and his face was thin and older. He didn't feel old, not a bit in his body, but he looked old, somewhat. Not that it mattered.

He was at the top of the world.

Being at the top of the world meant that he had everything—but it also meant he could lose everything. In the good times that was easy to forget.

When Nero was dethroned and the city was in uproar, Galba marched in from Spain.

Kallias played his hand swiftly in welcoming Galba. It was easy to disown Nero when he had no real love for him in the first place.

The Senate declared Nero a public enemy and he was dead. So, Ahenobarbus was right, nothing good came of that.

In the same year, Otho took over and Galba's own men killed him in the streets. But Otho was cut down very quickly after his announcement as emperor. The court had been a circle of rising and falling members. Poppaea Sabina died years ago, from complications when she was pregnant and Nero kicked her in the stomach.

Tigellinus had committed suicide. Half the freedman who used to run the empire had fallen some way or another. And a few of them stayed.

Titus Flavius Vespasian was the final contender for the throne.

He and Kallias were enemies.

Kallias arranged his escape to Greece.

He ordered a hasty breakfast, and had barely taken a bite when there was a commotion.

A servant burst in, laid a letter on the table and bowed low.

Kallias opened it, seeing that it was from Vespasian. The servant said something, but Kallias didn't hear.

"When I reach Rome, the Senate will name me emperor. You have worked for five Caesars, and maybe you have done well, in work. And sometimes not, in case of your personal character. The court will decide all of that, when you are summoned and tried for corruption and treason. I am not interested in your oath of loyalty."

"Calling me a traitor," he said out loud. "Very unnecessary."

Why would he stand in front of a court just for them to tell him what he already knew about himself?

He stood and threw the letter on the floor.

Aristocrat scooped up the letter, waddled to him, and Kallias picked him up. "These damned things," he said to the monkey, who was still playing with the parchment death sentence and waving it at him. But Kallias was too distracted to respond.

He would not have a trial. When the Praetorians saw him, or Vespasian's men—whoever reached him first, they would run him through just as they ran through Agrippina. They would cut him down in the street or his house and his blood would soak stones or the tiles beneath him.

He saw it as clear as a vision.

He hurried into his office, still carrying Aristocrat. But when he walked in, he dumped the animal on the floor. The monkey was agile enough to land on his feet. He made noises but Kallias wasn't listening.

He almost imagined that he could hear the Praetorians coming for him, that he could hear their footsteps thudding down the tiled hallway, although the letter had been delivered only minutes ago. There was wine on the desk, and he grabbed that and the dagger.

He rushed to the hot room of his baths carrying the wine in one hand and his dagger in the other. A few years ago, Murano had this made for him, with the fire symbol on the hilt, just as Kallias asked him to. The room was steaming. Kallias lowered himself into the water without bothering to undress.

He took a long, deep drink of the wine. He swallowed it so fast it gave him a coughing fit. He got himself together. He wasn't afraid. He had done too many things to be afraid.

He took the knife and made a long, neat cut on his left wrist. The blood bubbled up and lined across his hand. He cut very deep, and sucked his teeth for the pain. He cursed.

He cut the other wrist. He cut behind his right knee.

Then he lay back with his head against the marble, staring at the ceiling. The water bobbled under him and the heat nauseated him. He must have laid there for a long time. But he opened his eyes sometimes and he saw that his vision had blurred. It was taking too long, but he was used to that. In the background, his monkey ran around the room. He tried to tell it to stop, but the thing was running wild.

Kallias heard the servants passing in the hall, oblivious. The letter lay upturned on the floor, the seal on it very visible and broken. Aristocrat scooped it up and held it up to his face as if he were reading it. Kallias lay there with his face turned in that direction, but not really looking at the monkey or anything at all.

The blood would stain the bath and the water.

He understood it all now.

And he thought of when he was three years old, toddling around the atrium, and Lucius Spinther picked him up and held him high and spun him around and around and around.

Historical Depictions Disclaimer

Regarding the history in this novel, I generally tried my best to stick to the facts from my research when writing the story. But I'm not a historian, this is not a history book, and the appeal of historical fiction is that it's fiction. I deliberately took liberties with two things: Calvinus's governorship and the location of a centralized palace often mentioned where Kallias and other characters ran their schemes. The real fact is that Gaius Poppaeus Sabinus was the governor of Moesia for a few years longer than what he's credited for in my book. And Calvinus is obviously a fictional character. I didn't want to slander any real people who didn't actually have a lot of historical detail attached to them. And my entire depiction of the governorship in the story was just to represent Roman governors who had indeed been rapacious in their provinces.

As for the idea of a central imperial palace, I created a fictional place to keep the setting simpler.

I beg you not to flame me for these minor tweaks.

Finally, any other details not mentioned here are also simply my interpretation. If you want actual history books with detailed facts, please read the works of actual historians. They are numerous and they are brilliant. I'm just someone who loves fun stories and historical settings and sometimes combines the two!

Acknowledgements

I appreciate everyone who helped me put this thing together! Shoutout to: Morghan Decosta-Taylor for your invaluable developmental insights and perspective, Amanda Empey for providing so much patient feedback and help at every step, John Calligan for giving me crucial advice to help me improve as a writer, and Jodi Bracken for helping me brainstorm and encouraging me. Also shoutout to Robson Felix Dhliwayor and Anushay Tirmizi for reading and cheering me on.

About the Author

Rachel Cherry is from eastern North Carolina. She is a graduate of NC State University, where she majored in Communications and PR.

Rachel's favorite stories to read and write are always about power hungry people in historical or fantasy settings. In her free time, if she's not delving into some extremely esoteric interest, she's plotting her next story.

Inspiration

Growing up, I loved the story of Joseph. I was fascinated by this figure who, despite being sold into slavery by his own brothers, somehow found favor everywhere he went until he rose to become one of the most powerful people in his world. I thought (still do think) a lot about power and the ways different people interact within its structures, and eventually I was inspired with the story of Kallias.

The setting was key. When we think of Rome, we think of power, order, and patriarchy. We generally associate Rome with a vigorous type of structure that has been lauded in the West for centuries later. You can't write about Rome without mentioning power, and since power is my favorite theme, I knew there was no better setting to begin my thematic exploration than here.

When I wrote Master and Favorite my overarching thoughts were: What does it take to gain power? Who would most likely succeed in a patriarchal society? What kinds of abuse are the shadows that accompany power? Master and Favorite is simply an exploration of my opinion on these things.

NEXT BOOKS

Thanks for reading Master and Favorite! I hope to follow soon with two more historical releases. Check out the blurbs below and visit rachelcherry.com to sign up for my mailing list!

Note: blurbs subject to change.

THE SHOPGIRL

1880

Driven by daydreams of a lavish life, Lucy quits her job at a Cleveland textile factory and moves to New York City to work as a shopgirl—and find a rich husband. The shop allows her the opportunity to mingle with men of higher classes than her own lowly immigrant background, and Lucy soon lands a target: Jack Hall, who is not only well-off, but also adores her.

A hasty marriage reveals that Jack isn't as rich as Lucy initially believed him to be. And being the lady of a middle class household is just as exhausting as sweating in a factory. Lucy struggles to navigate a new society of new expectations while concealing her gnawing, overwhelming, discontent.

While Jack grapples with his own personal problems, Lucy concocts a scheme to bring an end to their marriage and finally pursue what she's still longing for—a rich husband who can hand her the world of her dreams. Social climbing is dangerous, and Lucy risks discovery and a crushing fall back to a life of poverty—but she didn't come to New York not to pursue her American dreams.

BEAUTIFUL HOUSE
1960

In a rural North Carolina town, Bernadette Smith works as a domestic help in wealthy white women's homes—while longing for better: a better job, a society without Jim Crow, a beautiful house. Things she can only have if she can leave the South. When Berry meets Josephine Walker, a family friend and girl her age, Berry finally has support for efforts too daring for someone with her skin color.

Jo, charming and headstrong, admires Berry's ambitions. Jo wants the same things Berry does—an equal world, a comfortable space to live. Their intense friendship soon turns to secret love. But a tragic incident forces them to abruptly flee North and eventually separate. A subsequent trail of events finds Berry homeless in a strange city and left to survive on her own.

But no matter how desperate her situation becomes, Berry refuses to return to the place that traumatized her. Or a house that haunts her. Convinced that nowhere else will ever be safe for her and determined to forget her feelings for Jo, Berry resolves to one day buy her own home. But first she will have to fight for a better education—and a good job.

Milton Keynes UK
Ingram Content Group UK Ltd.
UKHW010838220224
438295UK00004B/188

9 798990 007505